T0365023

CHERISH:
BEHOLD, I KNOCK

Debby L. Johnston

WESTBOW
PRESS®
A DIVISION OF THOMAS NELSON
& ZONDERVAN

Scriptures taken from the Holy Bible, New International Version®, NIV®. Copyright © 1973, 1978, 1984, 2011 by Biblica, Inc.™ Used by permission of Zondervan. All rights reserved worldwide. www.zondervan.com The "NIV" and "New International Version" are trademarks registered in the United States Patent and Trademark Office by Biblica, Inc.™

Scripture quotations marked (KJV) are from the King James Version

Poems ascribed to Opal Reese are the original work of *Cherish: Behold, I Knock* author Debby L. Johnston.

Art Credits:
DLJ logo designed by Kate Frick (*Frick.chick.designs@gmail.com*).
Church sketch by Maddie Frick (*Made Line Designs*).
Author Photo by Scott Johnston.

WestBow Press books may be ordered through booksellers or by contacting:

WestBow Press
A Division of Thomas Nelson & Zondervan
1663 Liberty Drive
Bloomington, IN 47403
www.westbowpress.com
1 (866) 928-1240

ISBN: 978-1-5127-6615-8 (sc)
ISBN: 978-1-5127-6616-5 (hc)
ISBN: 978-1-5127-6614-1 (e)

Library of Congress Control Number: 2016919788

Print information available on the last page.

WestBow Press rev. date: 12/21/2016

CONTENTS

LETTER FROM THE AUTHOR

Dear Reader,

I'm pleased that you've chosen to read more of Andy Garrett's story. In these pages, you'll reconnect with a host of familiar characters, and you'll meet new ones.

"Behold, I knock" is, of course, from Revelation 3:20, where Jesus says: *"Behold, I stand at the door and knock; if any man [or woman] hears my voice, and opens the door, I will come in... and will sup with [them]."* (KJV)

This verse illustrates the tireless and timeless nature of Christ. His grace is always available for the taking. It is not guarded or hidden from us. Jesus knocks, waiting to be let it in. The door is our heart—a door that can only be opened from the inside.

Sadly, many distractions work to drown out the sound of the Lord's hand at the door. Jesus, however, doesn't give up. He died on a cross to win for us a wonder-filled eternity in His company, and He's not willing to let anything stand in the way. In spite of the time it may take us to get past our pleasures, busyness, or pain, we'll find Him still there, lovingly waiting to reach in and heal our brokenness. Then, once we open the door, we wonder why we ever waited so long!

I've included in this book a tool to help you delve deeper into the themes found in the story. I hope you'll take time to review and think about what you've learned. The Readers' Discussion Guide provides questions to help you explore, alone or in a group.

Some of my story's characters have messed up ideas of who God is and what He expects from them. But circumstances, caring people, and the actual words of God, turn those wrong ideas around and replace them with the reality of Christ's redemptive love.

I pray this story will encourage and inspire you—and enlarge your discovery of all that Christ offers.

God bless you, my friend!

Debby

O AUTHOR OF IMMORTAL THINGS...

O Author of immortal things
And Designer of my heart,
Please touch the tattered part of me
With new Creator's art.

Reach down and sweep the depths of me;
Make sin's infections fly.
And when I feel Your pierced embrace,
Oh, make all sickness die.

Restore my form and breath, within,
As pure as Eden's air;
Erase the Serpent's curs-ed mark
And make my visage fair.

O sweep my clay with holiness
And turn my bones to gold,
And may I warm inside Your Grace,
And never more grow cold.

DEBBY L. JOHNSTON

Dedicated to my Lord Jesus Christ and to all those The Father loves—including Scott, who is my Andy.

PART ONE
FEED MY SHEEP

CHAPTER ONE

BATS (MID-MARCH 1979)

A gentle morning sun streamed through the stained glass windows and cast a golden haze over the filled pews of the Cherish First Baptist Church. Because of the bright morning light, there was no need to switch on the brass and crystal chandelier that adorned the dome; it was sparkling already. Beneath the sparkle, the seated blue-robed choir handsomely flanked the dark-robed Reverend Andy Garrett, who was just beginning his sermon.

Thankfully Andy's notes were well-prepared because this morning he found himself distracted.

Such distractions were rare. The usual sights and sounds of First Baptist's services routinely blended into the background of his thoughts when he spoke. He hardly noticed the tiny protests of little Luke Harkness (baby number four) or the inevitable whistle of Jack Butterman's hearing aid as the man comfortably nodded off.

No. Today, Andy's concentration was disrupted by something new, and it had to do with Junior Harris.

The modest farmer, who ushered at every service in stiffly starched and creased "Sunday bib" overalls, seldom volunteered an open-mouthed grin or spoke unnecessarily, because he refused—even for church—to wear his false teeth. This Sunday, however, at his station by the back door, Junior was unzipped from ear to ear in an abandoned and uncharacteristic exhibition of his gums. He even appeared to giggle once in a while. Andy was intrigued.

Junior's behavior struck Andy as especially odd because Junior was alone at the door. Fellow usher, Lou Webb, was out of town, and no one from the congregation remained to be seated.

Andy tried to ignore the usher's grin, but as he unfolded his sermon points on the initial call of Jesus to the disciples, Andy found himself smiling, too. He couldn't help it. And furthermore, Andy's pleasant demeanor stirred the people of the congregation to smile. People who normally sat motionless and expressionless during his sermon grinned up at him. Soon, the entire morning service was awash in a beatific glow of good will—all traceable to the atypical levity of Junior Harris.

Abbey Garrett puzzled over her husband's high spirits. Andy was always upbeat, but today he was unusually more so. She hoped that following the service he would share why he was in such exceptional humor.

Thankfully, today's message was upbeat and seemed to fit the mood of the morning. Andy smilingly explored all that was known about the twelve ordinary people Jesus had called into His extraordinary mission. Because of his own unusual call to the ministry Andy found the subject dear to his heart, and he drove home the point that God is never limited in who He can call and use.

Andy ended in prayer, and Music Director Marilyn Ingraham asked the congregation to sing "'Are Ye Able?' said the Master." As Andy sang, he decided to venture another look at the smiling usher. To his surprise, Junior now gave him a mischievous wink, and the man's belly bounced.

Startled, Andy lost his place and stopped singing. What could possibly have possessed Junior? He had to find out.

Immediately after the benediction, Andy swept down the aisle and blurted, "What ARE you laughing at?"

Junior's eyes twinkled.

"That." The usher giggled and pointed to the front of the sanctuary.

Andy looked but saw nothing. He shook his head.

"Look again," prompted Junior, and he pointed a little higher, to the top of the great circular window above the pulpit.

Andy scanned and rescanned the stained glass until he saw it. There, hanging upside-down and wrapped in its own leathery folds, was a tiny, sleeping bat. Andy doubted that anyone else had noticed it. He was surprised that Junior had.

With a laugh, Junior said, "I was waitin' for you to bang on the pulpit. I figured at some point that thing would come a-swoopin' down and set all the ladies to screamin'."

In the telling, the ample farmer imitated the bat's potential air raid with a sweep to the right and a sweep to the left. Junior's giggle grew, and his toothless grin gaped.

Andy tried to swallow his amusement. "So, Junior," he said, "you weren't worshipping with the rest of us, huh?"

Junior hung his head for a mere second. "No, Pastor. I guess my thoughts were just floatin' around elsewhere. Won't happen again, I'm sure!"

Andy chuckled and stepped into place to shake hands with members who were exiting the service. Junior couldn't help himself, however; he accosted everyone, to point out the bat, before they could reach the minister.

The church men laughed. The church women scurried out the door. And the church children were fascinated. (Deacon Stu Darrell caught his youngest son just before the boy lobbed a pencil from a visitor pew pad to make the creature fly; Stu herded the youngster outside.)

Abbey shook her head at the commotion. She thought the bat looked content to stay where it was, and even if it did take flight she couldn't imagine it could do much harm. She remained with Andy just inside the door to exchange pleasantries.

Oblivious to the stir it was creating, the little bat in the shadow of the window's rib slept peacefully. And it might have slept until nightfall, but a band of men, headed by Junior Harris, had other plans. The responsible fellows routinely dealt on-the-spot with problems, and this was no exception. Before they went home for lunch, the team armed themselves with the sanctuary light-changing poles and a half-dozen butterfly nets the children had used in vacation Bible school.

"It'll likely fly off at dusk," Church Moderator Luther Sharp intoned as they set to work, "but we can't have it making its departure during the evening service."

Junior giggled at the thought—a mere second before his waving butterfly net jerked the startled creature out of the sanctuary air.

———

Throughout the little town of Cherish, news of the church bat spread quickly. So did the story of its capture. But even after the announcement of the tiny creature's demise, Andy noticed that church members Elsie Trimble and Vivian Holladay never removed their hats during the evening service. Andy assumed it was because the retired spinster school teachers weren't convinced there were no other bats in the rafters.

The two women sat, as usual, in their south-section pew and never let their respectful attention waver from Andy as he spoke. Only their hats belied their concern.

Deaconess Ivey Webb and several of the younger ladies were more obviously distracted. They surreptitiously scanned the ceiling whenever they raised their heads from the Scripture passages. ("Where there's one, there's always more," Ivey had whispered when she had entered.) Every shadow of the light fixtures, the windows, and the curve of the dome drew inspection.

No more bats appeared, however, and Andy finished his devotional without incident.

Even so, bats dominated the conversation at the close of the service. The discussion unnerved Ivey. She put her hands over her ears as Luther expounded on the incidence of bat rabies. Gladys Briggs cringed at his suggestion that bats could not take flight unless they dropped down.

"A bat on the floor will try to climb anything, even your leg, to gain some height," Luther declared ominously.

Andy smiled. He knew that stories about the First Baptist Church bat would live on throughout the town for several days— maybe even weeks. He wouldn't be surprised to hear mention of the creature on the local news or see it referred to in the *Cherish Observer*. For a small town like Cherish, a bat in church was the perfect inspiration for a long special-interest feature on night-flying mammals.

Talk did finally wane after Junior Harris, Luther Sharp, and Danny Hart clattered among the church rafters and hollows that week. Although they carefully swept each recess with their flashlights and clutched their vacation Bible school butterfly nets, the men uncovered no evidence of other bats, birds, or mice.

It was a sad disappointment.

———•———

It would have taken more than a bat to dissuade the First Baptist faithful from showing up for church the next Sunday, especially since they were still celebrating Reverend Garrett's recent return to the pulpit. The congregation had sat under Andy's preaching for less than a year when he had become ill. Everyone had missed him during his surgery and weeks of follow-up, and they were glad he was finally back. There had been grave concern over his cancer diagnosis, and there had been more worry over the prescribed post-operative chemotherapy.

"Just a precaution," the doctor had said about the treatments. "We've found no evidence that anything has spread, but because of the aggressive nature of the type of cancer we removed, we'd like you to undergo a round of chemo, just to make certain."

The treatments had meant multiple trips to the hospital in nearby Harmony. And although the chemotherapy had ended and nothing more had been found, Andy was to report for checkups once a month for a year and then once a year for the next five years. The likelihood of anything showing up was said to be small, but the church continued to pray for no recurrence.

Andy was relieved that the treatments were over. His sermon delivery reflected it, with a renewed warmth and fervency. Andy was grateful that God had not allowed cancer to cut short his very first pastorate.

Andy often marveled to find himself in the pulpit. After all, he had not always been minister-material. When God had intervened in his life at age twenty-two (Andy had been happily tending bar in Old Town Chicago at the time), Andy had been inside a church only once, and that had been in childhood. He and his sister had spent a weekend at his grandmother's, where church attendance had been required.

Andy would have loved to have skipped school, too. From as early as kindergarten, Andy's disdain for education had doomed his future. As a rebellious underachiever, Andy had narrowly avoided flunking out of high school, and he had definitely flunked out of the first college he'd attended. At the end of high school, Andy would have been denied a diploma, except for his father's intervention. In an under-the-table deal, Mac Garrett had air-conditioned the school's administrative offices to gain the principal's handshake and a valid parchment for his son.

College had also been Andy's dad's idea. When the sons of the Garretts' country club colleagues had enrolled in college, Andy's dad had left no question that Andy would go to college, too. After a single-handed struggle to muscle his way from poverty to a place among the town's elite, Andy's father had refused to let his only son undermine the family's prestige. To ensure his son's acceptance, Dad Garrett had found a college that, for a price, would take anyone for a year. Andy had balked; he had not wanted to spend another day in a classroom. But he had been left no choice. Once at the school, Andy had made sure his dad's money was wasted: he had drunk his way through two semesters and then shown up at home to face his father's ire. It wasn't long after that, that he had fled to Chicago to take up bartending—a profession that had suited Andy perfectly. Tending bar had made few demands, and Andy had been content to go nowhere.

Why God had cared, Andy could not say, but one day God interrupted his nowhere life.

The miraculous intervention brought about a miraculous transformation—so miraculous that it caused Andy to seek enrollment in a small Christian college on the outskirts of his hometown. He had been certain the school would not accept him on a transcript of three D's and two F's, but he had been surprised. Nothing is impossible with God!

Unlike earlier in his academic career, Andy took his new liberal arts classes seriously and even excelled. And he found love. When he and Abbey Preston were married, he enrolled in seminary. Andy had wished his parents could understand God's call on his life, but they did not. His acceptance as pastor of the insignificant Baptist church in the nothing town of Cherish, Illinois drew only disdain. It was a matter of social shame for the senior Garretts. After all, they had finally become somebodies in Herndon, and their only son was proving, again, to be an embarrassment.

Andy, however, rejoiced in God's miracle. From a shiftless city-bred bartender, God had molded a humble small-town shepherd! And the First Baptist Church of Cherish had grown dear to his heart.

CHAPTER TWO

CONNECTIONS

From his first day in Cherish, Andy had been determined to get to know and shepherd responsibly the flock God had given him. Pastoral visits had proven to be invaluable in filling in family trees and building pastor-member relationships. Andy and Abbey had loved gathering in homes around the supper table or over a competitive game of Uno.

Some home visits had upset preconceived ideas. For example, the extreme clutter of the Fisher house had been shocking and difficult for Andy and Abbey to reconcile with the neatly dressed and handsome family that filled an entire pew every Sunday. On the other hand, the farm of Clifford and Louise Myers had proven to be surprisingly ordinary. Andy and Abbey had expected to find a broken-down, problem-littered place in keeping with the Myers' many unfortunate accidents and their permanent spot on the church prayer list. But it had not been so.

Unfortunately, illness necessitated home visits, too, like the illness that had stricken Jethro Peters. Lou Gehrig's disease continued to mercilessly rob the man's strength and independence, and his wife, Emma, hovered day and night with her expert and loving care.

Best of all were the home visits that were only a jog away. The large number of church members who lived in the parsonage neighborhood had been a welcome surprise. Neighboring church friends extended invitations to cookouts, home-made ice cream parties, and after-the-rain night crawler hunts with a swarm of children who scrambled by flashlight through everyone's backyards.

Andy and Abbey found that their church-friend neighbors were handy when you needed to borrow a lawn mower or a cup of sugar, and their neighbors generously shared rhubarb and too much zucchini when their gardens overproduced.

The genial Erica and Danny Hart, Betty and Stu Darrell, and Sylvia and Larry Potts had installed the Garretts into their two-block social circle without ceremony—and thought nothing of regularly beating the Pastor in pinochle.

Yes. It felt good to have friends from your congregation as neighbors.

———

While Andy was pastoring from his office during the day, Abbey was often entertaining neighborhood visitors, like Lizzie Potts, who needed some entertaining.

Lizzie tended to wander the backyards, alone. As the youngest of the neighborhood little ones and the only girl, Lizzie's solitude was not her fault. Her brother, Stevie, was either in school or in serious ballgames with his friends—where girls were tolerated only when parents said she had to be included.

Fortunately, Lizzie had a four-legged companion. "Hith name ith Butter," she would lisp when asked.

Clutched unceremoniously by his neck in the crossed crook of her arms, the oversized yellow tomcat never complained. Butter's eyelids were usually shut, and his back legs swung limply between Lizzie's feet. It was unnerving to people who saw the two of them for the first time. Only an occasional swish of Butter's tail and a lazy one-eyed peek to see who was there convinced adults that the cat was not suffering under Lizzie's strangle-hold.

Lizzie and Butter were regulars on the Garrett doorstep, and Abbey looked forward to their visits.

"Do you have any cookies, today?" Lizzie would ask. "Of course," Abbey would reply. "I always have cookies for my friends."

Sometimes Abbey and Lizzie would settle on the porch to munch and talk. And on other occasions, Abbey would invite Lizzie and Butter into the kitchen for milk to wash down their treats.

Abbey loved listening to whatever it was that had captured the little girl's heart that day, and she loved Lizzie's lisped thank yous and quick hugs.

When Abbey and Andy had first come to Cherish, their dream had been to fill a pew with their own little "Lizzies" and "Stevies." But it had not happened. An unexpected consequence of Andy's cancer had been that babies would never be theirs.

For weeks after the oncology doctor's pronouncement, it had been difficult to watch other women rocking infants in the pews. Abbey and Andy had cried. But with time, their disappointment had faded, and visits like Lizzie's had brought healing. Now, every child in the church was, in a sense, theirs. They loved them all. But secretly, Lizzie would ways be Abbey's favorite.

The move to Cherish had also made it possible to reconnect with Andy's sister, Molly Doaks.

Molly and Paul had settled near Chicago while Andy was away at college, but when Andy had shared the news of his new church, he had learned that Molly and Paul were moving, too—to Harmony, a town only thirty minutes from Cherish. Paul's dad had offered Paul the chance to take over the Doaks' family farm, and Paul had jumped at the chance.

The realization of their serendipitous nearness had brought whoops of joy from Molly and Andy. "I can't believe we're going to be so close to one another!" Molly had cried.

As youngsters, Andy and Molly had weathered much, together. Molly, only a couple of years older than Andy, had been her brother's protector during their parents' raging arguments. The children had often huddled among the shoes of their closet while their parents had screamed and denigrated one another outside the door.

Although the abuse had never been physical, it had nevertheless been long-term and damaging. Not only had the children suffered from it, but their mother had also sometimes ended up in the hospital's psych ward to recover. The emotional wounds from the fights might have severely damaged Andy and Molly had it not been for Grannie. Whenever the worst of the verbal storms had spent themselves, and while Rachel Garrett slept sedated at the Herndon Hospital, Rachel's mother had come to restore sanity.

The children's grandmother had originally hailed from the back hills of Kentucky. A small woman with a sharp tongue, brightly rouged lips, and a quick wit, she had suffered no nonsense. Grannie wasn't above using a willow switch when necessary, but she also wielded rewards of hugs and kisses.

With Grannie had come unconditional love and stability. There had never been any fear of stirring an unexpected upset or incurring a siege of wrath on her watch. Instead, Grannie had laughed at the children's stories and had regaled them with tales of her own. And on Friday nights, she had served bowls of hot buttered popcorn and goblets of cold grape juice while she and Andy and Molly had stayed up to watch televised professional wrestling. In front of the black-and-white console TV, the children had cheered whenever Grannie had cheered, and they had booed whenever Grannie had booed, and nobody had ever spoken ill of Gorgeous George. Grannie had been the blessed source of healing and happiness that had dotted their childhood.

Then, when Molly was in high school and Andy was ready to enter junior high, the Garretts had moved from the run-down old house of their poverty and taken up residence in a well-to-do section of town. Mac and Rachel had celebrated Mac's hard-won success as the area's first certified installer of gas-fueled home furnaces, and they had embraced the status of their new wealth. Their money had guaranteed entrance to the Herndon Country Club and a new car. Mac had hobnobbed with city leaders, and Rachel had taken up shopping on the top floor of Buckner's Department Store. A swimming pool in their backyard had glittered like a jewel and had made the children popular. But Mac and Rachel had continued to fight. And when they weren't fighting, they were pressuring their children to plug into their all-consuming social agenda. With every aspect of their teen years socially orchestrated and contrived to enhance the Garrett name, it was little wonder that days after graduation Molly had hurried to marry Paul, and a few years later Andy had escaped to Chicago.

Reunited in Cherish and Harmony—so unexpectedly and after so many years apart—brother and sister were now happily winding their lives back together again, free from the shadow of the dysfunction and control of their parents.

The Doaks now visited the parsonage on Thursday nights, and Andy and Abbey enjoyed Sunday dinners at Molly and Paul's. While at the farm, Andy and Abbey would pick up weekly cartons of fresh eggs, butter, bacon, and pickles. The farm was a wealth of produce and homemade goodness, thanks to the hard work and good management of its fields and livestock.

Andy had expected no less of Paul since Paul had grown up there, but Andy had marveled at how Molly had blossomed as a farm wife. It was as if she had been born to it. Here, her talents, long latent under the constricting oversight of her misguided parents (who had insisted that princesses were to attract wealthy husbands, not keep house), had finally gained expression.

Molly loved to entertain her brother and sister-in-law in her kitchen, where her cooking had come to rival Grannie's. It was not uncommon for Andy and Abbey to overstuff themselves on a Sunday pot roast and Molly's cakes and pies. And if the weather was warm, the Garretts and Doaks would have their dessert on the porch. If it was cold, they would gather for coffee around the fireplace. Either way, they would nod off and awaken just in time to decide on a supper of leftovers, before Andy and Abbey had to leave for home.

Andy and Molly relished their newfound closeness and grieved that their childhood hadn't been like this. Except for their Grannie-respites, the siblings had missed such contented and homey gatherings with family. It was good that they could make up for lost times together, now.

CHAPTER THREE

OPAL REESE

In his office with pen in hand, Andy contemplated the best way to bring his upcoming sermon to a meaningful close. Commentaries and annotated Bibles cluttered the space before him, and the cup of coffee on the corner of his desk was cold. He had just leaned back in his chair when a flash of short, frightfully flyaway dark hair appeared around the study door. A lethally sharp pencil followed, perched behind the sculpted ear of a face that appeared, last.

Church secretary Opal Reese wanted to know if Reverend Garrett had a sermon title, yet, for this Sunday's bulletin.

"'The Prodigal Son Returns,'" Andy announced. "Luke 15:11-32."

Satisfied, the secretary withdrew. Andy heard the peck of efficient fingers adding the missing title and Scripture reference to a page that was otherwise finished. Then, a crisp yank signaled the strip of the bulletin from the platen.

Andy could hear Opal at the mimeograph machine, now—and a sudden panic overtook him.

"Wait!" he cried. Andy nearly toppled his chair in his haste to reach the outer office.

"Wait!"

He couldn't remember if he'd given Opal the right hymn titles. He should have thought of that before he heard her tear the

17

page from the typewriter. Andy knew how quickly she worked, and it might already be too late.

He blurted out, "Do you have hymns 196 and 225?"

Puzzled, she replied, "Uh-huh…"

Andy tried to recover, nonchalantly. "Oh. Okay, then," he said. Then he coolly lingered and glanced over her shoulder, as if he had merely been interested in the operation of the mimeograph.

Opal smiled with a raised brow and kept cranking. He knew she knew he had panicked, and she knew he knew she knew. But it was okay.

By the time Andy had come shooting out of his office, Opal had already run a dozen copies and would have the remainder run and folded in minutes. The woman's proficiency never ceased to amaze him.

He knew he couldn't have had a better secretary if he'd served a church of thousands. Opal kept Andy apprised of everything he needed to know about the congregation, seldom made typographical errors, masterfully operated the office equipment, and made great coffee.

On top of that, she had a unique talent that Andy hoped to preview now that his emergency had passed.

At First Baptist, Opal had established herself as a kind of poetic celebrity. Her poetry was often mere doggerel, but Andy had found that she had a knack for mining a nugget of truth and lacing it with humor in rhyme. Andy felt Opal watching him as he casually passed her desk and thumbed through her monthly newsletter draft.

"It's on page three," she offered.

Andy nodded and thanked her. (It was humbling to be that transparent.)

Without looking up from the mimeograph, Opal added, "I have a friend who never goes to church. He used to go (when he was younger), but he now thinks he doesn't need to. He says he gets just as much out of the sermons he hears on television. I call it utter laziness! He's going to be sorry, someday, for neglecting his church attendance."

Andy grinned as he read:

TV FELLOWSHIP
By Opal Reese

Still dressed in striped pajamas,
On the sofa, you recline;
You're settled in on Sunday morn'
For "TV Chapel Time."

You set your cup of coffee down
On a nearby TV tray
And munch your toast and marmalade
Until it's time to pray.

No need to fill an offering plate
Or shush a baby's cry;
And from your favorite front-row seat,
My, how the time does fly!

No problem with the traffic.
When the services are done,
You're front-row parked on your sofa—
And kick-off time is One!

The preacher never stops to call.
You teach no Sunday school.
There is no one to gossip if
You break the Golden Rule.

And, best of all, if you miss it all
To give your car a lube,
There are no stares, next Sunday morn',
When you worship at the tube.

And when someday you're sick in bed
And alone and afraid you'll die,
Don't bother to call your TV church,
'Cause no one will stop by.

Then, when at last you leave this earth
For the "big one" in the sky,
Don't think your church will shed a tear—
A TV doesn't cry.

Andy's literary critique was a loud "Amen!" and Opal grinned broadly.

A previous pastor had not been as accepting of her talent. When the young Reverend Garrett had chuckled at her verses on his first day, Opal had known they were going to get along just fine.

Abbey appreciated Opal nearly as much as her husband did. Abbey knew that in some small churches, the pastor's wife served as the church secretary. She had not wanted the job. She and Andy approached things too differently, and it would not be good for them to work day-after-day in the same office. Abbey was content to take care of the Pastor outside of his office.

Today, she and Andy had a lunch date, and Abbey waited in an office chair for Noon to come. It gave her a few minutes to observe Andy and Opal on the job.

"Oh, yeah; I need another insert, too," Andy was saying.

Although Opal had just finished cranking the Bible study handouts, she didn't register the least bit of aggravation. Opal took Andy's last-minute change in stride—an attribute that deeply impressed Abbey.

Abbey also knew that, in spite of a scattered first impression (Opal unwittingly created a startling wild-woman look by habitually raking her fingers through her hair), Opal always had things under control. When Opal was in charge, everything in the office ran smoothly and efficiently. Only when she went to visit little Zephyr, her first grandchild, and left Andy alone did things sometimes get a little bumpy.

Andy had confided to Abbey that the mimeograph mocked him whenever Opal was gone. The machine had won an exasperating skirmish just last month. Andy's attempt to run off a single sheet of notes for a Bible study handout had taken him over an hour, and all the while, the telephone had rung nonstop. Andy had vowed never to be alone with the office equipment, again. He wasn't sure he could handle a repeat without "screaming into the sunset."

"Don't ever leave me," Andy had implored when Opal had returned, and the much-appreciated secretary had chuckled.

Now, the clock on the courthouse tower struck twelve.

Opal straightened the pile of freshly run handouts and scribbled a reminder about the additional instructions Andy had given her. Then she pulled out her purse, shoved her arms into her coat, and jangled her keys.

Andy hurried into his coat, too. As Opal locked the door, Reverend Garrett leisurely led his wife down the sun-strewn sidewalk to the Star Diner on the square for lunch. After lunch, they would stroll over to the Fourth Street Bakery for dessert.

"I love you," Andy murmured as he clutched Abbey's hand tighter. "I've got the prettiest wife in town!"

CHAPTER FOUR

HORACE SAUNDERS

As always at Noon, hungry Star Diner patrons jockeyed for seats. Andy and Abbey gratefully accepted Reverend Grassley's offer to share his booth. When the waitress swung by to fill Grassley's empty coffee cup, she expertly slid full cups in front of the Garretts and set out glasses of water. Andy ordered the baked steak and Abbey chose the fish sandwich.

After the coffee pot and pony-tail had retreated, Andy toyed with his cup. He uncomfortably wondered what to say if Grassley brought up the subject of Horace Saunders.

Horace had been Methodist only three months ago but now was firmly ensconced in the pews of the First Baptist Church. Andy hoped the Methodist minister knew that Horace's move had not been the result of proselytizing by the Baptists.

Sure enough, Grassley began, "Well. How's our friend, Horace, doing?"

Andy swallowed nervously. "J-Just fine," he stuttered. "Just fine. It-it was a surprise to see him at First Baptist."

Grassley laughed. "Relax," he said. "This isn't the first time Horace has done a little church hopping. He's been over at the Presbyterian Church, too. No doubt, he'll be back at our church before he's done."

Andy nodded. It was good to know there were no hard feelings. Andy did wonder, however, what had driven Horace to leave Reverend Grassley. He wondered if it had anything to do with Horace's intense preoccupation with the End Times. In case it was a different reason that had sent Saunders to the other side of the square, Andy didn't bring it up. But he did wonder how long it might be before Horace would leave First Baptist for another congregation.

Thankfully, the arrival of their food changed the subject.

———⟫●⟪———

Reluctantly, Andy cleared the half-finished sermon from his desk. Horace Saunders would be here any moment. It was the last Thursday of the month, and the courthouse clock had just chimed ten.

Andy had learned to expect a visit from Horace every last Thursday. At any minute, without an appointment, his formerly Methodist parishioner would arrive to drink a cup of Opal's coffee and engage in speculations and observations about "the rapidly approaching End of the Age."

Sure enough, one minute after ten, Horace knocked lightly on the study door. Andy nodded for him to enter, and he stood to pour his square-jawed guest a cup of coffee. Horace nodded yes for some cream and laid claim to one of the padded office chairs. He planted his elbow familiarly on its arm.

"Did you see the paper, last night?" Horace began.

Andy knew that every headline heralded an End Times milestone for Horace: the first test-tube baby, the Jim Jones suicide deaths, the peace award to Egypt and Israel, and the Iran hostage situation. The material for contemplation was endless.

Today, Horace had seized upon the price of gold. "Did you see where the price of gold has hit $850?" he asked. "That's what the Bible says is going to happen in the Last Days!"

Andy smiled. "I did read where gold prices have soared."

"But don't you see?" Horace responded excitedly, "It's just like the verse in that Larry Norman song, 'Wish We'd All Been Ready.'"

Before Andy could reply, Horace quickly quoted the line: "'a piece of bread could buy a bag of gold.'"

Andy wished Horace knew his Bible as well as he knew the song lyrics. Andy told Horace that he appreciated the sentiment of Larry Norman's song but he thought it was better to stick with God's Word on the subject.

"Actually," Andy said, "gold and its price aren't mentioned in the Revelation prediction."

Horace was going to protest, but Andy had opened his Bible and showed Horace the verses. "See?" said Andy. "Revelation 6:6 says that a day's wage will be required to buy enough wheat to make a loaf of bread. That means food is going to be scarce and expensive during the Tribulation period—but it doesn't say we should become fixated on gold."

Horace shrugged it off. "It means the same thing," he said. "You're going to starve without a bag of money. Isn't that awful?"

Andy was amazed at how excited Horace became over the Bible's predictions of tragedy. Horace seemed to think it was going to be like TV: the fires and earthquakes, plagues and famines, wars, and darkness would all be happening somewhere else in the world, and Horace would sit untouched and watch it in his living room. Horace would wisely expound to his neighbors about all that was happening—because he had read it in the last chapters of the Bible.

As always, Andy reminded Horace that the prophecies were warnings and that they were supposed to encourage people to turn back to God and avoid the End Time judgments. "Remember, Horace," Andy said, "Second Peter 3:9 says the Lord is patient, not wanting anyone to perish, but wanting everyone to come to repentance."

Horace smiled and nodded, "You're right, of course, Pastor. And isn't it a shame that people won't listen?"

Andy let the comment hang in the air. He did think it a shame.

Horace stirred sugar into his coffee and asked wistfully, "Pastor, do you think we'll get to see any of the big End Times doings—you know, the terrible judgments the book of Revelation describes?"

They had been over this ground before, but Andy knew he'd have to say it again.

"Well, Horace," Andy said as he leaned back in his chair, took on a scholarly scowl, and laced his fingers behind his head, "nobody but God knows the exact schedule of events. Many scholars think God's going to rapture His people before all of the judgments begin. That's because there are sixteen references to the 'Church' in the first three chapters of Revelation, but there's not one mention of the Church in the Tribulation chapters, six through eighteen. Perhaps that's because the believing Church has been snatched out of this world supernaturally before the Tribulation and judgments begin."

Horace's face dropped. Clearly, he was disappointed.

"Well, Pastor, I think that's a pretty skimpy argument for a pre-tribulation rapture. Actually," he sniffed, "I'm absolutely convinced we're in the midst of some of that stuff, now. Things are looking pretty bad, pretty bad."

As he often did, Horace shook his head woefully and took another long draw on his coffee.

Andy agreed that the world was continuing its downhill slide, but he observed that things didn't seem to be much worse than when the disciples were being tossed to the lions. The disciples had thought they would see Christ's return in their day, too, but God had evidently chosen to delay.

"Whether Jesus returns before or after the Tribulation," Andy said, "we can be glad that His delay lets more people seek His salvation and avoid the eternal wrath to come."

"And," Andy emphasized, "He expects to find the Church busy about His work whenever He decides to sound the trumpet call."

Horace nodded his head sagely, but Andy wondered if that part of the message sank in with him. Andy hoped so. More people needed to hear the Word.

As the hands of the clock approached eleven, Andy tried not to be too obvious in checking the time. Eleven was when Horace would leave for his standing appointment with Jim Kirby, the barber. Andy imagined that the barbershop walls and Jim's ears would re-echo with Horace's predictions.

Andy tried to remember: was Kirby a Methodist or a Presbyterian?

CHAPTER FIVE

PRAYERS FOR JAKE

From his chair behind the pulpit, just before the morning service began, Andy saw that inveterate talker Leo Ryan had waylaid Luther Sharp. Planted squarely in front of Luther's face and well into the church moderator's private space, Leo had effectively cut off all avenues of escape and had launched into one of his mind-seizing monologues. Mercifully, Leo's wife, Sybil, appeared and tugged on her husband's sleeve. When Leo paused to respond, Luther sprang away with the speed of an escaping cat. By the time Leo looked back, Luther had slid into the open seat next to his wife and had opened his bulletin.

In surprise, Leo opened and shut his mouth and then turned back to Sybil. The sweet-faced woman gently led her loquacious husband to a seat a few rows down. Andy didn't know how she did it; Sybil was the only person on the planet who seemed able to interrupt Leo's pauseless onslaughts and gain his attention. Plus she did it without saying a word. Sybil had no doubt saved many grateful subjects from death by talking.

From the vantage point of the sanctuary platform, Andy also noticed that Elsie Trimble was absent. It was most unusual for the spunky spinster not to be seated next to her friend, Vivian Holladay. Andy hoped Elsie hadn't become ill, and he made a mental note to ask about her, after church.

Now, after a grandly trumpeted crescendo, the organ prelude ended abruptly. In the dramatic silence that followed, all whispers and conversations throughout the room ceased. Deacon Danny Hart rose to extend the morning's greeting. The call to worship followed, and then came the opening hymn, invocation, *Gloria Patri*, gathering of tithes and offerings, *Doxology*, second congregational hymn, and choir anthem. The pattern was virtually the same every Sunday.

When it was finally his turn, Andy stepped to the pulpit, read the Scripture passage, and launched into the morning's sermon. Andy found it satisfying to see that the children were listening as attentively as their parents. Even the little ones knew this morning's parable. The story of the prodigal son was a favorite. Andy presented his three points from Luke 15:11-24 and then summarized:

"The profligate young man in Jesus' parable knew he did not deserve more than the place of a slave in his father's household. He had foolishly demanded his inheritance early—long before his father would die—and he had bid good riddance to his father, an older brother, and all the stifling constraints of home. The young man had moved far away and spent all his money in wild living. When finally penniless and hungry, he had decided to drag himself back to his father's house. He remembered how well-housed and fed his father's servants had been, and in his hunger, he was ready to serve his family in humiliation for the rest of his life. The young man thought to himself (as we read in verses 18-19), *"I will say... 'Father, I have sinned against heaven and against you. I am no longer worthy to be called your son; make me like one of your hired men.'"*

"But," Andy continued, "what the son could not have expected was that his father would gather up his robes and run out to meet him on the path when he saw him coming. With tears of joy and with arms held wide, His father welcomed him home and re-instated him as his son.

"Imagine, now, that you are the wayward child and God is the father," said Andy, "because we and God ARE the point of this parable. How wonderful to read that God pulls up the skirts of His robes so He can RUN to receive us when we finally come home. Yes, our God runs! Our Heavenly Father is not ashamed to show His feelings—even if it costs Him some dignity.

"But then, we already know He is like that. Our Father threw away all dignity when, in the form of His Son, He chose to hang naked and torn on a cruel cross on our behalf. If anything, this parable shows we must never think we are too sinful or have wandered too far away for our God to welcome us back."

Andy added that "earlier in that same chapter of Luke, Jesus tells of the joy of a shepherd who finds a lost sheep. Jesus says (in verse 7): *"I tell you that in the same way there is…rejoicing in heaven over one sinner who repents."*

"God loves you," Andy said, "more than you can imagine. And He is always eager to welcome you home."

It was lunchtime on Monday, and Andy was still eating when Hester Hall telephoned the parsonage. Andy didn't mind the interruption on his day off. Emergencies for the pastor's time didn't take a day off, and he knew that Hester would not have called unless it was important. She asked if he could come to her house.

"Of course, Hester," he said. "I'll be there in about half an hour."

When Andy pulled into the Hall drive, he marveled again at the smallness of the place. It always made him think of a cabin or a large shed. The shady, overhanging boughs of a giant catalpa tree made the home seem even smaller.

It was tidy, though. Andy observed that its only shrub had been trimmed, and the postage stamp of a lawn had been mowed recently. He assumed that the boys had done it, because he knew Kent Hall was too ill.

He parked and walked up the steps. Hester must have seen him coming because she greeted him at the door before he could knock. The saintly-looking woman was alone, and although she was composed now, it was evident she had been crying.

Andy followed her to the doily-decorated sofa and sat next to her as she gripped her apron with the news that Jake, her youngest grandson, had been arrested for theft at the service station along the highway.

"I need you to take me to the county jail," Hester explained stoically. "I would go myself, but our son, Will, needed our car to take Kent to his doctor's appointment this afternoon. I'm sorry to impose, but I was hoping you would pray with me and then we could go get Jake."

Andy assured her he was glad to help, and as Hester nodded her thanks, she stood.

Andy could see Hester's coat over the chair by the door, and he saw her purse and an extra hanky waiting there, but Hester did not move toward them. Instead, she tugged the sofa cushions to the floor and reached for Andy's help to her knees.

Andy realized the second cushion was for him, and he knelt beside her.

Hester bowed over the sofa, with hands tightly clasped at her forehead, and she began to pray. The little woman drew into God's presence with such familiarity and reverence that Andy was humbled, and she petitioned Heaven with such earnestness for Jake's soul that a lump formed in Andy's throat. When Hester asked Andy to close, he imagined the breath of God on the back of his bowed head. Surely, God had bent that close to hear this woman's prayer.

Before he rose from his knees, Andy wondered if Grannie's prayers for him had been like this. He had learned that she had prayed for his salvation, and he was thankful that God had answered. Andy prayed now that God would answer Hester's prayers for Jake, too.

Andy stood and helped Hester into her coat and into his car for the short trip to the county jail. It was a place Andy had been to only once before. He and Hester checked in at the front desk, and an officer led them through the various doors to Jake's cell. The clang of the officer's keys echoed through the hall as the cell door was opened.

Not caring what others might think, the 350-pound young man behind the bars crumbled in shame the minute he saw his grandmother. Jake wept, "I'm sorry, Grandma. I'm so sorry."

Tiny Hester drew his sobs into her shoulder.

Andy watched their tender exchange and wondered how this little woman could be related to such a giant. In fact, all of the Halls were big, except for her.

After a minute, Hester gently but firmly drew Jake to his knees. The young man sank limply and did not resist. He had been led like this, before. He knew his grandmother's ways.

Hester knelt beside him—this time, without the benefit of pillows—and although her arthritic knees suffered on the cement, she poured out her prayers, as before. Andy prayed, too. Jake could only cry out, "I'm sorry, God! Help me to do right!"

When they finished and Hester was ready to rise, Jake's assistance to her was tender. He lifted his grandmother as if she might break. Then, before she let go of his arm, Hester gripped the giant boy in a fierce hug and told him how much she and his grandpa loved him. "You need to get your life right, Jake!" she said. "Get yourself right with God and the law."

31

When the deputy escorted Andy and Hester out of the cell, Jake remained inside, bent over his cot in shame.

Back in the main entrance to the jail, Hester marched purposefully to the front desk. She opened her purse and dug out the money for Jake's bail. Andy observed that it was as if she'd done this a hundred times before. His heart ached as he watched her. He had heard that she had, indeed, done this before with her son and with another grandson, many years ago. Andy also knew that Hester and her husband had little in the way of earthly goods and that this money was a burden for them. But he also knew it was pointless to discourage Hester from making the sacrifice.

"This is what family does," she said as if reading his mind.

Andy knew that because of lung cancer, Hester's husband, Kent, had been on disability for some time from the fire department in Harmony. Danny Hart had said that although money was tight for Hester and Kent, they still had more money than their son, Will, or their daughter, Lou Ann. Jake and his brother Earl were Will's boys. And Lenny, Sawyer, Red, and Dexter were Lou Ann's. All of them were hard workers, but somehow they never managed to save a dime. It often fell to Hester and Kent to hold things together.

As Head Deacon, Danny had said, "The church is always ready whenever the time comes that Hester can't handle the need. Right now, she'll just say no."

When Jake finally walked out of the jailhouse, Andy overheard him vow to get a job and repay his grandmother as soon as he could. Andy imagined the young man would try.

That night, the way dreams sometimes do, Andy's dreams mixed the events of his day with the undercurrent of his past. Andy saw his grandmother on her knees, and he saw the results of her prayers: his spiritual awakening, his path to seminary, his call to Cherish, and his path forward, now, with God's hand leading him.

When he awoke, Andy wished Grannie wasn't 300 miles away. He wished he could hug and thank her. And he wished she could hear him preach.

She had come last Thanksgiving weekend expecting to hear him preach. But Grannie's visit, in the company of his parents, to see him and Molly had been cut short when they had all departed before Sunday. With Grannie in tow, Mac and Rachel had unexpectedly left Molly's and Paul's in the dark of night. No doubt, there had been some sort of a fight.

Andy doubted that his parents had any idea how their abrupt departure had hurt him. And he wondered if it had hurt Grannie, too. Grannie had been the only one from his family (until Molly's coming to the faith) who had understood and celebrated his calling. Andy wondered if his parents would ever understand.

When Molly had telephoned to say they had left, Abbey had comforted her husband with the words, "the next time Grannie comes, she will be in church."

Andy had impatiently waited for the "next time." He still wondered if and when the next time would be.

CHAPTER SIX

SLEDDING

Earlier in the week, Luther Sharp and Danny Hart had straightened the storage room in the church basement, and they had set a large pile of discarded items and trash by the parking lot for pickup on Friday. A few inches of late-spring snow had lent the collection a sculpted look that intrigued young Jimmy Fisher. The teenager wondered what the pile contained, and since there was time before the youth fellowship meeting would begin, he started to poke through it.

Jimmy was an expert on piles of things. It was Jimmy's home that had astounded Andy and Abbey with its clutter. The Fisher living room had overflowed with an enormous pile of "stuff." It appeared that whatever one had had in hand upon entering the house had been casually tossed down and seldom or never collected again. With eight people contributing to the stash, the pile had become considerable. As large as the collection was, however, the Fisher clutter contained no garbage (nothing perishable), and it was different from a hoarder's stash in that there were no stacks of newspapers or piles of things in groups by kind. The pile was simply a pile filled with everything from old toys to car parts, clothing to Christmas decorations, bird cages to old radios, and ever so much more.

Tonight, with the eye of a practiced pile picker, Jimmy bypassed things of little interest; but then, under his breath, he whispered, "Hey! What's this?"

He had come across a large stack of hard plastic food trays like those found in school cafeterias. How the trays had come to be part of the church trash, he couldn't imagine; but it didn't matter. All that mattered was that they were there.

Jimmy tugged at the stack until he worked it free from the pile. Then he dragged the trays, a few at a time, to where the ground sloped at the other end of the parking lot. Jimmy picked a tray from the stack, and just as youth director Chelsea Mitchell arrived, he launched himself onto the hard plastic surface and sped with a crazy spin to the bottom of the snowy hill. The fact that Jimmy landed upside-down didn't bother him at all. A soft drift had cushioned the end of his ride. Still hooting with pleasure, he grabbed the tray and started back up the hill for another run.

Chelsea clapped her hands. Harking back to an adventurous childhood, the youth director gamely approached the hill and grabbed a tray, too. Not as foolhardy as Jimmy, Chelsea carefully backed onto her slippery transport. When it threatened to take off without her, she dug in her heels and scolded it, but she finally managed to grip the tray edges and plant herself solidly for a run. The makeshift sled flew at a speed that left her breathless. It was faster than anything from her youth.

Exhilarated and safe at the bottom, Chelsea looked up to see other teens arriving. Suddenly she remembered her responsibility. "This could be dangerous," she thought, and she felt guilty for having let her fun urge take over before her I'm-the-responsible-adult-and-the-youth-director sense kicked in. She needed to end this now before other teens tried it and got hurt.

But it was too late. Following Chelsea's example, others from the youth group had already grabbed trays and were flying over the hillside with wild hoots and hollers.

Chelsea bit her lip and prayed that no one would break a leg. She hoped the kids' parents wouldn't think she had planned this.

Before that worrisome thought could fade, however, a very adult Benjamin-By-the-Way, who had come for the midweek service, grabbed a tray. Chelsea watched in shock as the grown man launched on the run and called out "Here I come!" His wife stood by, helplessly chewing her nails, as Benjamin swooped recklessly down the hill.

Chelsea gulped again when Bob and Ann Parks shoved off together on two trays, holding hands. The chubby couple collided partway down the hill and ended with backsides together in a pile of laughter.

Others would have followed, but several women intervened. They were sternly insistent that their husbands would kill themselves. "You'll break your neck!" Betty Darrell warned when Stu reached for a tray. Stu heeded his wife and backed off. But Danny Hart managed to get in at least one run before Erica gripped his arm and led him away from "foolishly courting disaster."

The teens continued to fly, however; and the hill grew slicker with each run.

Howard Thompson and Josie Fisher were hurtling down the bank for the fourth time when Pastor Garrett's car pulled into the lot. Before Abbey could blink, Andy had run to the edge of the slope, wound his muffler tighter about his neck, and shoved off on a tray. From an upside-down pile at the hill bottom, he laughingly roared up at her, "What a ride! Come on down!"

"I can't," Abbey yelled back. "I didn't wear my boots. Besides, it's time for church."

She was envisioning an emergency-room run and hoped that Andy would regain his sense. He needed to assume some leadership to get things back on track. Andy laughed because he knew she was worried he was going to break a leg.

And she was right, of course: the voice of reason. It was time to be inside.

"Awww! Can't we slide a little longer?" the teens (and a couple of adults) protested. But the fun was over.

Chelsea corralled her teens, and Andy trudged back up the hill to lead the adults indoors. The youth headed downstairs, and the Garretts shepherded everyone else through the overflow room and into the sanctuary.

———

Usually, the midweek Bible study was somewhat somber, but not tonight. With cheeks rosy from the cold and bodies pumped from sledding (or from worry, as in the case of the non-sledding women), everyone jabbered like the teacher was out of the room.

Bob Parks laughed and said how good it was to see the old food trays used for something productive. "We scavenged them from the cafeteria when the old high school was torn down," he said. "Never knew what to use them for, until now!"

The only one not laughing was Vivian Holladay. She wasn't sure how much levity was appropriate when in church, and at her advanced age she had not been among those "traying" down the hill. In addition to her exceptional reserve, Andy noticed that Vivian was sitting alone, again. He was concerned. Usually, her friend, Elsie, occupied the seat to her left. While the group continued to relive their sledding fun, Andy leaned in to ask Vivian about Elsie.

"Is Elsie all right?" Andy asked. "I see she's not with you this evening. Hasn't she returned from her visit?"

With her back characteristically ramrod straight against the pew and her hands folded properly in her lap, Vivian replied, "Elsie's still in Topeka with her sister. She's grown ill, and it's turned into pneumonia. They've taken Elsie to the hospital."

"Miss Vivian, I'm so sorry to hear that!" Andy cried. "We should add Elsie to the prayer list."

"That would be most appropriate," said Vivian with a half nod. It was the type of nod Andy felt sure she had conferred on bright students when they had recited correct answers years ago in her classroom.

Andy returned the nod and moved to the podium to begin the session. He was worried about Elsie. Pneumonia was nothing to take lightly at her age, and Andy hoped she would be able to fight it off and return home soon. It seemed wrong for Elsie not to be in her pew with her friend.

Prayers that evening were said aloud for Elsie—and silently for Vivian. The prayers for Vivian were silent, because although everyone knew how much Vivian missed her friend, they also knew that Vivian would not be inclined to have her emotional state discussed publicly, even in prayer.

Everyone knew that the two starchily proper women had spent their careers teaching at the same school, and they knew that Elsie and Vivian had remained close friends into their retirement. From their south-section pew in church every Sunday, the two women had continued to reign with an authoritative propriety, as if the entire congregation was their classroom.

Since nearly all of the middle-aged church members had passed through their tutorial molding at one time or another, it was understandable that the women were treated with respect. And it was easy to tell who the former students were because they always referred to Elsie and Vivian as "Miss Trimble" and "Miss Holladay."

Andy knew that things simply would not be right at First Baptist until Miss Trimble returned.

Following the Bible study, Abbey and several others made their way to the choir room for practice. Abbey had finally joined the singers.

Abbey had always known she was welcome, but she had wanted to sit in the pews during Andy's first months at the church. From the pews, she could smile up at him and encourage him as he spoke. If she sat in the choir loft, she would be behind him. Now, after nearly a year, Abbey was ready to vacate her pew.

When Abbey mentioned her intent to come to practice, choir director Marilyn Ingraham had pressed her hands together in joy. "We have a lot of solid altos," Marilyn had confided. "But we need someone like you, who the other sopranos can follow with confidence."

Marilyn's only regret, she said, was that Abbey didn't play the piano and organ.

"Sorry, Marilyn," Abbey apologized, "but I was an art major; not a music major. Voice lessons and college choir were electives for me. I can read the music, but I have no skill on the piano, and I wouldn't know where to begin on the organ. Besides, Theresa does a terrific job!"

"Yes, she does," agreed Marilyn. "But whenever Theresa's absent, we are without the organ and we are hard-pressed for a pianist."

It was true that Theresa Jackson could seamlessly slide from one instrument to the other and that she was the only one at First Baptist who played the organ. But Abbey knew the empty organ bench was not Marilyn's primary concern. "Hard-pressed for a pianist" meant that Lena Thorndike would be at the keyboard.

It was a sore spot with Marilyn.

Abbey was sympathetic but tried not to indulge Marilyn's discontent. Abbey knew that as a piano substitute, Lena could be a trial for any choir director. The problem wasn't that Lena didn't play well—because she did. It was that, at eighty-two, she was set in her ways—and Lena was nearly stone deaf. Only so much could be conveyed with hand gestures—and that was only if Lena was watching you. During choir practice, if Marilyn wanted to stop and run through a section they hadn't quite perfected, it was not unusual to have to wait for Lena to finish playing the entire piece before they could go back. On Sunday mornings, Lena often played all five verses of a selected hymn, even though Marilyn had just announced they would sing only verses one, three, and five. Spontaneity was virtually impossible when Lena was at the piano, and near chaos reigned if Marilyn or the pastor announced a last-minute hymn change from what appeared in the bulletin.

Abbey was actually in awe that Lena could play the piano at all without hearing it. Abbey could hear the notes, but she couldn't play much beyond *Chop Sticks*. Lena was a wonder!

Secretly, Abbey was relieved that she couldn't play piano because Abbey much preferred to sing. Also, Abbey knew how much pride Lena took in still being useful at her age.

CHAPTER SEVEN

GOOD-BYE, KENT

"Opal, did I possibly leave my green sweater in the fourth pew on the right on Sunday?" asked Ivey Webb over the phone. "I can't seem to find it, and the last place I remember having it was in church."

Opal put her hand over the mouthpiece and yelled in to Andy to see if, perhaps, he had seen the sweater.

"I'll go and check," Andy called. "I need to stretch my legs, anyway."

Opal told Ivey she would call her back.

Andy marked his place in the commentary and rolled away from the desk. With a great stretch, he yawned and pushed himself up from the chair. He'd been studying nonstop for a couple of hours. It was time for a break; he needed to move.

Andy made his way into the outer office. Opal was typing entries into the blank boxes of the next month's calendar for the newsletter. He nodded to her and then strolled through the door and down the hall to the sanctuary.

There, sure enough, in one of the pews on the right, he found a green sweater and a flowered handkerchief. He collected the items and turned. But instead of making his way back to the office immediately, Andy stopped. He stood for a moment in the sanctuary silence. It was wonderfully peaceful.

Unlike Sunday mornings, which were busy with corporate worship, it was quiet and still in this consecrated room. Andy basked in the moment. The sunshine through the stained glass cast rainbows of color over everything. It felt holy. Andy lifted his eyes and breathed, "It's good to be in Your House, Lord. Bless Your Name!"

As Andy lowered his gaze, he could visualize all the familiar Sunday-morning faces and where each member sat while he preached. Andy thought about them and their needs, and he thought about how special they all were to him. Slowly, he began to walk up the aisle. At each pew, he paused to say a prayer for the people who sat there.

"Bring healing for Charlene Fisher's mother," he whispered. "And help Benjamin By-the-Way get the raise he needs at work. Help Samantha Peerie through her latest 'blessing.' And help Elsie Trimble recover from her pneumonia and return home."

The list of concerns was long, and Andy took the time to pray for them all.

———————

Back in the office, more time had passed than Opal had expected, and after a good half-hour, she came to check on Andy. At the sanctuary door, she stopped. Opal watched as Andy moved with eyes closed from row to row and as he stopped to touch each pew post and pray.

The scene moved her. Opal knew that Andy was lifting up the concerns of the church members to God. She bowed her head for a moment to whisper a prayer of her own: "God, thank you for this dedicated pastor and how much he loves Your people. You've blessed us with Andy and Abbey, and I pray You will let us keep them in Cherish for a long time."

Opal then turned and withdrew. Without a sound, she walked back to the office to wait for Andy's return.

———

"Sorry I took so long," Andy apologized when he laid Ivey's sweater and handkerchief on Opal's desk.

Opal had busied herself. She looked up now and gave the impression that she hadn't missed him.

"No problem," Opal said. With her usual efficiency, she finished a line of type and then telephoned to let Ivey know that Andy had found her sweater. Ivey would collect it, later.

For some reason, Opal felt guilty for having spied on Andy. She now covered her awkwardness with some forced banter.

"You should be glad the parsonage isn't next to the church," she sniffed. "My cousin says their preacher complains that people call them day and night about something left in the fellowship hall, or to be let in for some reason or other."

Andy just chuckled. "I can see where that could be bothersome," he said. "I guess we live just the right distance away."

His response carried no hint that he had heard her in the hallway observing him. Satisfied, Opal relaxed.

When Andy walked back into his study to pick up where he had left off on his sermon writing, Opal turned back to her typewriter.

"God," she whispered over a blank page, "bless him."

———

At first, the ringing seemed far away in his dream, but with a start, Andy realized (at the same time Abbey did) that the sound came from the telephone in the kitchen. He threw off the covers and stumbled out of the bedroom. When he answered, his voice came out lower than usual, but he tried to sound awake.

It was Lou Ann Lamb, the Hall's daughter. Could he come to her parents' home?

Andy answered in the affirmative. He didn't bother to ask questions—partly because he was still half-asleep and partly because he assumed Kent had taken a turn for the worse. Kent's health had been precarious for many months, now, and it was inevitable that his time would come.

The hands on the clock pointed to twelve thirty-five. Andy had been asleep for only two hours.

He stiffly dressed, and Abbey followed him about, to hand him his jacket and find his keys. Then with a peck on his cheek, she sent him on his way.

When Andy arrived at the Hall's, he saw every light in the place turned on and three cars parked in the street. Yes. It was as he had expected. Andy braced himself for the tears that must be flowing on the other side of the door. He knocked and composed himself.

But suddenly—with a jerk—the door flew open. Instantly, the smell of fresh popcorn startled Andy's nose—and the noise was deafening! Andy recognized the sounds of all-star wrestling, but for some reason, the sound was turned up so high he couldn't hear a thing that Lou Ann was saying. He just followed her into the house.

The walls shook. Instead of the somber tragedy Andy had been expecting to find, the living room was alive with cheering men, women, and grandkids. Hester's husband, Kent, who held the prime spot in front of the television in an oversized recliner, couldn't yell because of his diseased lungs, but he was pounding

44

the arm of the chair with every up and down of the combatants on the screen. The din of the television's roar was drowned out only by the Hall family's thunderous yells.

Andy was sure he hadn't been called to watch the match. He was confused and tried to get answers from Lou Ann, but his voice could not compete with the living room noise. Amid more explosive shouts from the watchers in front of the television, Lou Ann lifted a finger and beckoned Andy to follow her into the kitchen.

Andy marveled as he followed Lou Ann, that like her brother and all of the grandchildren, she took after her father's side of the family. Towering two inches above Andy and weighing probably three hundred pounds, Lou Ann was the smallest of the giants in the little house.

As Andy had suspected, in the Hall's cramped kitchen and with the door closed, they could still barely hear one another. Andy nodded to Hester, who stood at the sink doing dishes, and Lou Ann yelled, "Pastor, we're all here, tonight, because Pa doesn't have much time left, and before he dies we want to let him know how much we love him. We just aren't sure how to go about it. We want to do it right, and Ma said you'd know."

Lou Ann said it matter-of-factly, and Andy's heart swelled at the gentleness and genuineness of it, even though it came out in a yell. He knew the deep love that all of the Hall children and grandchildren felt for Hester and Kent.

Because Andy knew his answer mattered, he thought for a moment and said a silent prayer that he hoped God could hear over the din. "Well," he yelled back, "why not tell him tonight? Is the wrestling match over soon?"

"It'll be over in ten minutes," Lou Ann hollered after she checked her watch.

"Okay, let's wait for it to finish, and we'll all gather in the living room," yelled Andy. "You can take turns sharing. It doesn't have to be long—just a sentence or two. He'll know what you mean."

Lou Ann nodded her approval. Andy sat in a chair beside the kitchen table while Lou Ann helped her mother finish the dishes. As soon as the match ended, they headed for the living room.

"Turn off the television," Lou Ann hollered at the top of her lungs (the boys were loudly reliving the match over the sound of a television commercial that was already deafening).

"Now move Pa's chair," she ordered. She pointed to a spot in the center of the room. Andy's eardrums still throbbed even though the noise was gone.

The boys obeyed. They set Kent's oxygen tank in his lap and scooted his massive recliner into place.

"Now," said Lou Ann, at normal volume, "Pastor says we can share something we want to let Pa know before he dies."

Andy noticed that the frankness of her statement caused no consternation. There was no offense in it, and none was taken. Instead, in virtual silence, everyone gathered around Kent and stood in a circle, waiting expectantly for what would come next. Lou Ann and her brother, Will, stood behind their father's chair, and as if coordinating their actions by some rehearsed plan, they slowly swiveled the chair to face the oldest grandson.

"Say something," said Lou Ann.

With no thought for having been put on the spot, Lenny nodded and took a step forward. He cleared his throat, thought for a moment, and then said, "Grandpa, I love you, and I don't want you to die. But because I know you're going to, I want you to know I'll always remember how we used to go hunting together. You showed me how to be patient and wait for the deer to come to us, and we always got one, didn't we?"

Dark circles and the fatigue of the disease lined Kent's face, but now his eyes crinkled, and his mouth grinned. "Sure did," Kent croaked pleasantly, and then he wheezed.

Lenny stepped back into place, and the chair was swiveled again. This time, it faced Sawyer.

The biggest of the boys, Sawyer was also the shyest. Although he hung his head, he stepped up. With a big sigh, he said, "Grandpa, I love you, too, and I'm going to miss you a whole lot. I'm going to miss our visits to the stock car races. Those sure were good times."

When Sawyer slipped self-consciously back into the circle, Kent nodded and wheezed. In a strained whisper, Kent said, "Those were good times."

As Andy stood and watched, the chair continued to swivel until it had faced each of the grandsons and each had shared a story and told their grandfather how much they were going to miss him. On the whole, tears were absent, held in check as if no one wanted Kent to see them crying.

Will came around to the front of the chair after the boys had finished. Andy could see his struggle. Unlike his sons, Will was unable to control his feelings. His tears came before he spoke, and he could barely share.

Finally, he sobbed "Pa!" And he knelt and put his cheek on his father's knee. Will's shoulders shook. From beneath his hidden face came the muffled words, "I love you, Pa!" Kent patted his head and whispered, "I love you, too, son." After a minute, Will got up and found a place in the circle. Everyone was wiping tears on their sleeves.

As emotional as her brother had been, Andy expected a torrent of tears from Lou Ann. But Lou Ann appeared peaceful as she came to stand in front of her father. "Now," she said, "we've all shared, except me, and what I want to share is this... Pa, I will always remember when you went on Bowling for Dollars on television in Decatur, and we all drove up to the station to watch you. Remember how we stopped at the Big and Tall at that J. C. Penny's on the way, and everybody bought a white shirt?

Remember how we stood in the parking lot and took out the pins and the cardboard and put those shirts on?"

The boys were smiling now and nodding. They all remembered the day. Kent's eyes were bright, and Hester clasped her hands in front of her with a look of joyful remembrance.

"When we got there," continued Lou Ann, "we were the biggest family there, and the show host came over to talk to us."

Andy knew she meant that Kent had more family represented than any of the other contestants—and that their matching white shirts had made it clear they were related—but Andy smiled at her expression "the biggest family." Who could have missed the Hall giants?

"And, Pa, remember how you WON? You won $500!"

The room erupted in claps and whistles as if Kent had just been handed the check. Andy found himself laughing, and Kent laughed, as much as his lungs would allow.

Lou Ann continued. "And," she said, "the best part was that you wanted all of us to celebrate the win with you. So, we went to a real restaurant—one with real chairs and white material on the tables and a fancy man (not a woman like Peggy at the Diner) who came to take orders. We even ordered dessert."

Andy saw that the family stood a little taller as if the experience had ennobled them and given them a standing among the wealthy.

Then Lou Ann said, "And then we all went to the putt-putt go-cart place. And nobody else was there but us, and we filled every cart and went round and round and round. Sawyer could barely fit in the seat, but he made it."

"And," said Lou Ann, "when we got home, you had seventy-five cents left!"

They all laughed at that, especially Kent. His shoulders shook, even though his lungs wouldn't let him guffaw like he used to.

"That was the best time, Pa. It's a time we'll never forget."

As she finished, everyone smiled, and tears coursed down their cheeks to think that this was their memory—a memory they would all share forever.

Lou Ann then turned to Andy. "Okay, Preacher. Is there anything else we need to do?"

Andy thought for a second and said, "Just let your Pa know that you'll take good care of Ma, so he doesn't have to worry."

As if Kent hadn't overheard their conversation, Lou Ann declared a little more loudly, "Pa, the Preacher says it's okay for you to die, now. We're all gonna take good care of Ma. We'll do the mowing and change the storm windows and shovel the walks. And if anything breaks, we'll fix it. We'll take good of her for you."

Andy had been startled by her announcement that "the Preacher says it's okay for you to die, now," but as he reflected on it, he realized it was just what Kent needed to hear. He had always taken care of his family, but he could rest now in the knowledge that his children and grandchildren would take over that role. He needn't linger on that account.

Each boy and Lou Ann now stooped before Kent's chair and kissed his hands. Hester was last, with a hug and a kiss for her husband, and then she stood at his side. Kent's breathing had become so labored, now, that it hurt to listen to him.

The time was growing late, and it would be morning in just a few hours. With the wrestling match over and their sharing done, it was time for the family to go home and sleep. One by one, the Halls and Lambs said their good-byes and left the little house.

Lou Ann remained. She was going to spend the night. She protectively curved her mother into her shoulder. Hester smiled.

Andy wondered how much longer Kent had with them. He saw deep exhaustion, now, in the man, and he knew that this patriarch had risen, just for tonight, to the energy required to share the wrestling and the good-bye experience with his children.

Andy told Lou Ann—in the language of the family—"You all did good," and Lou Ann smiled proudly.

Andy shared a prayer with them and thanked the Lord that Kent knew his Maker and that he had lived his life as an example for his children and grandchildren.

Then Andy bent over and shook the large man's hand. "Kent," he said, "you are a wealthy man. You are so blessed to have such a wonderful family. You and Hester have done a good job. Many fathers would be envious of what you have in your children and grandchildren. I'm proud to have known you. I only wish I had seen you and your family on Bowling for Dollars. That must have been something! God bless you, friend."

⸻⸻

Abbey hated it when the phone rang before six. She hurried to answer it. It had been after three in the morning when Andy had made it back to bed.

Because she knew that Andy had roused, Abbey opened the bedroom door just enough to announce that the Halls had taken Kent to the hospital in Harmony. They would call when they knew more. Andy didn't need to come right now.

Andy let his head fall back on the pillow, and he sleepily thought how unlikely it was that Kent would return to the little house under the catalpa tree. He was glad that Kent and his family were ready—as much as anyone can be. They had all said their good-byes. No doubt, Kent would soon be at peace in the company of His Lord.

CHAPTER EIGHT

WINSTON

Because Kent had died of cancer, it reminded Andy of his own cancer experience. He recalled how the diagnosis had caught everyone off guard, especially his parents. The news had prompted Mom and Dad to rush to Molly's house from their vacation in Florida, which meant they had arrived without Grannie.

Andy had wished Grannie had been with them. Unlike his scared and angry parents, Grannie would have been a comfort.

She couldn't have driven away the sickness with her backwoods remedies as she had when he was a child. (Grannie had poured foul-tasting stuff down his throat more than once, and she had trusted in the mighty but smelly powers of onions and garlic.) But Grannie could have made the nurses step lively, and she probably would have put a cold compress on his forehead at least once and held it there with the comfort of her warm hand.

Andy had felt sorry for his parents. They had wrung their hands by his bedside. Without God in their lives and lacking any element of faith, they had nothing to fall back on but panic; and somehow, although Andy was the hospitalized one, he had become their counselor. It had been difficult, especially when his dad had railed against "a God who would do THIS to one of His own!" Andy had tried to explain that no one was exempt from the problems of this earth, but that everyone could reach up to

God for comfort and help through the valleys. His dad had only become angrier, and he had communicated in monosyllables for the rest of their visit.

Thankfully, his parents' torment had been relieved when the surgeon had reported he'd found the tumor to be contained and he had removed it. Since they knew Andy was out of danger, Mom and Dad Garrett had departed. Their absence had brought peace and relief for Andy and Abbey, and Molly and Paul, and Andy had been able to go through his chemotherapy without the stress of his parents' neediness.

Why was it always so hard to be with Mom and Dad, Andy wondered? Why couldn't the Garrett family be like a normal family? Why did his parents have to be angry and fight all the time and make everyone miserable? Why couldn't they leave their children alone? For that matter, how had the two of them managed to stay married for so long? If they were so unhappy and hated each other so much, why had they never divorced? It was impossible to fathom.

Throughout his treatments and recuperation, Andy had spent a lot of time in prayer. Most of his prayers had been simple: "Thank you for Your love, Lord. And thank you for Abbey. And thank you for Your care and healing. And please, God, help Mom and Dad find your peace."

Andy loved it that Abbey was so predictable and steady. But today, his wife wasn't her usual self.

Abbey had a secret. And she teased him with it. Andy knew from experience how little Abbey liked surprises, but he loved them. It tickled him that, today, she had arranged a surprise for him.

While they were still in bed, Abbey had assumed a mysterious air and had told him that today was going to be special. Then she had smiled enigmatically throughout breakfast and all the while they had dressed.

Now, she insisted they take a ride in the car.

Abbey wouldn't tell him where they were going, but she made Andy drive. She read from directions scribbled on a piece of paper, and Andy made the turns according to her instructions. The further they went, the more Andy tried to guess their destination. He pestered Abbey for clues. "It's a surprise," was all she would say, and try as he might, Andy could not get anything more from her.

"Just take care you don't get us lost," Andy couldn't resist spouting. They both knew that Abbey didn't have the best sense of direction, so this was a low blow.

"You'll see," was all she would say.

It did surprise Andy that their route bypassed Harmony, because Harmony, with its grand population of 23,000, was the most frequent destination from its much smaller neighbor, Cherish. Harmony boasted a mall and a hospital that regularly drew Cherish shoppers and patients. At Abbey's direction, however, Andy drove past the Harmony turn off.

"Are you sure this is right?" Andy asked, unable to help himself. Abbey set her chin and insisted she had written the directions correctly. (His questioning, however, did generate a bothersome twinge of doubt. She did hope everything was correct.)

Andy bit his tongue for nearly an hour. When they finally arrived in Fort Marshall, he still held his peace, but he couldn't imagine that his wife could have knowledge of anything in Fort Marshall.

Suddenly Abbey said with excitement, "Okay, now—turn right here."

She directed him down several unlikely side streets, and Andy felt sure they were lost. He was preparing to say so when Abbey started to count houses and check house numbers.

They were nearly to the end of the block when Andy saw it. The sign in the yard of a well-kept tan bungalow told him all he needed to know. It bore a pugnacious outline and the words: ENGLISH BULLDOG PUPPIES FOR SALE.

Abbey covered her ears as her husband whooped. Coffee slopped into the cup holder of the console as he whipped the car to the curb.

"So you think you might want one of these?" Abbey asked with a grin, but Andy was already out of the car and charging up to the front door. Abbey hurried to catch up.

A woman answered Andy's eager ring, and Abbey explained that she was the one who had called. The woman invited them in.

It was impossible to miss Andy's excitement. "I take it you've had a bulldog, before?" Mrs. Hynds asked with an "I'm going to make a sale" smile.

Andy's head bobbed like a toy on a spring, and she replied, "Well, I have two puppies, and they have excellent papers."

She pulled their pedigree from a drawer and Andy dutifully scanned the words, but he could hardly bear the delay.

"When can we see them?" he asked.

Mrs. Hynds laughed again; she was definitely going to make a sale. She disappeared to fetch the dogs.

No sooner had the two pups been set on the rug, than Andy hit the floor. The puppies walked all over him, licked his face, and chewed his hair. He laughed and scooped them between his shoulder and his neck where they were warm against his ear. Their puppy-breath was intoxicating.

"Oh, I love these guys!" he cried.

Abbey asked which one he wanted to take home, and he frowned. He pulled them both close.

"I can't decide," he said. "I just can't decide!"

Because he had grown up with a female, Abbey thought he would pick the littler puppy, but in the end, Andy declared the male to be his favorite.

Andy scooped him up, and with a voice of ownership he announced, "I'm going to call him Winston."

Abbey knew that, when Andy was a youngster, his parents had bought a bulldog puppy, and Winnie had been Andy's best friend for many years. Andy had shared Winnie-stories with Abbey, and she knew he had always hoped to own another bulldog someday.

Abbey had known little about bulldogs, except that their snorts always sounded frightening and their protruding canines looked forbidding. Abbey's childhood had abounded with a series of unfrightening, unpapered mutts, and while she would have been happy with any dog, she knew that Andy loved bulldogs. Abbey was encouraged that nothing about the puppies in their arms foretold "frightening."

In added confirmation of the breed's sweet nature, Mrs. Hynds released Winston's parents. The adult dogs wiggled and licked, and although they had protruding canines and snorted, neither parent seemed to have a terrifying bone in their body. The dogs confirmed for Abbey the hope that Winston would be a sweet companion for her and Andy.

When they bid Mrs. Hynds good-bye and Andy carried his new little buddy to the car, Abbey slid into the driver's seat. She knew that Andy would be worthless behind the wheel, now; he was in puppy love, and there was not a single thought in his mind for her or the road ahead. Winston, alone, captured his attention.

Abbey retraced the way home successfully, without Andy's help, and she patted herself on the back that her surprise had gone so well.

Abbey didn't want to wake up. She glanced with one eye at the clock on the bed stand and confirmed that it was still early.

"I hope Winston learns which days are Saturdays, soon," she grumbled.

The puppy had been with them for five days, and he had already become patterned to rally them at the usual weekday time.

Andy rolled from under the covers to get up and let his dog outside.

Abbey knew that Andy would return to bed, but she also knew that it would do no good. The routine was set. Winston would stand on the rug and snort until they both got up.

"He has your personality," she quipped after Andy returned. She pulled the covers over her head.

"You do mean that he's sweet and lovable, right?" Andy shot back. He pulled the covers over his head, too, and searched for Abbey's lips to give her a kiss.

"Of course," she said, and she rolled into him for another kiss. Saturday mornings used to be their special snuggle times. Abbey wondered if they would ever get those back.

Winston was now jumping against the side of the bed and yipping in between snorts. He was willing them to get up so they could start the day with his breakfast and play.

In exasperation, Andy leaned over and scooped the pup under the covers, but it was futile. The puppy pawed and shook his little square head until Andy tossed back the blankets and roughed with him.

Abbey frowned. It was clear she couldn't sleep any longer. She kicked off her covers and paused to collect her thoughts, but it was impossible to think. The noise of puppy play filled the room.

Andy held Winston high and growled at him. "Whatever did we do before we got Winston?" he called out joyously.

Sleep, thought Abbey. Sleep.

Then, while Andy tickled the puppy's tummy, he added, "You should have seen him, yesterday, while you were at that Sunday school meeting. Winston met Ollie."

"You trusted Winston around the Hart's ferret?" Abbey responded with surprise. "He's awfully tiny to get in a tangle with a ferret!"

"Oh, I didn't let him off my lap," Andy said. "But Ollie didn't seem to care. I don't think it mattered to Ollie one bit that Winston was there."

Now Winston tugged at Andy's slippers.

"Roxy likes him, though," said Andy. (Roxy was the Darrell's terrier.)

"What did you do, take Winston on a neighborhood tour?"

"Yeah. Kind of. Winston and Roxy loved romping together."

Abbey watched as Andy chased the puppy into the living room. Winston growled, snagged a stuffed toy, and ran as he shook it senseless.

"And then while you were at the grocery store," Andy continued, "a couple of children I don't even know knocked on the door to ask, 'Can Winston come out and play?' So I took him out in the front yard, and the kids played with him for a good hour."

Before Abbey could reply, Andy jumped up and dashed across the room to steal Winston's toy. The puppy yapped in protest, tumbled head-over-heels, and the chase was on.

"Is that why he was all curled up, asleep, on the living room floor when I came home?" Abbey called over the noise. "I thought it was awfully early for him to have pooped out. Now I understand!"

Abbey couldn't help but smile at the sight of her husband and his puppy rolling on the floor and growling at one another. They were a pair. Although Winston had changed their usual

Saturday morning routine, the puppy was growing on her. Who could resist?

Like his owner, Winston was irresistibly winsome.

Perhaps the only creature to dislike Winston was Butter. The usually easygoing feline took one look at Winston's wagging welcome and drew up his back, puffed his tail, and punctuated his hissed warning with a little dance on his tip-toes. Winston hung his ears and scooted backward half-way across the room. Lizzie scolded the cat and tried to push the two animals together "to make friends," but nothing worked. Abbey suggested they take their cookies out to the porch and leave Winston inside.

After a couple of days of this, Abbey wondered if Butter would venture inside again for milk and cookies. She opened the door, and Lizzie walked in and called to the cat. Butter hesitated, at first, but then he quickly squeezed past his owner. The tom hugged the living room wall all the way to the kitchen. When he spied Winston, he made a leap for the kitchen chair next to where Lizzie usually sat.

Abbey was surprised. She didn't like cats at the table, but when Butter stayed glued to the seat and didn't venture any higher, she held her tongue.

The puppy didn't like the cat any more than the cat liked him. Winston kept Abbey safely between himself and the swishing tail and evil stare.

The truce seemed to work. Lizzie finished her cookie and slowly drained her milk.

Winston ignored the little girl's invitations to come for a pat on the head. Instead, he peeked at Lizzie over Abbey's foot. Although Winston shifted his feet, he never budged. It was obvious that he felt Lizzie was too near the throaty growls on the chair next to her.

When Lizzie and Butter finally left, Winston stood at the door and watched Butter circle Lizzie's legs. Lizzie reached down and clutched her kitty in her usual death grip for the walk home.

Winston continued to stare from the storm door, and Abbey wondered what the little dog must be thinking.

Abbey got a clue once Lizzie and Butter were out of sight. Winston dropped down and pranced into the living room as if to say, "Well, that's over!" Then he picked up one of his stuffed toys and shook the life out it.

Abbey laughed. "Oh, yeah," she said. "You're tough! You are one tough dog!"

CHAPTER NINE

JEFF

Andy thought he heard a knock on the outer office door. It was unusual. Most people didn't bother to knock. The outer door was either open or left ajar, and most people just pushed it open the rest of the way and walked in.

"Come on in," Andy called over his shoulder. He was doing battle with the recalcitrant mimeograph machine because Opal had abandoned him for a visit to her daughter. Andy had assured Opal he would be all right on his own, but now, with his page still not correctly set on the troublesome copier, he wasn't sure.

The young man who entered the office was hesitant and unfamiliar. Andy continued with one hand to coax the machine to accept his lesson sheet, and he reached over the counter with the other to shake the stranger's hand and introduce himself.

"You're the pastor?" the fellow asked in disbelief.

Andy knew that most people thought he looked young for a minister. He was thirty, but he had a youthful face and he sometimes came to the office in blue jeans like he had today. Other pastors in town wouldn't be caught dead at their church, even during the week, in anything but a suit. (One minister even helped with a teen car wash in his suit and tie!) As the youngest pastor in town, Andy represented a cultural transition where ministry was still formal in the pulpit but more casual off the platform. He assumed this was confusing the visitor, who didn't look twenty, yet, himself.

"Sure am. How may I help you?"

The young man's brow furrowed, and he nervously stuffed his hands into his pockets. It made his stubble-bearded face look gaunter and his thin form appear more dejected than when he had entered. His body language shouted that he might run out the door at any moment, but his jaw said he was going to stay. His deeply creased T-shirt was stained, his jeans were threadbare, and his belt had run out of holes and had been folded over the buckle. The only things that looked oddly new and somewhat clean were his tennis shoes.

The visitor finally stammered his reply. "I, uh, I... I'm tired of being on drugs."

Andy stopped the mimeo adjustment in mid-crank. He left the master half on and half off the cylinder, and he locked the drum in the up position. Then he suggested they go into the study to talk.

The young man settled uncomfortably into a chair by the door. Andy bypassed the desk and sat in the chair next to him. When Andy inquired, he learned that his visitor's name was Jeff Archer.

"How long have you been on drugs, Jeff?" Andy asked.

"'Bout a year." The voice was calm, but Jeff's eyes swept the office nervously until they locked on a bare corner of Andy's desk.

"I went to Florida after I graduated and my mom died. I wanted a job where it was warm," Jeff said. "When I got there, my work friends had parties and passed around drugs. They're the ones who got me started. And it cost me my job. Now I'm back in Illinois, and I want to quit."

"I'm glad to hear that you want to get off drugs," Andy said. "But I'm curious as to why you've come to me."

"I can't afford to pay for help, and I don't have a car to go over to Harmony for counseling or treatment. I thought maybe a church could do something. My dad lives a couple of blocks over, and your church is the first one I came to," he said.

Andy could see the dilated pupils when Jeff finally looked him in the eye.

"Do you help people like me?"

"Why don't we ask God for help?" Andy suggested, and when he indicated he was going to pray, Jeff awkwardly bowed his head.

Andy's mind and heart whirled. "God," he prayed silently, "please help me to know how to help Jeff." Then he prayed aloud and asked God to help the young man.

After the prayer, Andy commended Jeff for taking the first step—deciding to quit. Andy knew it wasn't going to be easy for him to go cold turkey. He hoped Jeff would be able to do it. Andy had had friends in Chicago who had kicked drugs, but it had been a long and painful process—even though they had had professional help.

The withdrawal effort without such help was going to be agonizing. Andy told Jeff so, but Jeff seemed to know that, already.

Next, Andy said, "Quitting is no good if you keep putting yourself back into the settings that got you hooked in the first place. There are going to have to be some changes in the places you go and the people you see."

"I don't have any friends here," Jeff pronounced glumly. "They've all moved away. And the few people I know in Harmony sell drugs, and they aren't my friends."

"Well," Andy said, "it's time to make new friends. Come to Sunday school and church and meet lots of people who don't use or sell drugs."

"Oh," Jeff said with a shocked expression. He seemed about to say something but couldn't find the words. Finally, he offered,

"I don't want to say this wrong, but I don't know if I can be like them."

"Like who?" Andy asked (although he understood well what Jeff meant).

"Well, you know... I've been through a lot of stuff and these church people have never had to go through all that."

"By 'all that' I assume you mean lying and swearing and drinking and drugs—and what else, Jeff? You might be surprised at what some of these people have come out of, with God's help and some godly friends."

"Aw, you don't get it!" Jeff grimaced. "People like me have never had it easy. We get into accidents and fights, and we get sick and lose our jobs, and... Well, people like you always make it sound easy. But, the truth is, you've always had it good! You've never had to deal with hard stuff, like no money, or cancer, or..."

"Whoa!" Andy shot back. "Stop right there. You think I'm making assumptions about you, but I'm hearing you make wild assumptions about me—things you don't have any idea about. I want you to know that God can do anything. He has in my life!"

The intensity of Andy's response startled Jeff.

"To begin with," Andy bored in, "I HAVE had cancer, and I go every month for a checkup to make sure it hasn't come back. Second, I used to be pretty close to being an alcoholic. Since it's my own estimation, I'd say I WAS one! I went to bed drunk from parties five and six nights a week and drank at home alone the rest of the nights. I was to the point where I 'needed' a drink to get me going during the day. And talk about temptation: I was a bartender in downtown Chicago!"

Jeff was transfixed.

Andy continued, "So, don't tell ME that I don't know about hard times and temptations, just because I go to church. Furthermore, it was God who turned me around, so I'm talking from experience, here, and I'm telling you: if God could do that for me, He can do it for you."

Jeff was blown away by Andy's unexpected revelations. He sat with his mouth half-open and his eyes wide. "Boy!" he finally said. "I got goose bumps just then."

But then Jeff pulled back and squirmed a little. With a guarded glance, he hazarded, "You don't look like any drunk I ever saw. And you look awful good for having had cancer."

Andy responded quickly, "But isn't that what you want, Jeff—to be young and active and cured of drugs?"

Jeff had to admit that it was what he wanted, and Andy began to see the hope form in his eyes.

Then Andy said, "Jeff, I don't believe God brought you into this church at this particular time by accident. He wanted you to meet me—at this time in my life—and to hear the story of where He's brought me so that you would know He's big enough to handle YOUR situation. Six months ago I couldn't have told you that I'd had cancer and was now free of it. Eight years ago I couldn't have told you that God could take away old habits and give you a new life. But now I can! God brought you here TODAY because He knew that, at this point in my life, I would be able to tell you what He has done for me and can do for you. You need to know that He CAN help you, Jeff!"

Andy paused. "Have you ever asked God to forgive you for the things you've done and to wipe the slate clean so you could start over?"

"No..."

After his whispered response, Jeff was silent, and Andy waited. Finally, Jeff ventured, "He would do that—give me a clean slate? After all the stuff I've done?"

"He absolutely will," said Andy. "He did for me."

"But He won't make ME into a preacher, will He?" Jeff objected.

Andy laughed. "Would that be so bad? Especially considering what you are now?"

Grudgingly, Jeff grinned and admitted, "No, I guess not."

The grin was like a shiny crack that afforded Andy a glimpse of the real Jeff, underneath.

"When you ask God to forgive you and wipe everything clean in Jesus' Name, He does it. You get a clean page to start writing down a new life, and God is there to help you."

Andy said it quietly and let Jeff think for a moment.

"You make God sound so real," Jeff frowned. He kept looking at the floor.

"Don't you want Him to be real?" Andy asked.

"I-I guess I do," Jeff said. He glanced up, and Andy thought that maybe Jeff was beginning to understand.

"He is real," Andy said, "and He hears you when you tell Him you're sick and tired and want to change. If you let Him, He'll be a better friend to you than any of your drug buddies has ever been."

Jeff shifted in his chair. "So what do I have to do?"

Andy nodded and said, "Just tell Him thank you for being God and for being a REAL friend. Tell Him you're sorry for messing up and that you want a clean page to start over again. Tell Him you want His help to write on your life-page from now on. Tell Him you want His Son, Jesus, in your heart, and you want Him to help you live right every day for the rest of your life—and forever."

"You're going to have to help me say all of that!" Jeff said. Andy asked if he meant it, and Jeff said yes.

Andy moved his chair a little closer. Jeff didn't seem self-conscious this time when they prayed. His head hung nearly to his lap.

Andy poured out the Sinner's Prayer and Jeff repeated it. Before they finished praying, Jeff was adding his own words to tell God the things from which he wanted to be free. Then when he said "thank you" to God for taking it all away, Andy could tell that it had become real to him.

"What is that?" Jeff asked as he patted his heart.

Andy smiled. "That's God," he said. Andy knew that God's Spirit had come inside of Jeff, just like He had in his own life, only a few years ago.

It was clear that Jeff hadn't expected to be emotional, but when he tried to put his feelings into words, the closest he could come was to say that he felt clean for the first time in a long time, and a tear escaped and coursed down his cheek. He said he felt hope.

"I'm not sure what happens next," Jeff said, "but I think I can do this, now."

Then Jeff asked wistfully, "Will you meet with me and keep praying for me?"

Andy assured him that he would. "And I'll do better than that," Andy said. "When things get tough, here's my phone number. Call, and I'll come to see you. Or you can come and see me here, anytime."

"Maybe you could tell me a little more about God, too," Jeff said quietly.

"And about Jesus," Andy replied.

Jeff seemed excited. He pumped Andy's hand, and he stammered several thank yous before he backed out of the office door and left.

That night, Andy told Abbey, "I'm not sure what God has in mind for Jeff. But I think he's like I was. I think God has every intention of turning his life around. We need to pray for him."

———⟫●⟪———

The Garretts—and all of the First Baptist Church members—did pray for Jeff, every day, and sometimes several times a day.

The drugs fought leaving the young man's system, and Jeff's struggle was hard to watch. As promised, Andy spent time with him—often many hours a day until Jeff's father could be home from work. Andy prayed and encouraged him. He assured him that he was not alone and that God would not abandon him. Jeff leaned on God and Andy, hard.

Sometimes, Jeff was wringing wet when Andy arrived. Jeff's battle was fierce against the cruel giant that dominated his body and twisted his cravings. He shivered as his will pushed back and he fought the lies in his mind.

"I want the stuff so bad," Jeff told Andy, "but I keep saying no. And when I shout 'No!' and say 'Leave me, in Jesus' Name,' I can't explain it any other way than to say that I feel the dark fingers ease up. God helps me!

"But I need you to pray with me, too," he insisted. "When you pray with me, I feel even stronger, and I hurt less. It's like I get the window in my mind to open wider against the dark. And even though I sometimes can't see the light very well, I can at least see it! That's God, isn't it?"

Andy assured him that it was indeed God.

"I'm glad," Jeff cried, "because the drugs can't have me! I belong to Jesus, now. I want to be clean! I just wish this wasn't so hard!"

Andy knelt with Jeff, and together they battled in prayer against the demons of addiction.

The toughest nights of spiritual battle with Jeff always made Andy appreciate, again, the miracle that his own youth had not been scarred by drugs. As a teenager, he had seen the power that drugs had exerted over some of his friends, and it had made shooting up and sniffing scare him. He was grateful, now, that unlike much of his generation, he had been spared the whole drug experience. Alcohol had been bad enough.

Watching Jeff wrestle with his addiction had taught Andy something else. It had taught him that God doesn't always work the same way in every situation. Each person and each situation is unique and receives His singular attention. Although God was with Jeff and He was working in his life, He was dealing with Jeff in a way he had not dealt with Andy.

Andy recalled God's touch a few years earlier, and he remembered how God had immediately taken away his desire for alcohol and cigarettes. It had been simple, and Andy had never gone back to either vice. But now Andy watched as Jeff—who had also become a believer—struggled in pain through the long withdrawal process.

No. God was not dealing with Jeff in the same way He had dealt with Andy; but, thank God, He was dealing with Jeff, and He was helping him.

Andy also knew that his prayers for Jeff were important. Andy prayed that Jeff would not become discouraged. He was thankful that, so far, he hadn't.

Andy bowed his head, now, and prayed, again.

CHAPTER TEN

THE LADIES' CIRCLE

Andy heard the clack of Opal's typewriter as he approached the office door. He had just retrieved his Bible from the pulpit.

The noise stopped when he entered. Opal had correction fluid in hand and was blotting out a comma. Then she smiled a satisfied smile.

When she saw Andy observing her celebration, she rolled back her chair. "Have a look," she said. "I think you'll like it."

Andy reached over and picked up the page.

101 WAYS TO SERVE IT
By Opal Reese

Here, have a little "Manna Soup"
or "Manna on a Stick."
I've mastered "Manna a l'Orange"
(here, have a little lick!).

There are "Manna Crackers" on the shelf,
"Creamed Manna" in the 'fridge;
There's "Scrambled Manna" in the pan,
And "Home-Made Manna Fudge!"

"Crockpot Manna" might be good,
and "Manna a la Mode."
You might like "Manna Balls with Sauce"
or "Manna for the Road."

"Manna Slush" is nice to slurp,
or "Manna Mocha Mix."
I might just set some "Manna Tea"
out in the sun, for kicks.

I've mastered "Manna with a Wok"
and "Manna Fricassee."
And you would like my "Manna Split"
(I swear no calories!).

You like my "Manna Meringue Pie?"
(The crust is "Never Fail.")
But now I hear we'd better find
some recipes for quail!

"Manna Tea?" he inquired with the rise of an eyebrow.
Opal shrugged her shoulders, and Andy laughed.

~ ~ ~

Later that morning, Andy and Opal made their way downstairs
to the fellowship hall. They found that in spite of an invitation to
come down for refreshments, the ladies were running late. The
women of the missions circle were still milling about, passing
items along an assembly line.

Spread on half of the room's rectangular folding tables were rows
of open bath towels. The rest of the tables contained piles of personal
grooming items: combs, toothbrushes, toothpaste, soap, washcloths,

mouthwash, dental floss, lotion, nail files, nail clippers, and shampoo. The women, including Abbey, edged forward in single file to collect one of each of the items from the piles. At the end of the line, each woman deposited her collection onto an open towel. She added a small New Testament and a witnessing tract and gathered the corners of the bath cloth with ribbon. Boxes of the bundles would be shipped to an inner city shelter for homeless men and women.

After a little more activity, the women stopped for prayer and sent Andy and Opal to the head of the refreshment line. Abbey smiled as she served. She placed a slice of the orange Bundt cake and a couple of cream cheese mints on Andy's crystal dessert plate. His eyes lit up. But his smile faded over the dainty cup of punch.

Abbey knew that Andy could never fathom why women served such small amounts of beverages. She would get him more, if there was punch left over.

By the end of the line, a small amount of punch remained unserved. Abbey retreated to the privacy of the kitchen and poured the punch from the bowl into a tall drinking glass. Then she set it quietly by her thirsty husband's plate and took her seat. She was wedged between her talkative Andy and the ever-silent Sybil Ryan. Abbey doubted that anyone had even noticed her wifely good deed.

But as Abbey took a bite of cake, she was startled to feel a tug on her sleeve. It was Sybil.

Abbey leaned over to hear Sybil murmur quietly: "Good for you! My husband hates those little cups, too. 'They're hardly worth the bother,' he always says. He'd rather have a paper plate and a full tumbler any day." Sybil smiled.

Abbey was speechless. The affirmation of their husbands' shared dislike was the most words Abbey had ever heard Sybil Ryan utter! Leo always did the talking for the two of them.

Abbey returned Sybil's smile. Then Sybil resumed her silence. The two women turned again to eating their cake, and Andy finished off his glass of punch with a contented sigh.

CHAPTER ELEVEN

THE COUNTRY, AND AN UPDATE ON JEFF

Meadowlarks and red-winged blackbirds tossed their songs from sunny fence posts and telephone wires, and June twirled her verdant skirts across the countryside. Rows of beans had leafed out, and knee-high corn stretched for the sky. Amish horse-and-buggies dotted the byways between Cherish and Harmony, and a warm and clement sky stretched away forever above the Garrett's car on its way to Molly's.

The windows were rolled all the way down, and Andy filled his lungs. Air in the city, upstate, had never smelled like this. Here, sheets hanging on clotheslines took on the perfume of new-mown grass and fresh breezes, and the warm earth wafted a loamy richness. Andy pictured Molly rolling out pie crusts in the farmhouse kitchen with the curtains fluttering in the breeze, and he could imagine Paul pausing on his tractor in the field to draw an intoxicating spring breath.

Days like today made it easy to understand why farmers shunned city life. Andy knew this was what had pulled his brother-in-law to return to his childhood farm after his father had retired.

Molly had told her brother how much she loved having meaningful things to do in a beautiful setting. At the farm, in addition to cooking, she fed the dogs, cats, and chickens; and she collected eggs, tossed kitchen scraps to the pigs, and took her turn at milking their six Jerseys.

More than anywhere else in her life, Molly felt at home in the nearly centennial farmhouse. It exuded character and held Paul's family history—a happy history. Molly loved it whenever Paul's dad, Phillip, came for dinner because Phillip told stories of what the farm had been like when his beloved Olivia had been living. Now, Dad played checkers with friends and visited his brother in Ohio.

Molly always marked how like his father Paul was. Paul was steady and capable and had a ready smile—the three things that had drawn her to him. But she also marveled at how very different Phillip Doaks and Paul were from her parents. How grateful Molly was that Paul had brought her a contentment and peace that she might otherwise have never known. And he had brought her to the country.

———⋙◉⋘———

After many weeks, it was a joy to see Jeff in church, clean-shaven and neatly dressed in a wrinkle-free T-shirt and crisp blue jeans. Jeff looked healthy, and he had put on weight. His eyes were clear, and his smile was pain-free. Abbey was surprised at the change in him. She also noticed that he was not alone.

"This is my dad, Bud Archer," Jeff said for Abbey's benefit at the door following the service. "And this is his fiancée', Doris." (Andy had met Bud when he had visited Jeff so many times at his home, but Bud and Doris were new to Abbey.)

Abbey noted that Jeff was taller and less stocky than his dad, but he had his father's eyes. Bud looked like the factory worker he was—and Bud was beaming.

"Thank you for what you did for my son," Bud told Andy. "Jeff has been a new person ever since he met with you—even before he completely kicked the drugs. I was so angry when he came back from Florida in the shape he was. But then you helped him, and I want you to know that hearing him talk, and seeing how you worked with him, made me pay attention. Jeff told me what you said to him about God, and it reminded me of things I learned about Jesus when I was a kid in Sunday school. We never went to church much, back then, but some of it kind of stuck, you know?"

"Anyway, Pastor," he said, "you need to know that I prayed with Jeff two days ago, the way he said he prayed with you. And now we're both Christians! His mother would be happy. I feel like I not only got my son back but we both also got a new start, together."

Bud pumped Andy's hand. "I can't thank you enough, Pastor! Thank you, again, for taking the time to talk and work with my boy. It was a wonderful thing you did—for both of us."

CHAPTER TWELVE

VIVIAN

Abbey ran to the television room to get Andy. The caller had said Elsie Trimble had died at her sister's home in Kansas.

Although Elsie had remained frail after her pneumonia and had stayed in Kansas, her death was unexpected. Andy grabbed his keys, and he and Abbey drove immediately to Vivian's. The loss of Elsie would certainly crush her dear friend—or so they thought.

They had forgotten that Vivian was still Vivian.

When they got her house, Vivian greeted them stoically and invited them into her formal sitting room.

"I'm so sorry!" Andy told her. Abbey's eyes brimmed, but Vivian's remained dry, and her response was unemotional. Vivian's only concession to mourning was a stern black dress that Abbey didn't recall having seen before. Vivian sat in a severe straight-backed chair facing Andy and Abbey, who perched uncomfortably on an ancient horsehair couch. The room reminded Abbey of a silver print from a bygone era; everything was in somber shades of grays and blacks.

"It was simply her time," Vivian steadily stated as if she were lecturing a class. "Elsie insisted on taking that trip, but I think it was too much for her. All in all, it was a blessing that her death happened when it did because she was with family."

75

"Of course," said Andy, unsure what more to say to someone who did not believe in displays of emotion.

"The funeral will be held in Topeka," Vivian continued matter-of-factly. "I'll be flying there to attend, which means I won't be in church on Sunday. I know that, as pastor, you worry when people aren't in church. I don't want you to feel you have to call and check on me when you see I'm not there."

"Certainly. That's most considerate," Andy heard himself say.

What he wanted to say was that he felt certain the death of her friend must be very difficult for her and that he and Abbey would keep her in their prayers. But he couldn't say it. Vivian Holladay's unemotional reserve was her public way of handling the situation, and Andy knew she would frown on his sentimental familiarity.

Before Abbey thought, however, she asked, "Will you be all right, traveling so far by yourself?"

Vivian rose an inch and starchily replied, "Of course. I'll be fine, thank you." A brittle edge to her voice warned that a line had been crossed.

Andy quickly interjected, "Of course, of course. We'll see you when you return. If you need anything in the meantime, you know you can call."

In respect for her privacy, Andy and Abbey didn't stay long.

Vivian accepted handshakes—no hugs—when they stood to leave.

When they got in the car, Abbey sighed. "I do hope she's going to be all right. It must be hard to guard one's feelings so closely when you are grieving."

Andy assured her that Vivian's grief would be private and not in public.

Abbey speculated again on whether Vivian would be okay to make such a long trip by herself.

"Anything Vivian puts her mind to, she'll be able to do," Andy said. "She's a very strong woman, even at her age."

"I guess so," said Abbey, "but just like Elsie, she is getting up in years."

Andy smiled. "Somehow, I doubt that Miss Vivian would like to hear that said about her."

On Sunday, with Elsie and Vivian's south-end pew vacant, there was a pall of sadness over the congregation. Members of the adult Sunday school class stopped at the exit after church to recall with Andy and Abbey their remembrances of Miss Trimble. Each member expressed deep sympathy for Miss Holladay. They regretted that she would be very alone, now.

———◆———

Andy watched to make sure Vivian got back safely from Topeka.

When he spied her in church, he breathed in relief.

Vivian still displayed no emotion over Elsie's death, but Andy felt she must be pleased that so many of her friends and former students were stopping by her pew to express their condolences and to welcome her back. Although he was too far away to hear, Andy knew that Vivian was acknowledging each person's gesture of sympathy with a formal "thank you" and their name.

As the organ prelude began, those gathered around Vivian hurried to their seats. The outpouring of sympathy would resume, following the service.

Vivian now removed her hat and scanned her bulletin. Her customary habits never varied. It was as if Elsie were sitting with her.

Andy's heart broke to see her all alone.

But then, Andy noticed Amanda Smith slip wordlessly into the pew next to Vivian—exactly where Elsie used to sit. When the song leader announced the hymn, Amanda reached over and offered to share her hymnal. Without a word spoken—just a

nod and a nearly imperceptible softening in her countenance—
Andy could see that Vivian accepted and appreciated Amanda's
company.

A few Sundays after her return to Cherish, Miss Holladay
took a misstep on the way to her car, and she fell—hard.

Out of breath, Andy asked, "Miss Vivian, are you all right?"
He had run to help.

Andy could see at a glance that the thinly-boned woman
wasn't going to get up and shouldn't be moved. While Andy and
others hovered over her, Luther Sharp raced to call an ambulance.

Although Vivian was in pain, she was also embarrassed by
it all.

"Good grief," she groused. "You'd think you'd never seen
anyone take a little spill."

Sirens heralded the arrival of help, and the crowd parted to let
the medical technicians through to do their job. They efficiently
set about evaluating Vivian's condition and how best to move her.

"That doesn't look like a good place to take a tumble,"
quipped one of the medics in an attempt to make a connection
with his patient.

"And what exactly would be a good place to take a tumble?"
snapped Vivian.

The technician swallowed. Andy could see him mentally
backpedaling. The young man now had the measure of the
woman he was here to help. "You're absolutely right," he said,
"it's never good to take a tumble."

Slowly and gently, he and his co-workers stabilized and lifted
Vivian into the vehicle. Once they had settled her inside, the
young tech grabbed a clipboard and pen and began to question
her. He moved down the list of blanks on the form and jotted

down her name, address, and insurance carrier. Vivian alertly answered every question—until he asked her age.

Andy, who was hoping to get Vivian's keys so he could take the car home for her, was standing by the open vehicle door as the tech checked off the answers to his questions. When Vivian didn't answer the query about her age, the young man leaned in and stared at her face. Andy pulled his head in, too. He wondered if Vivian had had a sudden stroke or had passed out.

But, no, there she was, propped up with a serene look on her face as if the tech had never asked the question. The tech asked it again:

"Ma'am, could you give me the year to go with your date of birth?"

Again, Vivian sat serenely, as if oblivious to the man's query. The tech finally passed his hand in front of her face, to which she snapped smartly, "I can see you, young man, and I can hear. You do realize, however, that it is impolite to ask a woman her age! Also, it is Miss and not Ma'am."

She drew herself up and crossed her arms indignantly. Andy's eyes grew wide, but the tech had learned from his earlier exchange with her. He remained unruffled.

"I see," said the young man. Then he leaned in and softly, conspiratorially, said, "Miss Holladay, I must say that as much as I dislike breaking with convention, my job requires that I fill in that line on this questionnaire. I could get into trouble if I leave it blank."

Even more quietly, almost whispering in her ear, he asked, "How can we resolve this difficulty?"

Vivian hesitated, and then she leaned over and whispered her age into his ear.

He whispered back, "Thank you, young lady!" and flashed his most handsome smile.

She blushed! Andy was sure of it.

"She blushed, and then she started twittering on and on to the young man as the ambulance doors closed," Andy told Abbey. "It was so unlike her. The way she was going on, she probably talked to him all the way to Harmony."

"She must have been reacting to a pain-killer—or maybe she was in shock," Abbey suggested.

———⟫●⟪———

Once the ambulance took off for the Harmony hospital, Andy handed Abbey his keys and asked her to follow him. He would drive Vivian's car to her house. From there, the two of them could head to the hospital.

It was a good plan, and everything went fine until the two cars approached the stop light (the only stop light in all of Tobler County). The light turned red. Instead of stopping, however, Andy continued through the intersection, and Abbey screamed.

A Decatur theater critic had once described Cherish as a town where one rarely has to look both ways before stepping off the curb, but at that moment there happened to be a blue pickup entering the intersection from the cross street. As Andy sailed through the light, only inches ahead of the truck, the driver laid on his horn and swerved. How they missed one another was nothing short of miraculous.

Deafened to all other sounds, the truck's blast continued to reverberate in Andy's ears, and he forced his vehicle to the side of the street. Against his will, Vivian's car continued a slow roll before it stopped. Andy sat in stunned silence.

Behind him, Abbey jerked to the curb and ran to Vivian's car. She nearly yanked Andy's car door from its hinges. "Why didn't you stop?" Abbey yelled. Her voice shook from the near-disaster she had just witnessed.

Andy was still in shock, and he blinked at her. "She doesn't have any brakes!" he managed to squeak.

Abbey gasped.

Andy's voice quaked as he explained how he had "put his foot through to the grill" but nothing had happened. He had been sure the pickup was going to hit him, and he couldn't believe, even now, that he had escaped unscathed.

"My whole life flashed before me!" he shuddered.

"Your life flashed before me, too," insisted Abbey. "You can't keep driving that car."

Andy nodded weakly, but then he shook his head, which was beginning to clear.

"I think we can get it to her house," he said. He exhaled to calm the erratic beating of his heart. "But I'm keeping my hand on the emergency brake, this time!"

Abbey finally conceded. There were no more intersections to cross, so Abbey climbed into their car and Andy slid behind the wheel of Vivian's brakeless road hazard.

At a snail's pace, the two cars inched around two corners and into Vivian's narrow driveway. Still praying—now with effusive thanks—Andy shoved Vivian's keys into his pocket. He headed, a bit unsteadily, to his car.

Typically, Andy would have taken Abbey's place behind the wheel, but not this time. Andy's nerves were shot. He collapsed into the passenger's seat and let his head fall back. Abbey took charge and put the car into gear for the drive to Harmony.

By the time they got to the hospital, Andy had recovered enough to be angry. He chided Miss Holladay.

"Vivian," he began. "You don't have any brakes in your car!"

"Oh, I know," she said dismissively. "I could tell I was due for a replacement but thought I could wait until next week. I didn't expect anyone else to be driving my car."

Andy bit his tongue when she asserted, "You no doubt drive faster than I do."

From her dais of pillows, Vivian continued, "I always drive slowly, and to keep from going too fast, I keep one foot on the brake. I'll have you know that I've never received a ticket in all my years of driving."

Andy was speechless. How do you lecture a hospitalized woman who's never had a ticket and tell her she's ruining her brakes for no good reason?

He had to let it slide. After all, Vivian seemed to be doing all right, and Andy didn't want to bring on any upset, now.

Andy and Abbey stayed by Vivian's side in the emergency room until early evening. Around seven, the staff transferred her to a room. Because of her medications, her eyes had already closed.

Although Andy felt sure Vivian couldn't hear him, he prayed aloud by her bed before he and Abbey left: "Dear God, mend Vivian's bones and set her on her feet again, soon. Keep her from pain and complications. Guard over her tonight as she sleeps. In Jesus' Name. Amen."

In the morning, an alert Vivian greeted them with a proper nod. Andy handed her a fistful of cards from First Baptist members who had dropped them off at the office for him to deliver. "Get well, soon!" the cards cheerfully commanded, and Vivian dutifully read every line.

Throughout the day, various church members dropped in to visit and deliver their encouragement, personally. By the end of the day, Vivian's room had bloomed into a garden of colorful bouquets.

⸻⸻▶◀⸻⸻

Although Vivian remained alert and responsive, an infection pushed back her surgery slot by a few days. The delay seemed to frustrate her, but she said little about it. At least she wasn't in pain.

Then one day, when Andy and Abbey passed down the hallway on their way to Vivian's room, a nurse pulled them aside. Usually, the nurses at the station were too busy completing reports to look up, but this one had jumped up the minute she'd seen them coming.

"She's not eating," the nurse confided. "Do you think you could encourage her?"

The Garretts were surprised and promised they would try. Surely Vivian realized the importance of eating to build her strength before the surgery.

During their visit, however, they noticed a change: Vivian's usual stern manner was noticeably subdued. She was alert, but she was uncharacteristically passive. There was no fire or fight in her eyes. Vivian rested, reserved and formal, on the pillows stacked behind her, but she did not rise to their challenges.

At their urging, she did drink a little juice, but Vivian barely touched the food on her tray.

In case she wasn't eating because she didn't care for the bland-looking mashed potatoes and the gray meat (whatever it was), Abbey asked, "Is there something different you would like us to bring you for lunch? We could bring you something from outside of the hospital. What are you hungry for?"

"No, thank you," Vivian demurred. "I'm not hungry."

"Vivian, you've got to eat to get your strength back for your surgery," Abbey urged, expecting a terse reply for being so forward.

But Vivian didn't reprimand Abbey's manners. Instead, Vivian remained silent for a minute. Then quite peacefully she announced, "I won't be leaving the hospital, you know. This is my time; the infection has just confirmed it."

"Oh, Vivian, that's absurd!" Andy now blurted before thinking. "You're a strong woman, and it's just a hip fracture. People get them all the time, and with surgery, you will be good as new."

The old Vivian would have risen an inch or two from her pillow and contradicted her pastor in no uncertain terms. But the new Vivian settled herself a bit and smiled serenely.

"I know you mean well," she said, "but some things are destined. This is my time, and that's all there is to it."

Andy and Abbey continued to protest, but Vivian refused to respond. It was as if the Garretts had no voices.

When they left, the nurse caught Andy's eye, and Andy shook his head. The nurse sighed sadly and went back to logging something on a chart.

———

After that day, Vivian's strength faded with every visit.

"I just don't have a purpose, anymore," Vivian told Andy one day. "All of my family and friends are in Heaven. I think it's time I make that trip, too."

Andy couldn't deny Vivian her thoughts. She was resigned and ready to go. Vivian had lived a full life and had no regrets. Unlike many people who didn't know the Lord, Vivian knew exactly where her soul would rest.

Nevertheless, Andy tried to change her mind.

His subtle attempts only irritated her. "My mind is made up," Vivian insisted with every discussion. And she continued to refuse food.

If only her antibiotics would work faster and the surgery could be scheduled sooner, Andy thought. Maybe she would regain her will to live.

He prayed, but as Vivian's course did not change and she continued to fail, Andy bowed in defeat. He finally prayed that Vivian wouldn't be too uncomfortable and that there would be no painful complications.

It was those prayers the Lord answered. Vivian suffered no physical or mental distress that anyone could see. She simply spent more time sleeping, and she grew thinner and paler.

Andy thought he would bear her passing without emotion, but his tears came unbidden one day when Vivian whispered, "Today, I'm going to visit Jesus and Elsie." Andy bent his head to hide his tears and to hear better, and he was surprised to feel Vivian patting him.

"It's okay, you know," she said. "I know where I'm going."

Later that afternoon, Vivian made the trip to Heaven without the slightest stirring. It was hard to tell when she had stopped breathing, but something had spurred Andy to check. When he couldn't see the rise and fall of her chest, he pressed the call button for help. The nurse he now knew well came running and checked Vivian's pulse and heart. She confirmed, with regret, that Vivian was gone.

Andy sat in the room for a while. He reflected that Vivian was one of the last of her generation from the church. As her friends (especially Elsie) had passed on, Vivian had become lonely here; but Andy knew she was not lonely now. He imagined a reunion with her friends and family members who Vivian hadn't seen in years. In his vision, it was a joyous homecoming, complete with hugs and laughter, unlike their restraint on earth.

Then the scene changed. In his imagination, Andy caught a glimpse of a stately and whole Vivian properly shaking the hand of Jesus! Jesus' posture matched Vivian's formality, and His nod was gentlemanly. It was evident that He knew her well. The propriety of it prompted Andy to chuckle, and from that moment on, Andy shed no more tears for Miss Holladay.

⸺⸻●⸻⸺

Andy knew that Vivian's funeral would be well-attended. The service would be in the church sanctuary, and Vivian's many students would pass by and nod politely to the figure lying composed and regal upon the silk. The south-end pew that had been the exclusive territory of Miss Trimble and Miss Holladay over the years would be bare—except for the two ladies' hats. Abbey had suggested it, and it had seemed the perfect tribute to the memory of their propriety and presence. No one would sit in that pew for a long time. It would remain empty out of respect for its beloved occupants.

To avoid interruption, Andy left all inquiries for Opal to field, and he worked on the funeral message at home. Winston curled up next to him on the sofa in the television room, and Abbey kept his coffee cup filled.

Around suppertime, Abbey brought him scissors and the newspaper with the obituary. Andy wanted to read it as part of the service. He shook out the folds of the *Cherish Observer* and turned to page four. There, as expected, he found Vivian's picture and the paragraphs describing her life. The first line, however, is what caught his eye.

In black and white—for all the world to see—the *Cherish Observer* had most impolitely announced: "Vivian Holladay, 91, of Cherish, Illinois..."

Out of habit, Andy drew in a breath, as if Vivian were reading over his shoulder. But then he chuckled. Andy knew that Miss Vivian no longer cared. After all, she had graduated, and proprieties had changed.

Unlike the temporal manners of Earth, the etiquette of Heaven had no strictures regarding revealing a woman's age. Besides, Vivian was now ageless!

CHAPTER THIRTEEN

EMMA PETERS

It sometimes seems that death comes in twos or threes. This time, it was twos. Only a week after Vivian's home-going, Jethro Peters also went to Heaven.

Like Vivian's, his was a quiet passing. Emma reported that she had been out of the room for just a couple of minutes. She had slipped downstairs to start the laundry, and when she returned, there was a smile on her husband's face. His eyes were closed as if he were daydreaming. She had been amazed that he had been able to smile; because of his ALS those muscles hadn't worked in a long time. She asked him what he was thinking about, and when he didn't respond, she looked closer and saw that he was gone.

"You know," Emma said, "I believe Jethro smiled because he was walking! He was walking unaided through the pearly gates."

It had been three years since Emma had seen Jethro walk. Three years ago she had become his full-time caregiver. He had protested, at first. He had insisted that he had married her to take care of her and not the other way around. Month after month, Emma had watched as Jethro's muscles had deteriorated and he had lost the ability to move, eat, and talk. Jethro had loved his wife's cooking, and it had broken Emma's heart not to be able to cook for him.

Now that Jethro was gone, Emma radiantly shared at his funeral, "I know there are feasts in Heaven, like the banquet in

Revelation, and I delight in imagining Jethro not only tasting, but also chewing, swallowing, and washing down all of the wonderful things set before him!"

As Andy listened to Emma share, he let imaginary scenes of Heaven play through his mind, as he had at Vivian's death. He imagined a cordial meeting just inside the Golden Gates, where Elsie Trimble, Vivian Holladay, and others greeted Jethro.

Then, Andy thought, who knows? Maybe Kent Hall would be there, too, to invite Jethro to a round of heavenly bowling.

Across the screen of Andy's imagination, an agile Jethro toed the line and released his ball with accuracy and speed. In celebration, Kent Hall lustily called "Strike!" in a voice devoid of wheezing or coughing.

CHAPTER FOURTEEN

FANNIE'S GUESTS

For the first time in her life, Abbey thought she might not have what it takes. It had seemed simple—a request to substitute for the secondary grades teacher in Sunday school while Shirley Anderson and her husband joined their family for a vacation on their houseboat on Lake Shelbyville.

But now Abbey stood in shock. Despite her demands that they sit, she watched Alan Horn and Brady Shook dance on the table in the classroom. After the Bible relay, all of the other children had sat. All of the other children were busy answering the questions in their workbooks—but not Alan and Brady.

Abbey had tried to catch them, but they were faster and jumped from table to table like little mountain goats. She had shouted, but they had merely squealed louder and ignored her commands. Nothing Abbey said or did seemed to work.

Dru Lillian looked at the boys in disgust as she dutifully completed her assignment. Abbey despaired. Why couldn't Alan and Brady sit and do their workbooks, too?

Worst of all, Abbey was sure the noise was filtering down to the lower level classrooms and was probably reverberating in the hallway. She had no idea what to do.

In defeat, she decided to go and find the boys' parents. It would be admitting she had lost control. Nevertheless, something had to be done. Abbey started slowly across the quaking room and sighed.

Suddenly, just as Alan was starting a new jig and Brady was finishing one, Abbey noticed Brady jerk to a stop and begin to wither. With eyes wide and locked on the door, Brady punched Alan, who glanced up in mid-twist and also stopped stock-still. The two boys instantly scrambled from the table top and slid with lightning speed into their seats.

Abbey followed their gaze. Danny Hart stood at the door.

Danny hadn't had to say a word. His glare had been enough to put the fear of Judgment into the boys. Once Alan and Brady were seated and had grabbed their pencils and workbooks, Danny stepped into the room.

"Thank you!" Abbey breathed, and Danny gave her a grin.

"I wondered if you might need a little help," he whispered. "Those two boys can be a real handful. I think they figured you were new, and they could get by with their shenanigans."

"I was going to get their parents," Abbey whispered back.

"That would have worked, too," Danny said. "It's been done before."

Abbey was glad to know it wasn't just her. She had despaired of ever substituting again.

Danny patted her arm. "I'll stop by in another fifteen minutes to see if they're still behaving."

———⊰●⊱———

Abbey was emotionally wrung out from Sunday school and hurried to put on her choir robe. No one seemed to have noticed the noise the boys had made (at least they didn't mention it), and she was glad to have the peace of the morning service ahead of her.

Today's organ prelude was, thankfully, reflective. It calmed Abbey's spirit and lifted her heart. She was ready for worship, and she opened her hymnal with the congregation to the first hymn. As the introductory measures played, she filled her lungs to sing—and that's when she noticed someone sitting in Elsie and Vivian's pew.

No one from the church had sat there since Vivian had passed away. Now there were two young women in the south-end pew. Abbey wondered who they might be.

Her speculation was cut short when Fannie Weller slid in beside them. Abbey decided the women must be staying at Fannie's bed and breakfast during rehearsal and production of an upcoming play at the Cherish Playhouse.

Like a plump mother hen, Fannie had served as hostess to theater underlings in her spacious and multi-roomed house for the last twenty years. A production's supporting cast could number in the dozens for musicals or just a handful for dramas, and there would always be a need for housing and meals for the actors. The headliners stayed in Harmony hotels, but the chorus and bit-part players could not afford hotel rooms. It was Fannie's house, along with a few other Cherish homes, that provided affordable accommodations. And Fannie kept women, only.

Abbey wondered what parts the two young ladies sitting in church, today, might have in this season's performance. Abbey wasn't even sure of the title of the play or who the headliners were this year. It was a little early for the announcement in the newspaper.

Abbey and Andy were still getting used to the idea that tiny Cherish had a professional off-off-Broadway theater. It astonished them that well-known actors and actresses like Mickey Rooney, Robert Conrad, Forrest Tucker, Eve Arden, and more would come to such an out-of-the-way venue to perform.

According to First Baptist Church members, Connor Wilson, Sr. had started the Cherish Playhouse for his son. Soybeans had made it possible; the senior Wilson was the owner of the processing plant in Decatur.

Connor Wilson, Jr. had studied acting and played in several New York City productions. But an unexpected illness had sent him home and had sparked in Connor the idea of building a professional playhouse in the corn. His dream was realized when top talent from Broadway had squeezed Cherish into their cross-country itinerary. Theater-lovers from across the state and beyond began to patronize the playhouse and critics extolled its rare offering of the professional art in an intimate rural setting.

After nearly thirty years, the theater's fame continued to expand, and its seats were always filled. Connor Jr., who now lived in Decatur, refused to enlarge the stage or add seating. He didn't want the town to change—and it didn't.

From her vantage point in the choir loft, Abbey observed that other church members had also noticed Fannie's guests. The theater ladies were the subject of pokes and side-glances all across the room, and Fannie, who sat proudly next to them, was acutely aware that she and they were the center of attention.

Abbey thought that staying at Fannie's must be a treat. Over the years Fannie had spurned suitors, who were usually more interested in her money than in Fannie. Instead, the spinster lavished her devotion on her many boarders. And Fannie's life was full. She maintained a lively correspondence with her famous and not-so-famous guests and she had a treasure of scrapbooks, letters, and photos to prove her connections in New York and across the country.

Against the distraction in this morning's service, Andy did his best to hold everyone's interest. He masterfully recounted the story of Joshua, the faithful man of God who had encouraged the Israelites to drive the Canaanite giants from the Promised Land.

Only Joshua and Caleb had believed God could help them against daunting odds. In a rousing close, Andy challenged the members to "always remember that our God is bigger and mightier than any of the giants you and I will ever face!"

The Bach fugue that bounced from Theresa Jackson's fingers on the organ seemed to speed the decided detour of vacating members who veered toward the south section of the room, first. Virtually everyone swung by to say a word or two to the visitors.

The swell of well-wishers gave Abbey time to slip off her choir robe and arrive at Andy's side before the ladies exited.

"This is Lisa and Serena," Fannie announced. "They're staying with me while they rehearse for *Star-Spangled Girl*."

Abbey could see, now, that Lisa was lithe and was likely a dancer, and Serena had the sculpted look of an Egyptian statue.

"They're both drama students at the University of Illinois," explained Fannie.

Andy and Abbey shook their hands.

"Is this your first professional engagement?" Andy asked the girls.

"It is for me," said Serena. "Lisa performed in Champaign last summer in *Guys and Dolls*."

"I love musicals," Lisa interjected with enthusiasm.

Abbey did, too, and said so. Abbey added, "We're happy to have you here, today. We hope you'll come back to worship with us, next Sunday."

The ladies assured them that they would.

PART TWO
THEY HEAR MY VOICE

CHAPTER FIFTEEN

GRANNIE

Abbey loved that when Andy was pleased, his voice rose by half an octave. Today, he had burst into the house with a high and resounding, "Guess what!"

"What?" she asked.

"Grannie's coming to visit!" Andy was practically levitating.

"When do they arrive at Molly's?" Abbey asked in excitement. She was happy that Grannie was coming again, and she assumed that Andy's parents were driving down to Harmony.

But Andy said, "There's no 'they.' It's just Grannie!"

Before Abbey could process what he was saying, Andy added, "And she's going to stay at our house!"

Abbey was puzzled; she knew that Grannie didn't drive. How was Grannie going to get to Cherish from her Chicago suburb if Andy's parents weren't bringing her?

The answer burst like a party-popper from Andy: "She's taking the train! Grannie's coming all by herself on the train."

Of course, thought Abbey! Of course, Grannie could take the train. And what fun it was going to be to have Grannie all to themselves!

"The train gets in at ten minutes after one, tomorrow," Andy said. "We can pick her up at the station. And this time, Grannie will be in church to hear me preach on Sunday!"

From the look on Andy's face, Abbey knew he was already imagining Grannie smiling up at him from the pews.

———⊱⬥⬥⬦⬦⬦⊰———

Andy and Abbey arrived at the depot in Decatur a little late, and they saw Grannie before she saw them. Of course, she had on a hat, and amid a pile of variously shaped suitcases and bags, she was intently crafting something in her lap from rose-colored thread. Grannie looked tiny and frail sitting there—every bit of her eighty-four years. Andy had trouble accepting how she had aged. He still thought of her as vibrant and feisty—Southern-backwoods-spry—as she'd been in his youth. He wanted to see her as he remembered her: arms akimbo—the Kentucky spitfire who had tamed the wildest parts of his upbringing. Now, instead, Andy worried that she had traveled alone.

But she had made it!

Grannie looked up before they called her name. It took her a second to process that they were here. When the realization came, she tossed her crochet onto the seat and stood to gather their hugs. Her lips had been freshly rouged, as always, and she lavished her love marks on their cheeks.

"I made it!" she cried. "I just couldn't wait any longer. Mac and Rachel were always too busy to bring me, and I started thinking why do I have to wait for them? Years ago, I used to go everywhere by train, and I figured a train still had to come to Decatur. I was right!"

Her eyes danced with triumph.

When Andy hugged Grannie again, she dropped a cane he'd never seen her use before. His heart hurt to see her supporting herself and moving slowly. When had this happened? When had Grannie grown old?

"Did they give you lunch on the train?" Abbey asked.

"Absolutely not!" she said. "I brought my own. No need to spend all that money for a bought lunch."

No, indeed, thought Andy. Grannie would have been indignant to have wasted six dollars for a chicken salad sandwich and a cup of coffee.

"And," she announced, "I had enough to share with two other people."

Andy salivated. He tried to imagine what she must have had in her lunch basket. Surely there had been some of her incomparable fried chicken, all-day beans, sweet cornbread, and perfect apple pie—all the things he remembered from childhood.

He and Abbey gathered up Grannie's luggage and started to make their way to the door.

Andy was weighed down. How had this little woman been able to manage all of this luggage, he wondered? But he already knew the answer. Grannie had no doubt charmed half of the people on the train, including the porters, probably tipping them with a piece of apple pie instead of bills—and they had loved it.

In the car on their way to Cherish, laughter made the seats bounce. Grannie regaled them with stories of the big dance at her high-rise a few weeks ago. She described in detail the formal gown she had sewn for herself (Andy could just picture her in it), and she clucked at the fact that the women in her building wouldn't let their husbands dance with her or the other senior women. Andy and Abbey imagined that men were in short supply there, and they pictured Grannie dancing with other aging widows to spirited polkas and the wheezing of accordions.

By the end of their drive to Cherish, their sides ached. Grannie's mind was as sharp as ever, and her exploits smacked of the joy of life.

Once at home, Grannie's presence diverted all attentions to her. Even Winston fell under her spell. His welcoming snorts abandoned Andy and Abbey, and he gravitated immediately to

Grannie. Throughout her visit, Winston never left her side. The adoring dog even stationed himself at her place at the dinner table to beg. (No one ever fed him from the table, but Winston was always hopeful.)

"What time is church tomorrow?" Grannie demanded over dessert.

"Andy will go early, and then you and I will ride with the Darrells, at nine," Abbey told her.

"Molly and Paul will come over to attend our service, too," added Andy. "And we'll all have lunch, here."

The plans satisfied her, and Grannie stood to help clear dishes from the table.

To Andy, she instructed, "You go and polish up that message. I'm expecting to hear a barn-burner!"

Andy promised, "Yes, ma'am! I'll be giving everyone Heaven!"

In the morning, as if she had birthed him herself, Grannie proudly smiled up at Andy from the third center pew. Gem-colored halos from the stained glass washed over Molly, Paul, Abbey, and Grannie. (Abbey had left the choir loft as soon as the anthem had ended.)

Andy introduced his grandmother to the congregation, but everyone already knew of her from his stories. They were eager, however, to meet her, in the flesh, after the service.

"This is the first time Grannie gets to hear me preach!" Andy announced, and the congregation applauded. Grannie beamed.

Then she nodded when Andy held up his Bible, with a forefinger planted inside to mark the page of his sermon passage, and he announced, "Please open the Word to Matthew 18."

As the pages rustled across the congregation, Abbey noticed that the Bible Andy held was not his usual, much-underlined, leather-bound volume. Instead, it was a thin, inexpensive, and stiffly bound Bible with pages seldom-turned. Abbey felt sure there must be a reason for her husband's use of this Bible, instead of the other.

Her observation was rewarded when Andy explained.

"You'll notice," Andy announced, "that I'm reading Scripture, this morning, from a Bible that's different from the one I usually use. The Bible I hold in my hand is very precious to me. It is the first Bible I ever owned.

"This Bible was purchased for me when I was six years old. My sister and I were visiting Grannie, and Grannie had bought and given each of us a Bible so we could go to church with her—something we had never done before. Sadly, although I proudly carried it, I never bothered to open this book, that day.

"In fact, I didn't open this Bible until I was twenty-two years old. That's when God and I finally became acquainted; that's when God was able to get my attention and turn me around. I remember well the night I dug this Bible out of my storage shed (yes, for some reason I had kept it all those years!) and I began to read it."

As Andy spoke, tears filled Grannie's eyes.

Andy continued: "This is the most important book ever written. I stand before you today because there is LIFE in this book! I am proof that God and His Word can change lives. These pages tell a powerful story of love and sacrifice! I wish that everyone could read and memorize this message, so they would see how much God loves them, and so they could keep His words with them always.

"Sadly," said Andy, "there are whole countries filled with people who do not have—and may be forbidden to have—the life-giving words found here. How blessed we are to have God's Word in front of us, today. Thank you, God!"

"With that in mind," Andy continued, "let's read, together, Matthew 18:10-15."

The congregation read aloud the parable of God, the Heavenly Shepherd.

Andy then reiterated, "Jesus said that although God owns and cares for a flock of hundreds, if even one lamb wanders away, the Shepherd goes in search of it. He brings it back into the safety of His care.

"God is not willing that anyone should be lost or perish," Andy restated.

Grannie nodded in agreement and smiled, and Andy continued to expound from the passage.

As he spoke, Andy wasn't surprised to hear Grannie murmur an occasional "yes" to several points, and he saw her head bob decisively.

He had anticipated that she would have a hard time keeping quiet. He knew that Grannie's idea of church was participation, with a capital P. He also guessed that, to her way of thinking, this congregation was unacceptably passive. After all, her grandson was imparting The Word!

Finally, Grannie could stand it no longer. As Andy articulated a particularly sound point, Grannie practically shouted an "AMEN!" that startled the couple behind her. Her outburst woke up others who had fallen into a listening lethargy, and her energetic spirit awed the children—especially Alan Horn and Brady Shook.

Andy loved it. He knew that Amens were common in Grannie's church, and he liked hearing them ring out.

By her third Amen, Horace Saunders and Leo Ryan had joined her. A couple of others who didn't have the confidence to let their agreement ring out were beginning to mouth silent

Amens. Marlene Horn and Lula Shook, however, sternly plastered their children's mouths shut with a look that only a mother could give.

Andy started to respond to the outbursts the way pastors from Grannie's church did: he acknowledged them. "I heard that Amen; thank you!" he said spiritedly. His words emboldened Grannie, Horace, and Leo. Now, even Lou Webb managed to make his Amens audible.

People all across the sanctuary listened to Andy's message more intently if only to anticipate what might occasion the next exclamation. Even Jack Butterman adjusted his hearing aid and stayed awake for the whole sermon.

After the service, Grannie held court with such pleasure that Andy decided not to rush her. She praised her grandson's preaching, and she delighted the congregation with asides about his childhood. She captivated them all with her wit and humor.

Andy finally stepped in when it was Leo Ryan's turn to greet her. Andy knew that if Leo got to talking, they would all be there for another half-hour.

Leo saw Andy approach and roared, "Amen, pastor! Great sermon!" Then Leo launched into how nice it was to have Grannie here, today, and how nice it was that she got to hear Andy preach, and how his grandmother had been a great woman, too, and how his visits to her house had been his favorite moments when he was a child, and that it was at her house that …

In mid-sentence (there were no breaks once Leo started) Andy loudly announced that it was time to get some lunch. "I'm sorry to break up the fun," Andy apologized firmly, "but we have a pot roast waiting at home and five hungry people."

Leo said, "Sure enough, I hear ya!" But then Leo launched into a description of his wife's pot roast and how he also loved her cherry pie, and...

Thankfully, Sybil Ryan pulled on her husband's sleeve. At her tug, Leo said, "Oh, yeah. We need to get going." He looked like he was going to say something else, but Sybil tugged again. Andy didn't know how she did it. As usual, Sybil always got Leo's attention without a word.

"Well, it's been nice to get to know you," Leo called over his shoulder. Gently but firmly, his silent wife hooked her arm in Leo's elbow and led him out the door.

Family stories punctuated Sunday dinner and supper at the parsonage. Some stories were sad, but most evoked laughter. In some, Abbey learned about relatives she'd not heard about before. One of those was Aunt Mabel.

Grannie leaned forward in her best storytelling posture with her hands on her knees. She recalled how Aunt Mabel had once driven up from Kentucky to visit Mac and Rachel, and she had picked up Grannie on the way.

"But by the time we got to Herndon, we were in trouble," Grannie announced in her you-won't-believe-this voice. "Mabel couldn't feel her legs, and I don't drive!

"So, Mabel steered, and I'm the one who had to work the gas pedal for miles (which is hard to do when you're in the passenger seat). You should have seen us! I was never so relieved as when I stomped on the brake in Mac and Rachel's driveway.

"Well, we all figured Mabel had had a stroke or something, so Mac carried her into the house and put her on the bed. Then he went to call for help. As you can imagine, Rachel and I were in a panic, and we fussed and clucked over Mabel. We put a compress on her forehead, and we loosened her clothes—and that's when we discovered she didn't have anything more wrong with her than sense!"

Grannie snorted. "Imagine a woman vainer than Lucifer," she sniffed. "Mabel was so skinny she couldn't get wet in the rain—but she was so vain she STILL had to wear a girdle! Well, that day it all caught up with her."

Grannie paused before her grand finale.

"So what happened?" Abbey urged.

"What happened?" Grannie said. "Why, that crazy skinny woman had put both legs in the same hole of her girdle!"

Only Grannie could tell such a thing with the drama and twist to make them all howl.

As the hours passed, and the stories faded, Abbey began to realize how few stories there were about Mac and Rachel or about the children's turbulent childhood.

Grannie's stories always evoked laughter and poked fun at herself and her family members (like Mabel). As far as Abbey knew, her stories never touched on tough things, including Grannie's past. No bitter tales ever crossed her lips. Instead, Grannie emphasized wise things and the bright side of life. Apparently, she always had. From what Abbey could tell, her sassy humor and carefully selected family legends had shaped Andy and Molly and transported them above the difficult circumstances of their youth.

Abbey was glad. Abbey couldn't imagine what Molly and Andy might have become without Grannie. Grannie's indomitable outlook and stories had buoyed the children up and made their troubled moments fly. Over the years, their happy Grannie-memories had overlaid their fears and their scars. And that same Grannie-power was still as strong as ever. It had woven such delight into their time, today, that it was hard for Molly and Paul to say good night.

"Chores come early on the farm," Paul apologized.

Grannie countered with, "Don't you think a thing about it, young man. I'll be here for several days, so we'll see each other again. It's just wonderful to see all of you kids! Being here is good for the soul."

Good for all of our souls, thought Abbey. How wonderful it was to have Grannie here.

—————⇒●⇐—————

When Andy and Abbey awakened the next morning, they realized that their furry alarm clock had not gone off and they had overslept. No doubt, Grannie had opened the bedroom door, and her canine subject had resumed his adoring escort.

It had been nice to sleep in, and Andy and Abbey snuggled like they used to in the mornings before Winston had come with his demands. Finally, after one more kiss, Abbey decided she'd better get up and get some breakfast for everyone. Before she could move, however, Andy suddenly threw back the covers.

"Can you smell it?" he cried, with his nose in the air.

Abbey did smell something, and she started to say, "It smells like..." when Andy cried out, "It's a Grannie Breakfast!"

Andy's nose had caught the aroma of bacon frying, and he had guessed that there were also scrambled eggs, biscuits and gravy, and sticky fried apples. It was Grannie's specialty breakfast, and it conjured up the Grannie mornings of his youth.

"Only Grannie makes sticky fried apples and a pan of 'speckled bet' to pour over your biscuits," he told Abbey excitedly, and he swept past her and down the hall. Abbey threw on her robe and hurried to catch up.

"You didn't have to do this all by yourself, Grannie!" Abbey protested when she got to the kitchen. "How can I help?"

But the meal was ready.

"There's nothing more to do, but eat," Grannie asserted. She filled their plates and made them pour their own coffee (brewed so strong that the spoon nearly stood up in it).

Andy could hardly contain himself to pray. With his eyes closed over the smells of his favorite breakfast, he lifted his hurried thanks.

———

After breakfast, Andy delayed going to the office as long as possible. He wouldn't have gone at all, but there were appointments to keep, including a lunch meeting of the Cherish ministers. He hugged Grannie and kissed Abbey, and he promised to be back in early afternoon.

Grannie and Abbey washed the breakfast dishes, pulled a few weeds from the vegetable garden, selected a jigsaw puzzle to work later, and served cookies and milk to Lizzie and Butter. Then as the two of them lunched on the patio, Abbey asked Grannie to share her breakfast secrets.

"Andy loves your speckled bet," Abbey said. "Maybe you could tell me how to make it?"

"Nothin' to it," said Grannie. "You just save the bacon grease (or ham will do, too) and add some coffee. If you want red-eye gravy, you add some red pepper."

"Really?" said Abbey. She was sure it wasn't healthy, but she said nothing.

Then, Abbey asked about the sticky fried apples.

"No secret there, either," Grannie said. "Just sugar 'em and cook 'em down slowly in bacon grease."

Abbey decided that bacon grease must be the secret to everything, and she sighed. It couldn't be good for you—and yet, it didn't seem to have affected Grannie. Perhaps the experts didn't know everything?

Besides, it certainly did taste good!

⸺➛●◄⸺

After lunch, Abbey turned on the television.

Normally the parsonage television wasn't on during the day, but Grannie had announced it was time for her program: *A Brighter Tomorrow.* Abbey had taken the hint and said she'd do the dishes by herself if Grannie wanted to go and watch television. Grannie hadn't argued. She had let Abbey run the dishwater while she settled into the cushions of the television room sofa.

But then, Grannie came stomping back into the kitchen and declared, "Nearly forgot to make my tea!"

Abbey was surprised. Grannie pressed against the counter and urgently pointed at the teakettle. Abbey quickly pulled out the tea bags and turned on the burner.

"Don't you have any instant tea?" Grannie countered.

Puzzled, Abbey asked, "Don't you want hot tea?"

"Yes. But I make mine with instant," Grannie insisted impatiently. Abbey didn't question her. She pulled out the jar of instant that she usually used for iced tea, and Grannie nodded approvingly. They could hear the program starting in the other room, and Grannie was impatient to get back to it. The minute the water was hot, Grannie spooned in the tea crystals. Then she shrugged off Abbey's offer of help and took off with her cup for the other room.

Abbey cringed as Grannie gripped her cane in one hand and dribbled her tea with every step. Hot tea splashed from side to side in the cup, and the overflow hit the floor. For the first time since they had moved into the parsonage, Abbey appreciated the multi-colored brown and gray of the shag carpet, and she tried to remember the color of Grannie's carpet.

108

When Grannie had settled again, Abbey returned to the dishes in the sink. Abbey could hear angst-in-the-afternoon turned up a little too loud, and she could tell that someone was confiding to someone about being in love. But since she didn't know the characters, Abbey didn't pay much attention.

After a few minutes, the volume increased for the first commercial interruption, and Abbey decided to see if Grannie needed a warm-up on her tea. She grabbed a potholder and carried the kettle to the other room. At the door, she stopped and snickered.

The all-important tea had been virtually untouched, and Grannie (with Winston on her lap) was sound asleep. Grannie's head was back, her jaw was relaxed, and her mouth gaped. She looked comfortable, and her cheeks puffed in and out in a light snore.

Grannie had unquestionably slept through the entire drama—loud commercials and all—and she would no doubt sleep through the second half, too. Abbey did not disturb her but tip-toed back to the kitchen.

Abbey did not check in again until the theme music signaled the end of the program. As the credits rolled, Grannie roused. When she noticed Abbey in the doorway, she knew she'd been caught.

"Well, I never!" Grannie exclaimed, and she pulled herself upright and straightened her hair. "The very idea!" she chided herself.

Finally, she indignantly confessed, "I fell asleep again, didn't I? Hmm!"

Then she inquired abruptly, "You didn't happen to see if Vince and Stella got engaged did you?"

Abbey had to apologize that she hadn't been watching, and Grannie scowled. "Well, I guess I'll have to call Gloria to find out what happened."

From what Abbey overheard of the phone call, Abbey gathered that Grannie seldom saw her program. The nap and subsequent call to her friend, Gloria, seemed to be part of Grannie's usual afternoon routine. Thankfully, Gloria was able to inform Grannie that Vince and Stella were not only engaged, but they were going to be married in Hawaii.

That night, Abbey found herself drooping. It was nearly eleven-thirty, a full hour past her bedtime. The 1000-piece interlocking puzzle of the Pella, Iowa Tulip Festival was only partly complete, and Grannie refused to stop.

Andy had long-ago said good night. In fact, the minute they had dumped the pieces out of the box, Andy had disappeared. "That stuff makes my brain freeze up," he had declared. Now Andy was sleeping peacefully, and Abbey was struggling to stay awake. Perhaps if Andy had helped with the puzzle, they might have finished it by now, Abbey thought uncharitably.

Around midnight, Grannie triumphantly set the last pieces on the table in place; but then she frowned.

"There's a piece on the floor somewhere," Grannie announced.

Abbey could tell by her tone that the puzzle would not be complete without that last piece.

Abbey sighed.

She and Grannie pushed back their chairs and searched everywhere. Abbey got on her knees and felt along the carpet, the two of them shook out the folds of their clothes, and they both checked the box one more time. But the missing piece was nowhere to be found.

"Must have got lost in packaging," Abbey suggested with an all-to-obvious yawn.

It was a hint that it was time to turn in, but Grannie's lips formed into a thin line, and she declared loudly, "Fiddlesticks! I don't believe it!"

Then, before Abbey realized what was happening, Grannie grabbed her cane, snatched up a nearby newspaper, and pounded her way down the hallway. Grannie threw open the door to the master bedroom and marched over to the bed. Without bothering to turn on the light, Grannie lifted the rolled-up newspaper and smartly swatted the figure lying there.

In dismay, Abbey turned on the light.

"Wha-? Ouch! What are you doing?" Andy cried, as he blinked against the newspaper onslaught and the sudden light.

"Where is it?" Grannie demanded.

"What are you talking about?" Andy protested.

"You know what I mean, you stinker!"

Abbey wasn't sure what to think—until she saw Andy grin.

Sheepishly, he reached under his pillow and pulled out the missing puzzle piece.

"I knew it! I knew it!" Grannie exclaimed. "Still pulling the same old stuff! Too bad I don't have a green willow switch right here, my little man!"

Andy laughed. He was hardly her "little man" anymore. She couldn't spank him now.

Muttering under her breath, Grannie stomped back to the card table and self-righteously pressed the last piece into place. It was then that Abbey caught the twinkle in her eye.

"I don't know how you live with him," Grannie declared. "And him, a man of the cloth!"

Grannie's visit came to an end far too soon. Sadly, in the same way that the anticipation of her visit had sparked euphoria, the end of her time with them spurred depression. Andy was surprised at the flood of old feelings that surfaced.

As a child, Andy had always mourned Grannie's last day with them because uncertainty always moved in whenever Grannie moved out. No one knew when Mom and Dad would take up fighting again, and Andy's young tummy had ached with it.

But now, he was grown. His parents weren't here, and there was no need to fear their hateful exchanges. Andy fought back the old feelings. He refused to let the darkness dominate him. Instead, the adult-Andy distilled his childhood dread into questions he had always asked himself:

Why had his parents always fought so much? Why were they so contentious and dissatisfied? Had they ever been kind to one another? Had they ever loved one another? (Surely they must have, or they would never have managed to have had two children.) Why wasn't Grannie like them? Why weren't they (especially his mother) more like Grannie?

Then for some reason, today, right in the middle of Andy's list of questions, a new thought struck him. It flashed straight to the forefront of his mind: Grannie knew something!

Grannie had lived through the times when his parents had met and married and borne children. She knew the Garrett saga and could tell him the story. She could recreate the past for him and supply the insights he had always wondered about.

His excitement grew. He could finally learn what had shaped his parents' lives and sharpened their anger. The time had come, and the opportunity was here, to ask.

Andy knew the stories wouldn't be happy ones. That had to be why Grannie had never shared them, before.

He knew that when they were children, he and Molly had needed happy stories. Stories of hurts and sad things they couldn't understand would not have helped them. It would have only added to the fog of insecurity that already enveloped them. Grannie had been right not to mess with their tender grip on goodness.

But now, Andy and Molly were adults. They could handle hard things. Andy could bear the truth, no matter how difficult it might be.

It was time to hear the Garrett story. It was time to ask.

Once the car had reached the highway, and miles of fields lined the way to Decatur, Andy prepared to ask Grannie his questions. Here, there would be no distracting telephone calls or knocks on the parsonage door. Andy knew he had one exclusive hour with Grannie before she and her wisdom would be gone.

He turned off the car radio and cut off the news anchor they had been listening to. He needed new news.

"Grannie," Andy began. "I need to ask you some things I've never asked before—some things about our family that I'm sure you know."

The car was still. Andy continued.

"I need you to tell me about Mom's and Dad's past."

When there was no response from the backseat, Andy went on. "For years we've all suffered from Mom's and Dad's fighting, and it's never made sense. I've always thought something must have happened to make them so bitter and mean. What happened, Grannie? What happened to them?"

Andy expected Grannie to respond, now. But she did not.

After days of nonstop reminiscences and humorous tales, Grannie was now strangely silent. Andy knew she had heard him. He could see her frown in the rearview mirror. But she didn't answer. Why was Grannie quiet?

She seemed to search the stretched fabric above her as if the answer were posted there. Then after a sigh, Grannie very slowly and deliberately said, "Son, your parents went through some unbearably rough times. It messed them up. I don't know if they'll ever get over it."

Andy waited for her to continue—to elaborate, but she did not. Now he bitterly whispered, "We ALL went through some rough times."

He then added sourly, "And I'm still not over it."

Instantly, Grannie sat forward and countered. "But you have gotten over it!" she said.

Then she declared more solidly, "God answered my prayers for you and Molly. You have both grown up and married happily."

Then she added, "And your parents can't hurt you anymore. They just hurt each other."

She pushed back into her seat. There was finality in her tone, and Andy was surprised. He could tell by her face in the mirror that she was finished and was not going to share anything further.

He was stunned to think she had nothing more to say. Andy's mind whirled over Grannie's sparseness. Why had she said only the little she had said? What did it mean? Had her words told him anything?

From the front seat next to her husband, Abbey sat in silence. She knew that Andy was struggling to sort out the puzzle of his past.

Indeed, he was replaying Grannie's statements. He continued to turn them over in his mind and weigh them against everything he already knew. It wasn't a lot. But as he processed her words, Andy could see how Grannie's responses mirrored answers he had already shaped for himself. Her words, few as they were, provided confirmation of at least three things.

First, she said he had gotten over his pain. Andy had to agree that he had grown out of much of his childhood pain. He had not forgotten it; he probably never would. But he agreed with Grannie that he and Molly had escaped lasting damage, and they were now miles away from the effects of their parents' craziness. So, he decided, it was true that he had "gotten over it."

Second, Grannie had mentioned her prayers for him and Molly to marry happily. He had not thought of her praying for that. He had known of her prayers for him in seminary and before his spiritual conversion, but he had not envisioned her pleas for him and Molly simply to grow up and form healthy and happy relationships. Thankfully, God had answered those prayers. Paul and Abbey were the proof of it.

And finally, Andy recognized that Grannie was also right about his parents not having escaped their terrible hurt. He still didn't understand what drove it, but it was true that his mother and father were still locked in some unaccountable combat, and they were still battering and bloodying each other's souls. Andy had grown up fearful of them, but now Andy pitied them. He envisioned his parents as weak and vainly clinging to their sick relationship in an attempt to—survive?

It still made no sense to him. But Andy knew, now, from what little Grannie had shared, that something had indeed happened that had set his parents on this course. And although he had no idea why Grannie remained silent about it, he could pray that God would save his parents from whatever it was that had caused them so much pain.

CHAPTER SIXTEEN

KIDS AT THE THEATER

As time passed after Grannie's departure, so did the number of Amens that had marked her Sundays with them. Leo Ryan and Horace Saunders kept them alive but with less frequency.

Attendance fluctuated, now, because the school year had ended and vacation had begun. First Baptist Church members scattered to the winds to find adventure.

The By-the-Ways flew to Florida and Disney World, the Darrells drove to see relatives in Texas, and the bumper sticker on the Webb's car announced that they had been to Wall Drug.

Emma Peters traveled the farthest; she was on her way to Egypt.

Years ago, Emma and Jethro had saved up the necessary money for a trip to Egypt, but the trip had never come. Jethro had become ill, and their only visits had been to the hospital in Harmony. In an acknowledgment that his ALS would take him early, Jethro had made Emma promise to make the trip after he was gone. Andy was glad she had done it. He and Abbey looked forward to talking with her when she returned.

Andy and Abbey had made their own summer trip early in June to visit Abbey's parents in Iowa. Abbey had already pasted the snapshots into her treasured family album. The summer trip had held no worries of ice and snow like their many perilous

Thanksgiving and Christmas trips from college and seminary had. Their decision, a couple of years ago, to visit Iowa only in summer had proven to be a good one. It was nice to sit on the Preston porch and admire Abbey's mother's flower beds while drinking coffee and eating fresh strawberry pie. Yes, summer trips to Iowa were the best.

Today, Andy and Abbey stopped at the Cherish Post Office to pick up their mail. As expected, they found a pile of bills and half-dozen postcards from vacationing church members. In the stack was an air-mailed envelope postmarked "Egypt" that Andy tore open immediately.

It contained a letter and a photo of Emma Peters in tennis shoes, a pith helmet, and a bright scarf. Also dressed in a big smile, Emma was riding high on a gangly-looking camel in front of the sun-kissed Pyramids. "Having a great time!" she had written. "Am keeping a journal and will tell you all about it when I get back."

Emma added that as she experienced each adventure, she was carefully describing it aloud, just as if Jethro were with her. "Some of my fellow-travelers think I'm possibly deranged to be talking to myself," she wrote, "but that's okay. They don't know that I need to share with my life-partner all the things we had planned to do together. When I get back home, I'll shut that door and won't bother Heaven, anymore—until I can see Jesus and Jethro, face-to-face."

Andy smiled. Emma was doing well.

⊷•◦•⊶

Practices for *Star-Spangled Girl* were nearing an end. Andy and Abbey weren't familiar with the names of the lead actors, but from their experience with *Shenandoah* last year, they were certain the play would be excellent, whoever the stars were.

Lisa and Serena had been in church nearly every Sunday, and Jimmy Fisher had shown more than a little interest in them. And although he was young (not yet sixteen), the young actresses had graciously indulged his attention. Jimmy's mother told Abbey she'd never seen her son so concerned over what he was going to wear to church. Charlene had then laughed when Abbey had pointed out that Jimmy was not alone in his fascination with the ladies. Once they had seen that the theater girls were approachable, Donny Cain and other male teens (who were far too shy to initiate conversation on their own) had flanked Jimmy to participate vicariously in his interaction with the beautiful celebrities.

While the boys were lavishing their attention on Lisa and Serena, the girls of the youth group sniffed at how childish the guys were behaving to think that full-grown women would pay any real attention to mere boys. Only Josie Fisher had ventured close enough to ask a question. She had been dying to know how Serena had arranged her hair. Serena had kindly shown her the secret, and Josie had spent the next two hours at home with hairpins, hairspray, and a mirror. As only a brother could do, however, Jimmy had snickered at the result, and Josie had angrily torn out every hairpin and thrown them at him. "You thought it looked great on HER," she had shouted and slammed the bedroom door.

When Jimmy got an invitation to come to one of the *Star-Spangled Girl* final rehearsals, the news flashed through the youth group. Suddenly everyone wanted to go, including the stand-offish girls who had pooh-poohed Jimmy's attentions to the actresses. Chelsea came to the rescue and talked with Lisa, who assured her it would be okay if all of the kids wanted to come one afternoon. They settled on the coming Saturday at three o'clock.

Of all the church kids, only Jimmy and Josie had ever been to the theater. They now flaunted their knowledge of how to enter and find seats in the dim light. Throughout the rehearsal, the director and actors paid no attention to the audience. But at the end of the session when the little group tentatively clapped, Serena interrupted the departure of the cast and director to announce that the visitors this afternoon had been the First Baptist Church youth group, "including special theater-lover Jimmy Fisher." The cast smiled and bowed, and several women called out "Hi, Jimmy!" Flushed with their attention, Jimmy hesitantly stood and bowed back. The cast broke into applause, which only caused his face to turn redder.

"Why don't you all come up, and we'll give you a backstage tour?" called the director.

In awe, the teens wandered behind the curtain and into the world of props and backdrops. Then they visited the dressing rooms, where Serena did a quick makeup demo for the girls.

Just before they left, each teen received a handbill for the play. Cast members had signed each one. Josie clutched hers to her heart with a near-tearful "thank you!" and Serena, who hadn't yet removed her stage makeup after the demonstration, planted a perfect red kiss on Jimmy's handbill. He nearly swooned.

The director called out, "Hope to see you and your families when we raise the curtain, next week!"

CHAPTER SEVENTEEN

MOM: STAR-KISSED

Once again, things at the parsonage were in a dither.

Evidently not be outdone by Grannie, Andy's parents had called to say they were coming for a quick visit. They also announced they were going to stay with Andy and Abbey—instead of Molly and Paul. They would be coming straight from their Florida time-share, and their flight would arrive two days from now. Andy and Abbey would have to meet them at the airport in Decatur.

As low-key as the preparations had been for Grannie's visit, the imminent advent of Mom and Dad Garrett sent Andy and Abbey into high gear. Once again, Andy turned the television room into a guest room, and Abbey obsessed over dusting and polishing every corner and surface. Winston scrambled onto the living room sofa where he could safely watch and not be run over in their haste. The bewildered dog wasn't sure what had gotten into them.

"Pillows!" cried Abbey, less than an hour before they were to drive to the airport. "We don't have enough pillows!" Grannie had only required one pillow, and they didn't have a second spare.

"You finish mopping the kitchen floor," Andy huffed, "and I'll go buy a couple of pillows and pillow cases."

He raced to the store and back, pulled the plastic off his two inexpensive purchases, pulled new cases onto them, and plopped them onto the fold-out sofa bed. Then he held open the door for Abbey, who climbed into the car for their drive to Decatur.

———————

In the middle of the preparation rush, Abbey had called Molly and Paul to tell them about the visit.

"Oh, you lucky people!" Molly had exclaimed.

"Do you have any hints for entertaining them?" Abbey asked.

"Sorry," said Molly. "They are impossible to entertain. You just try to avoid all controversial subjects and never leave them alone in the same room for too long."

"That's what I was afraid you'd say. Would you at least say an extra prayer for us? We have no idea how long they're planning to stay. Mom and Dad were very vague when Andy asked them. I imagine we'll have a chance to have you two over."

"Don't worry, Abbey. Of course, we'll come," Molly assured her. "You two came to support us when they stayed here last fall. Just let us know what the plans are as they develop."

Then, even though she doubted it, Molly encouraged her with, "It'll go all right. You'll see."

———————

As they turned in at the airport drive, Abbey joined Andy in a loudly offered prayer: "Lord, help this visit to be a good one. We pray that everything at the house is acceptable and that Mom and Dad won't be too uncomfortable."

Neither Andy nor Abbey could keep from worrying. Who knew what Andy's snobbish parents would think of their tiny town and little parsonage?

With their hearts beating an uncertain rhythm, Andy and Abbey left the car in the short-term parking lot and hurried to the baggage area. Andy's parents were waiting.

"There they are!" Abbey called out cheerfully. She and Andy put on their best smiles and offered hugs and kisses.

"Did you have a good flight?" Andy asked.

"Not bad," answered Rachel. "Thankfully it's a short trip. Not much can go wrong."

"That's fine for you," grumped Mac. "The guy behind me kept kicking the back of my seat."

"Of course there would be something for you to complain about!" spat Rachel.

Mac snorted loudly and balled his fists as they strode out of the terminal.

It's going to be a long ride in the car, thought Abbey.

Andy tried to deflect his dad's belligerence with the mention of a vintage car that he and Abbey had seen in short-term parking when they'd arrived; Andy hoped it was still there so he could show his dad. Also, because Mac and Rachel hadn't yet seen Winston, the dog would be another topic to safely broach to keep the prickly pair from goading each other.

As Andy had hoped, the vintage auto hadn't moved, and it provided conversation for the first twenty minutes on the road.

"Nineteen fifty-three, pristine," his dad whistled. "What a beauty!"

The gleaming black Packard Caribbean convertible was perfect in every way, from the white interior and the spotless whitewalls to the detail of the continental motif on the back bumper. Andy and his dad had been tempted to wait for the owner to return, but they knew it wasn't likely to happen soon.

"I would have loved to have had a look under that hood," his dad said.

Andy peppered his father with questions about other automobiles from that era. Mac swelled with his expertise and spoke at length about "the way cars used to be." His every comment disparaged newer models that "could not compare with the style and distinction found in the cars of the past."

"You can hardly tell one car from the other, now," Mac said with disdain. "Look at the new T-bird. All the beautiful lines have begun to melt away."

Andy valiantly kept up the conversation, but Abbey panicked when the subject of cars eventually waned. She knew that any lull in the conversation could result in the resumption of the heated jabs and loaded barbs that marked Mac and Rachel's habitual discourse. She quickly introduced the topic of Winston and began to regale everyone with some of the dog's more memorable antics.

"I can't wait for you to see him," Andy interjected enthusiastically.

The miles hummed by, and Cherish finally appeared. Andy slowly drove past the church and took a quick scoop around the town square. He had no idea what his overly critical parents would think, but he held his head high and introduced his church and town proudly.

Suddenly Rachel shrieked.

Stunned, Andy pulled over in a panic. "What's wrong, Mom?" he called out.

"It's Rory Duke!" she cried.

"Where?" asked Andy. "Is that somebody you know?"

"Is he really going to be here while we're here?" his mother asked excitedly, as she pointed to the marquee on the Cherish Playhouse.

It dawned on Abbey that she was talking about an actor whose name appeared in the lettering above the theater entrance.

"Yes," said Abbey. "He's playing here for another three weeks."

"Who's Rory Duke?" Andy asked, and Abbey was just as glad that he had because she didn't know who Rory was, either.

"He plays Vince Barrett on *A Brighter Tomorrow,* every day at one o'clock," Rachel cooed. "And he's sooo handsome."

"What?" Mac snarled. "I thought we'd run over somebody back there! Instead, it's just you, screaming over some soap opera star."

Rachel snapped back, "At least it's not some stupid football player!"

"Would you like to go to the show?" Andy asked quickly, to interrupt the spat. He was also hoping they'd found a night's entertainment for his parents' visit. He and Abbey hadn't yet seen the production, but he imagined it might be perfect.

In response, Rachel pushed Mac out of the car and made him pick up tickets for the next evening. "For all four of us," she specified.

Grumbling like a bear fresh from hibernation, Mac trudged to the counter inside and got the tickets.

The whole time he was away, Rachel chanted over and over, "I can't believe we're going to get to see him in person. I just can't believe it!"

When his dad returned, Andy poured out praise for the little theater, and he said silent praise to God for providing an activity that would entertain his parents for at least one whole evening.

"Why, you cute little thing!" Rachel cried when everyone entered the parsonage. Winston cooperated immediately with Andy and Abbey's hope that he would take center stage. He welcomed Rachel with a "who are you; please pet me" snort and body wag.

Mac squatted and roughed Winston's ears. "Reminds me of when we got Winnie," Mac said. "Now there was a good dog."

Andy felt relief to hear his parents recall his childhood dog with affection. Mom and Dad had liked Winnie when Andy was growing up, and he had hoped the sentiment remained.

"She certainly did love the boy, didn't she?" recalled Rachel.

Abbey marveled. It was so unusual to hear Andy's parents agreeing on anything agreeable.

"Remember how much Winnie loved Dairy Queen ice cream?" asked Mac.

Rachel laughed. "Oh my, that's an understatement."

Abbey remembered the story as Andy had related it to her and said, "Am I right that she generated a little slobber?"

Andy replied, "Imagine a Winston three times this size, and think of the slobber a dog like that can toss around! Mom and Dad always put Winnie in the back seat with Molly and me, and we were always sticky and soaking wet by the time we got home."

Abbey cringed, but she suggested bravely, "Maybe we can introduce Winston to the Dairy Delite while your parents are here."

"I'll sit up front," Mac announced emphatically.

"Oh, you fool!" Rachel spat and turned her back on him.

Time to divide and hopefully conquer, thought Abbey. She left Mac with Andy, to be entertained by Winston, and she drew Rachel aside to tell her about the Hemple lamp and antique table at the front window. These were Abbey's prized possessions because of their history.

"They're beautiful!" Rachel cooed, and Abbey felt proud. She sensed that Rachel truly did admire the fine old items and their provenance: a silver print of the lamp and table in a room in Abbey's great-grandparents' home. Rachel remarked how nice it was that Abbey had such a proud family history. Rachel's family had been poor, and they had owned little. There had been nothing to pass down but a handful of brittle photographs.

———◆———

"Your mom is downright giddy!" Abbey whispered to Andy, the next evening, as the curtain of the Cherish Playhouse lifted.

"Can you believe it?" Andy whispered back.

Unlike last year when Andy and Abbey had sat near the back for *Shenandoah*, their seats for tonight were in the second row. It wasn't a large theater, but Dad had shelled out good money for the tickets, and it was a treat to be close enough to see every expression on the actors' faces.

Even so, Andy's dad sat with his arms crossed. He appeared determined not to have a pleasant time. The play, however, proved to be a witty farce, and Mac laughed in spite of himself—he even doubled over and howled a couple of times.

Too enraptured by her soap opera star to notice her husband's reactions, Rachel sighed whenever Rory Duke took the stage. Her applause was the longest when the curtain finally fell.

"Wasn't that marvelous?" Rachel gushed.

"It was pretty good," Mac admitted.

An elderly audience member behind them, who'd overheard the exchange, asked Rachel, "Isn't Rory charming? I couldn't take my eyes off him all night." Then the woman tapped Rachel's elbow, "Do you watch him on A *Brighter Tomorrow?*"

With eyes glowing, Rachel exclaimed, "I know! I know! He's just wonderful! I watch him every day."

Mac rolled his eyes, but he held his tongue.

Abbey leaned over to whisper in Andy's ear: "It's like watching a couple of school girls with a crush on some cute kid."

Andy agreed, and grateful for the lack of bickering between his parents, he murmured, "We couldn't have planned a better evening."

Rachel suddenly turned. "That woman said we can wait by the stage door and get autographs!"

Mac rolled his eyes, again.

"Sure, Mom, we can go around to the alley," said Andy. "Come on."

Andy and Abbey led the way to where a long line of theater-goers stood. The Garretts were last in line, but Rachel didn't seem to care.

It was a full twenty minutes before the supporting players emerged and autographs began, and it was close to an hour before the stars came out. Rachel jockeyed for an opportunity to see those who were signing the playbooks ahead of her. She was impressed that Serena and Lisa knew Andy and Abbey. And as the line dwindled, Rachel grew more excited.

When she finally handed Rory Duke her program, she said, "I watch you every day!" Then she lowered her voice and whispered, "And I don't think Vince is nearly the scoundrel he's being made out to be."

Rory, who had to have heard that same thing twenty or thirty times that night, was charming.

"Well, thank you! Did you say your name was Rachel?" Rory grinned as he signed her program. "You waited a long time—sorry I couldn't have hurried more. Thanks for watching *A Brighter Tomorrow* so faithfully."

Then Rory did the unexpected. He bent over and kissed Rachel's cheek.

Andy thought his mother was going to faint! Her hand flew to that cheek and lingered long after Rory waved and joined his stage friends.

Even Mac was tickled at her and said affably, "She'll be the hit of the beauty salon back home when she tells them about meeting Rory Duke in person—and that he kissed her! She'll probably have that theater program framed."

With stars in her eyes, Rachel said to no one in particular, "Who would have thought that I would meet Rory Duke in Cherish, where my son and daughter-in-law live!"

"My!" observed Andy quietly into Abbey's ear. "Cherish has just engraved its name into the Garrett social registry."

CHAPTER EIGHTEEN

WORN-OUT WELCOME

As they had promised, Molly and Paul dutifully came to the parsonage the following night. Molly brought two pies: a coconut cream and an apple.

"I know Andy loves coconut cream, but I know Dad loves apple, so I brought them both," Molly said.

When Molly and Abbey were alone in the kitchen, Molly gave Abbey an empathetic look and mouthed the words, "How's it going?" Abbey shrugged a "not bad," which took Molly by surprise.

Then, because Rachel was coming through the door, Abbey said out loud, "We all went to the play last night and had a great time. Have you ever heard of Rory Duke?"

At that, Rachel clasped her hands and closed her eyes. "Oh, it was a delightful night!" she said.

Molly was incredulous. Her mother had praised something about Cherish.

"Do you know Rory Duke, from *A Brighter Tomorrow?*" Rachel asked. Before Molly could reply, Rachel said, "Well, he was in this clever play, and it was just marvelous. I even got his autograph."

"And he kissed her!" Andy called from the other room.

Involuntarily, Rachel reached up to touch her cheek. "Yes, he did," she said.

Laughter wafted in from the living room, where the men were playing with the dog.

"You seem to have the gift with them," Molly whispered, a few minutes later. "These are the most pleasant few moments I've spent under the same roof with my parents in years."

"It's all a wonder to me, too," Abbey whispered back. "I think I love Rory Duke."

<hr>

After dinner, Andy took Winston outside and started to collect the plastic drinking glasses they'd left on the picnic table earlier that afternoon. Paul was in the bathroom washing spilled coffee from his pants, and Molly and Abbey were finishing up the dishes in the kitchen. Rachel stepped into the guest room to get her playbook and Mac followed her so he could change into some slippers.

Suddenly, there were shouts from behind the guest room door.

"Why didn't you pack my slippers?" Mac was demanding.

"I probably couldn't find them!" Rachel defended herself.

"You know these shoes hurt my feet and I hate to wear them around the house," Mac charged.

"Well, take the stinking things off and walk in your stocking feet!"

"I guess I'll have to!"

Mac roared out of the room with a string of epithets. He slammed the door behind him and sank heavily into the recliner in the living room. He kicked off his shoes. Winston slunk behind the sofa, not sure what was happening.

Molly stuck her head around the corner from the kitchen and thought, "Well, the enchanted carriage has reverted to a pumpkin."

Rachel cursed and continued to berate Mac, even though he was gone. Objects in the guest room hit the floor as she apparently continued to search. All of a sudden Rachel emerged, slippers in hand.

"Here are your stupid slippers!" she yelled.

With intent to hurt, she threw them at Mac. One caught him in the chest—and the other smashed into Abbey's grandmother's lamp and sent it to the floor.

Molly gasped. She knew the lamp was Abbey's prized possession, and she knew that it was irreplaceable. Now it was in pieces, all over the carpet!

For a moment there was not a sound. Then Rachel began to sob. She fled to the guest room and slammed the door.

"Oh, great! Nice job!" yelled Mac, and he stormed out the front door in his stocking feet.

They both knew they were in trouble.

Andy had missed it all. When he and Winston came in from the yard, he found Molly on the living room floor collecting pieces of glass. Dad had disappeared, and Mom was crying hysterically in the guest room. Watching, dazed, in the middle of the living room was Abbey, with dish soap dripping from her hands.

Except for the muffled sobbing behind the guest room door, there was not a sound.

"What in the world happened?" Andy cried. "I've only been gone for a couple of minutes."

Paul emerged from the bathroom with a soapy wet spot on his pants. "I could hear it, but I had to put my pants back on and wasn't quick enough," he said.

Molly's voice was a monotone. "It happened so fast," she said. "Dad couldn't find his slippers and accused Mom of not packing them. She finally found them and threw them at him, and one of them hit the lamp."

Andy looked, then, from the pieces of glass on the floor to Abbey's frozen expression. "Abbey's precious lamp!" he breathed. He took his stricken wife in his arms.

Then Paul demanded, "Where's your dad?"

"Out there somewhere in his stocking feet," said Molly.

With that, Paul snatched up Mac's shoes and started out the front door.

"I'll find Dad," Paul said. "You can deal with Mom."

After Molly and Paul left, Abbey retreated to the bedroom and did not come out the rest of the night. Mac and Rachel hid in the guest room, where it was obvious they were packing their bags. They were surprisingly silent. Andy didn't bother to look, but he thought he heard a noise in the living room once the lights were out. He felt sure his dad spent the night in the recliner.

Cold cereal was laid out on the kitchen table, but no one ate in the morning. Abbey hadn't even made coffee. Andy finally brewed a pot, while Abbey stayed in the bedroom. Mac drank half a cup, and Rachel had nothing.

Around ten, Molly and Paul arrived. Even though Mac and Rachel hadn't called, yet, to get tickets for a flight home, they piled their bags into the car so Molly and Paul could take them to the airport.

Just before they left, Abbey came out of the bedroom.

Rachel couldn't look at her. Mac attempted an apology. "I know we can't replace it, but we'll get you a new lamp," he muttered in his shame.

"I am so sorry, Abbey," Rachel then sobbed into a handkerchief.

Abbey simply said, "I understand."

But she didn't really. How could anyone understand fully-grown adults who behaved the way these two did? It didn't make any sense. They hadn't been in the house two full days.

"We need to get back home, anyway," said Mac, and he and Rachel practically fell over each other to get out the door.

Andy was grateful that Molly and Paul were driving his parents to the airport. He didn't think he could be civilized with them for an hour in the car. Why did their dysfunction always have to ruin everything?

He and Abbey didn't even wave as they watched the car back out of the driveway.

CHAPTER NINETEEN

AMENDS

Abbey cried on the phone when she told her mother about the lamp. "I should have put it in a safer place—perhaps our bedroom," she lamented.

Abbey felt she'd let her family down. She had been entrusted with this treasure of their past (it had been left to her in Grandma's will), and she had let it break.

Her mother gently reassured her: "Honey, it's surprising it's lasted as long as it has. Old things become fragile with age and don't last forever."

Then she added, "Besides, you still have the table and the photo."

It was true. Abbey still had the photo—a browned image of Abbey's great-grandparents and children in their Sunday best— and Abbey still had the table that had always held the lamp. In the photo, the Hemples posed stiffly in their parlor, some sitting and some standing in a somber row. Above their heads, in the style of the day, paintings on the wall hung tipped down for viewing. Hand-crocheted doilies covered the arms and backs of chairs and a loveseat. And there, to one side, decorating an ornate occasional table (the one now in Abbey's living room), was the globed, hand-painted lamp.

Abbey had turned the picture to the wall after Andy's parents had left, and she could barely bring herself to look in the direction of the antique table. Finally, Abbey put a long cloth over the table, and she took down the photo. She buried the picture under her sweaters in the dresser.

Hiding the evidence did nothing to make her anger go away, however. Abbey harbored it in her belly like a frozen stone.

A knock on the door a few days later announced the delivery of a box from Herndon. Andy opened it and found his parents' peace token: a new lamp. Abbey gritted her teeth and refused to let Andy unpack it. Money and gifts, no matter how beautiful, could not repair her loss. She let the gift feed her anger.

The broken lamp had been a treasured antique and had represented decades of family history. This one, although similar in style, could not be more than a few months old and was sterile: it had no story. Its incandescence had never bathed loved ones on quiet evenings as they had conversed, read, and perhaps sewn in its light.

For nearly a week, Abbey sulked and refused to put the new lamp on the table. The box sat out-of-sight behind the sofa, and the weight of her pent-up anger pulled her down.

Abbey found she had no joy in her devotional times. Her heart bore no songs or laughter, and she was short with Andy and Winston. Andy, of course, understood her crossness, but poor Winston didn't.

Andy said little about it, but Abbey could tell that her behavior was wearing on him. He left her to herself to brood. He and Winston spent the evenings with a book in the living room; she sat alone in front of the television. The screen's images flashed by, but they brought little comfort.

Finally, one evening when Andy announced he was taking Winston for a walk, Abbey felt particularly abandoned. Abbey knew it was her fault. She was the reason for the separation between her and Andy, and a sigh caught in her throat. This was not how she wanted things to be. Tears dripped down her cheeks.

"God," she cried out, "help me to forgive! This anger is killing me, and it's making me into something I don't want to be. I'm ashamed to be spending this much emotion over a silly lamp, but I need your help to get rid of the disappointment. Help me to get my perspective right. Help me to be more concerned for Mac and Rachel than I am for my feelings over my lamp."

When Andy returned from his walk, he found her curled in a ball on the sofa clutching a pillow that was wet with tears. He knew his wife's heart was softening. Andy gathered her up and kissed her, but he said nothing. He knew this was between Abbey and God, and he shouldn't interfere. He just sat with her.

Abbey knew he had been praying for her healing. She was only sorry she had held onto her anger for such a long time.

"I'm sorry, Andy," she said, and Andy replied gently, "I'm sorry for your lamp, honey." Then he offered, "I can put the new one away in the garage if you want."

Abbey blew her nose and took a deep breath. "No," she said. "I need to put it up and start fresh with this. Let's get it out."

Andy helped Abbey draw the new lamp out of its box. He put together the base and hand-painted globe, and he held the hurricane glass cylinder while Abbey inserted a light bulb. She added a second bulb, a four-watt night light, to the inside of the lower globe. The lights could be switched on separately, or they could both be on at the same time. Each light gave the painted lamp a warm softness.

Abbey took Andy's hand, and they stood back to get the full effect.

"It is a lovely lamp," Abbey said evenly. "It almost looks like an antique—like something out of *Gone with the Wind.*"

She knew it must be expensive—a thought that only made her shake her head. She deliberately pushed the anger away; the other lamp had been priceless.

Abbey tried to put on a happier face. Maybe tomorrow she would feel better about it. She prayed it would be so. Abbey stooped and gathered up Winston and gave Andy a kiss. It was time to get ready for bed.

―――>●<―――

On Sunday, when Andy invited the little ones of the church to come forward, fifteen children gathered at the bottom of the platform steps and peered up expectantly. It was just as he'd imagined it—a host of cherubic faces upturned and waiting for him to speak. He had decided to add a children's sermon this morning because he believed a simple story could be instructive not only for the children but also for the rest of the congregation.

Andy settled on the top step and leaned forward. With a benevolent smile, he posed a rhetorical question—or so he thought. Andy had definitely intended it to be rhetorical. But instead, when he said, "Sometimes things happen that can make us upset, and we get angry, don't we?" that's as far as he got.

Before Andy could say another word, four-year-old Lizzie Potts immediately piped up with, "Yeth! Just like the day when Daddy came home late, and Mama took all the food off the table and told him it was cold. And he was hungry. And Mama went and shut the bedroom door, and…"

The story went on and on. With rising panic, Andy tried several times to interrupt, but Lizzie had a lot to say.

It was amazing how her voice carried. Even those sitting in the back pews were doubled over with laughter. Larry and

Sylvia Potts had slouched down in their seats in an attempt to be invisible.

"… and Daddy made hisself a sandwich and ate it at the sink," Lizzie finally said, in bringing her story to an end.

All of the air had left Andy. He swallowed and was afraid to look at Larry and Sylvia. He finally ventured, "Well, as I said, we all have times when we get angry."

The congregation howled. It took a minute for the hilarity to settle.

After laughing with them, Andy forged ahead with his address to the children: "I think we all know we shouldn't let our anger go on and on. Jesus tells us to be careful not to let our anger get the best of us. He tells us in Matthew 18:22 that we are to forgive, and that we must forgive not just once, but over and over again, as many as 'seventy times seven.' That's a lot, isn't it? That's as many as 490 times!"

The children whispered, "Wow! That's a lot!"

"So," Andy said, "if you are ever angry at anyone, don't forget that you need to forgive them, okay? Let's pray about that, now."

After the service, Andy couldn't apologize enough to Larry and Sylvia. "I'm terribly sorry!" he said. "I realize, now, that I should never ask questions when children are involved. I hope you two are okay after your little incident?"

The Potts laughed sheepishly.

"That's Lizzie!" Sylvia said. "We should be used to it by now. We never know what she's going to come up with."

As Abbey stood by Andy's side, she smiled at Sylvia and shook her head in sympathy. When Sylvia and Larry exited, Abbey turned to Andy and gave him a hug. He returned her hug and kissed her forehead.

"That was a great lesson, Honey," Abbey said, "even if it did get high-jacked a little. I needed it."

Then she added, "I love you, Andy Garrett."

CHAPTER TWENTY

THE ARCHER BAPTISM

~ THE PLAN ~

It was a beautiful early October evening when Jeff Archer, his dad, and Doris gathered in Andy's office.

"We all want to be baptized and join the church!" Jeff announced.

Andy was thrilled.

"And the two of us want you to marry us before the end of October," added Doris. Bud blushed and gripped his fiancée's hand. They reminded Andy of kids in their twenties—so much in love and so shy about it.

Andy told the couple he couldn't wait for the big day.

Doris asked, "Could the baptism be this Sunday? My family will be here, then."

Surprised, Andy checked the service plans for Sunday. He was glad to find nothing that would interfere with a baptism. "It looks clear," he said. "We should be able to do that."

Then Andy asked, "Have any of you ever seen a Baptist baptism?"

As he suspected, none of them had. "But I've seen lots of baptisms at the Lutheran Church," Doris offered confidently.

Andy smiled and sat back in his chair. He ventured, "Are you aware that Baptists do not sprinkle or pour?"

Doris looked puzzled, and Andy explained, "Baptism in a Baptist Church is by 'immersion.' It comes from the New Testament word for 'baptize' that means to be taken completely under the water."

"Really?" said Jeff in astonishment.

"Yes," Andy laughed. "You'll get a total dunking!"

Doris's eyes grew wide.

"But," said Andy, "it is a beautiful experience. It not only affirms but is also very symbolic of a believer's new life in Christ. When those who are baptized are taken under the water, it symbolizes death to their old life—like Jesus dying on the cross and then going to the grave. And then, when the baptized person is raised up out of the water, it is a symbol of their new, redeemed and resurrected life—just like that of Jesus! It is a witness to the fact that, in Christ, the believer has died to sin and been raised up, free from sin's eternal power over them."

Doris was excited, now. She loved the symbolism of baptism by immersion, and she exclaimed, "It must feel wonderful to rise up out of the water, just like Jesus rising from the dead!"

"Exactly!" Andy replied with a smile.

"I love it, man!" said Jeff.

Doris did ask about the danger of baby baptisms by immersion, and Andy explained that Baptists "dedicated" babies, and they only "baptized" people who were old enough to declare their faith in Christ.

Doris nodded. "I wondered," she said.

"But where do the baptisms take place?" Bud asked. "Do we go to the river, or what?"

"Good question," said Andy. "Some people do want to be baptized in a river or a lake, and some people have been baptized in a swimming pool. But we also have a baptismal pool right here in the church and can do the baptism during a Sunday morning service."

Jeff wondered, "Where is the pool? I've never seen it in the church."

Andy explained, "You've never seen it, because when it isn't in use, the baptistry is empty and has a cover over it. It's just behind the curtains on the platform in back of the pulpit. Do you want to see?"

Andy led the three soon-to-be-baptized believers from the office and took them on a tour of the baptism facilities. They viewed the baptistry pool in the sanctuary, its access stairs, and the other set of stairs that originated in the basement where the dressing rooms were located.

"Deacons always help the men get ready," Andy said, "and deaconesses help the women. Special robes are provided to wear for the baptism, so you don't have to worry about wet clothes. We do ask that you wear a bathing suit underneath. We'll also have towels for you. You just need to bring a hairdryer if you want one."

The three baptism candidates liked the idea that, after their baptism, they would be brought back upstairs to finish the worship service.

"I love this!" Jeff said. "I can't wait!"

Andy was glad to hear their excitement, and after they left, he scribbled a note for Opal to remind Lester Wiley to fill the baptistry on Saturday.

———⟶●⟵———

In the crisp early morning on Saturday, Lester filled the baptistry and turned on the gas jets under it, to begin heating the water.

An expert on preparing the baptismal pool because of many years on the job, Lester measured the water temperature as it came from the spigot (it ran only cold water). He then calculated how many gallons were needed to fill the cast iron pool, guessed how cool the sanctuary air was likely to be in the morning, and determined how warm the water would have to be to prevent shivers from the baptism participants as they were submerged and then raised up. Without some heat, the water would be too cold for dipping in a toe, let alone the whole body—and the whole body was required for a proper Baptist immersion.

Based on Lester's calculations, the gas should be turned off around five or six that night. That left him a few hours to make a quick trip to Harmony to get his lawn mower blade replaced. The jets would have to be turned on again during Sunday school to counteract any cooling from the night before.

As the chest-high water heated in the four-foot by eight-foot cast iron pool, Lester's wife, Bernice ("Bernie"), made her arrangements. Bernie was in charge of the baptismal robes and towels.

She set out three robes in the downstairs dressing rooms, and she polished the mirror in the women's dressing room. Then Bernie brought the pastor's black baptism robe and full-length waders into Andy's study. She worked quietly, because Andy was in the office today, even though it was a Saturday. She stacked a couple of towels for him, because after he'd completed the dunking, Andy would need to remove the wet waders and black baptism robe. He would dry himself and slip into his suit and preaching robe, and then he would have to quickly make his way to the pulpit to deliver the morning's message. Bernie knew Andy didn't have a lot of time for the change, and she wanted to make sure everything was ready for him.

Satisfied to have completed her task, Bernie left Andy in the study and went to see how Lester was coming along with his other maintenance chores. They needed to hurry if they were going to get to Harmony and back before Andy left the office at five. It wasn't good to leave the jets going without someone there.

"We'll be back, soon," Lester called in the office door to Andy, around two, as they left the church.

———◆◆◆———

Just before eight o'clock, Bernie called the parsonage.

"We're both all right," she began. Before Andy could panic over what might have happened to them, she said, "Just something under the hood. The car stalled on our way back to Cherish and we sat for a while until someone stopped and promised to send a tow for us. We're at a gas station just outside of Harmony, waiting while they fix the car. Lester's in the garage with the mechanic, but he said I should call to make sure you knew we'd got stuck and wouldn't be back in Cherish until much later."

"Thanks for letting me know, Bernie. You two take care, and I'll be praying you get home soon. If you need someone to come and pick you up, let me know."

Andy wasn't too surprised that Lester's car had broken down. He was just sorry it had happened on the highway with Bernice riding along. He'd often wondered what kept the scrappy little auto going. It was an old model with a rusted panel by the left rear wheel. Andy was sure the Wileys could afford better, but Lester was stubborn and very tight with a penny. He would probably drive the old Chevy until it dropped from total exhaustion. Andy prayed for a quick fix and that the Wileys would get home without more difficulty.

After he had prayed, Andy added another illustration to the sermon he had nearly finished in the office earlier, and he rehearsed again what to say during the baptisms. How thankful Andy was for God's working among the people at First Baptist.

The baptisms tomorrow would bring to five the total since he had come to Cherish. His first two had been the young people who had responded to his very first sermon while he and Abbey were just visiting and hadn't yet been called to minister there.

Satisfied that all was ready for tomorrow, Andy yawned and closed his books. After he brushed his teeth and pulled on his pajamas, he gingerly climbed under the covers so he wouldn't awaken his sleeping wife.

———

Unfortunately, Andy didn't know that he should have gone to the church before he went to bed. Not only was he not aware that Lester had left the jets on, but Bernie Wiley had also neglected to mention that important fact to him when she had called. The relating of the drama of the car's breakdown had caused her to skip over the real purpose of her message. Lester had specifically asked her to find out if Andy had thought to turn off the baptistry jets before he had left the office. If Andy hadn't turned the jets off, Doris was to ask him to do it, now, because Lester wouldn't get back in time to do it, himself.

Andy might have put two and two together if he had known that Lester had left the jets on. But he didn't know, and the gas jets continued to heat the baptistry for several hours longer than they were supposed to.

As Andy slept, things were getting hot. Anyone who might have been in the church would have seen that by eight o'clock the tank was bath-water warm, and by midnight it was simmering like a stock pot.

~ OH, DEAR! ~

When Andy arrived at the church around seven-thirty the next morning, he opened the door from the hallway into the sanctuary and was hit in the face by a thick wall of steam. Andy also heard the ominous sound of splashing, boiling water.

"What in the world...?" he cried.

When he realized it wasn't smoke and that the boiling sounds were coming from the baptistry, it came to him what must have happened: Lester had left the gas jets on and then couldn't be there to turn them off when his car broke down!

Andy kicked himself for not realizing the reason for Bernice's call. Of course, Lester had wanted him to turn off the jets. Andy raced now to make things right. He charged down the basement steps to the gas controls in the room under the baptistry, but when he got there, they were so hot they burned his hand.

It served him right, he chided himself. In a panic, Andy searched for a rag among some old paint cans on a shelf in the other room. With the cloth wrapped protectively around the control, Andy managed to turn off the gas, but there was still danger. Everything was searing hot. A spot on the cast iron of the tank was glowing red. Andy didn't dare touch anything more.

Taking two steps at a time, Andy raced back up to the sanctuary. When he opened the hallway door, he again faced the wall of fog that filled the sanctuary from top to bottom. Andy couldn't see into the room even after he turned on all the lights. He could barely make out the twinkle of the chandelier hanging in the center dome.

With the door open, some of the steam began to waft down the hallway, but Andy knew the best way to clear the sanctuary air would also be to open the front doors of the church, located at the back of the room. He started down the foggy center aisle, carefully feeling his way. With arms outstretched, Andy's fingers sought the post of each pew he passed. It was slow going, but he was making progress.

Suddenly a swift WOOSH of air pulled steam past Andy from behind and sucked it down the aisle in front of him.

"What?" he cried. It took him a second to realize that the sudden rush of steam was because someone had thrown open the outer door toward which he had been walking.

Andy hadn't known that steam had started to seep to the outside, curling upwards from the cracks under the front doors. To those passing the church, it was easy to mistake it for smoke. In the belief that the church was burning, Aaron Bueller, who lived across the street, had called the volunteer fire department. Andy had been in the church basement and hadn't heard the two county engines roar to a stop next to the building.

The firemen, with hearts racing at the sight of so much smoke, had assumed the worst. With hoses in hand, they had thrown wide the front doors.

Then they had gasped at what they had seen. Although the firemen had expected to see a fire, they had not expected to see someone calmly walking in the inferno.

Against a pale orange flicker, a shadowy figure with arms majestically outstretched was moving calmly—angelically—toward them, through the smoky blaze. The fire chief, a devout Catholic, crossed himself and fell to his knees. Those behind him froze and swore softly. It wasn't until the steam had dissipated a little that they realized the "flames" were simply the glow of the chandelier bulbs above them and that the angelic figure was only a man feeling his way down the line of pews.

Unaware of what the firemen had thought about him, Andy broke free from the billowing steam. It surprised him to find the men there, and he shouted, "It's not a fire! It's only steam!"

The fire chief, embarrassed to be found still on his knees in prayer, scrambled to his feet and called out, "Are you sure? It's an awful lot of steam! I think we'd better check it out."

With the increase in visibility, Andy walked the chief quickly to the baptistry and showed him the source of the steam. The fireman, who was all business now, asked why it was boiling, and Andy told him about the gas jets that had been left on all night.

"I need to see those jets," the chief ordered, and Andy took him to the basement.

The fireman pushed back his hat and whistled when he saw how hot the cast iron was, and he exclaimed, "You don't realize how lucky you are that this thing didn't burst or catch something on fire, for real. The heat from this thing is still dangerous. You need to keep that door open to help cool things off down here."

The men from the first fire truck were instructed to stay until the cast iron glow had faded from the bottom of the tank in the basement. Everyone else was allowed to return to the firehouse.

Abbey arrived when many others did. She had ridden, as usual, with the Darrell's. Her heart had constricted when she'd seen the fire truck. A little steam still trickled from the front door, and the fire hose lay unwound at the church entrance.

Abbey was relieved when the hose-tenders reported that there didn't seem to be anything to worry about; it was only steam and not smoke. They didn't bar anyone from entering the church.

Trying to make sense of it all, Abbey and the Darrells went in.

It felt clammy. Abbey instinctively braced herself against the back pew and discovered that the pew varnish had dissolved and was tacky. She could see that the sanctuary walls were dripping wet and that drops of water dappled the stained glass. When she reached the front of the room, Abbey feared for the piano and the organ. The thick humidity couldn't be good for them.

Before she could test the keys, however, her husband and a fireman walked in from the hallway door.

"You're going to have a pretty big mess to clean up," the chief was saying, and Andy was agreeing.

When Andy saw Abbey, he explained: "The baptistry gas jets were left on all night. Lots of steam!"

"I guess so," she said. Stu Darrell whistled behind her.

Andy also told them, "Mr. Bueller thought it was smoke and called the fire department."

As they talked about the damage, the fireman decided that his job was done. He tipped his hat and departed.

"What are we going to do?" Abbey asked in wonder. "Surely we can't have a service in here. Feel these pews."

Betty Darrell agreed and ventured, "Maybe we could cover the pews with plastic drop cloths. There are a few downstairs with the paint cans, and I think there are some old bed sheets stored with the Christmas costumes in case there aren't enough paint covers."

Several women went with Betty to search for possible pew covers.

"Won't the water be too hot for the baptism this morning?" someone asked Stu and Andy.

"No problem," said Andy. "We'll just drain a little of the hot water and add in some cold."

Stu Darrell thought that sounded reasonable and he went downstairs to open the tank drain.

"Protect your hands!" Andy called. "The cast iron is still searing hot. Don't burn yourself!"

Stu assured him he'd be careful.

Andy walked to the edge of the pool in the sanctuary to turn on the water spigot, but he stopped. His plan wasn't going to work.

Looking down into the bubbling turquoise depths, he could see where the paint had slipped off the sides. The water had boiled for so long that it had loosened the acrylic paint all the way around the pool. Sheets of blue had peeled and floated downward, and they were blocking the drain.

By now, Danny Hart, Bob Parks, and Lester Wiley had arrived. Andy apologized profusely to a very surprised Lester about not turning off the gas jets. Lester stood, stunned, looking down into the steaming water. He was temporarily unable to formulate a plan, so Danny and Bob took charge.

Because they could not drain the tank, they discussed how to cool the water in some other way.

No sooner had Danny suggested, "We just need some ice," than Bob called out, "I'll get it" and hurried off to the gas station.

What Bob brought back looked like a lot, but, "We're going to need a lot more," said Lester. The five large bags of ice lasted barely a second in the tank and made no noticeable difference in the water's temperature.

"Wow!" Bob exclaimed. "That was all the ice the gas station had, and nothing else is open."

Everything in Cherish was closed on Sundays.

During Sunday school, Danny and Bob called everyone they knew for ideas, and they were tempted to send a pickup truck to Harmony, or farther away, to see if anyone had vast quantities of ice. Fortunately, they connected with Leroy Cranz from the Methodist Church, who was the manager of the Dairy Delite.

"You need dry ice," Leroy said, "and I happen to have a lot of it at the moment because of our church festival in the park. I can let you have part of what I have. I'll bring it over after our church service ends. I'm in a men's quartet that's providing special music this morning, and we're also to sing later at the festival. I can come after this morning's service."

Danny confirmed the arrangement and asked Andy if they could postpone the baptism until the evening service. Andy telephoned the Archers and explained the dilemma. Doris laughed, and he could hear her relaying the situation to Bud and the rest of her family.

The out-of-town Lutherans who had come for this occasion agreed to stay in Cherish and come for the evening service. They were especially eager, now, to see a Baptist-style baptism. Things like this never happened when you sprinkled.

~ TEMPORARY FIXES ~

Marilyn Ingraham stood wringing her hands when she realized the instruments could not accompany the choir. After she had pulled herself together, she rustled through some past choral pieces to find an *a cappella* arrangement. The choir was instructed to leave Sunday school and gather in the practice room fifteen minutes earlier than usual so they could go over the replacement song and re-familiarize themselves with their parts.

Then, just as the impromptu practice ended, Luther Sharp came to announce that the morning service was moving to the downstairs fellowship hall instead of the sanctuary. Immediately, a frazzled Marilyn reverted to the original choral piece. Theresa Jackson could accompany them on the fellowship hall piano.

It was no surprise when the town newspaper showed up. News of the boiling baptistry had traveled fast. Before the close of the service, a reporter from the *Cherish Observer* arrived and took photos of the congregation listening to Andy from their folding chairs in the church basement.

Afterward, the newspaperman introduced himself to Andy and jotted down the comments of several church members. He even got a picture of Luther Sharp pointing to the gas jet ring and the bottom of the baptistry tank.

"This is where it all started," Andy overheard Luther expounding.

The best photo, however, was taken upstairs, where the camera captured a little steam still rising dramatically from the baptistry waters. To complete his story, the reporter said he would return later to cover the baptism. Born a baby-sprinkling Catholic, he was intrigued by this practice of the Baptists.

Church members knew that the story would likely be a two-pager when it rolled off the presses on Monday. This was real news! The *Observer* was sure to run a few extra copies for keepsakes. That way, people who attended First Baptist could mail copies to former church members who had moved away from Cherish but liked to keep in touch.

After the morning service, the men of the church assured Andy they would deal with the baptistry tank and have it ready for the evening service. Andy didn't need to stay.

"You go home and eat, and rest up for tonight," Stu told him.

Andy felt like he should be doing something, but he finally took Stu's advice and headed home.

If only he had realized last night what Bernice had been trying to tell him! If only it hadn't caused such damage! If only…

As Andy and Abbey sat down for lunch, the telephone rang. "Turn on the radio!" Bob Parks cried. "We're on the news!"

The Garretts hurried to catch the story before the segment ended.

The "boiling baptistry" dominated the Cherish on-air patter throughout the afternoon. Andy doubted that the words "First Baptist" or "immersion" had ever had so much coverage in the community before.

The Decatur station also picked up the news. How they learned about it, Andy didn't know. But he did hear that a phone call by Ann Parks to relatives in San Bernardino had spread the day's episode all the way to California, long before the evening service would begin.

Impatient for the dry ice to come, the First Baptist churchmen tried to dislodge the paint clog from the drain with broom handles but as quickly as they freed the original blockage another one formed from other blobs of paint.

"We need to get down inside the tank to remove that stuff," Bob Parks said. "But I'm not ready to be stewed."

Finally admitting there was nothing more to be done with the baptistry until the dry ice was delivered, the workers turned their attention to the rest of the sanctuary. They wiped down the walls—at least as high as they could reach—and they dried the floor-level stained glass windows. Hopefully, their efforts would reduce the streaking when things began to dry.

After a quick break for lunch, the dry ice came. And as Leroy Cranz had predicted, the water was finally cooled.

Bob Parks tested the temperature carefully before he slipped into the tank. From inside, he worked to remove the turquoise clogs at the bottom and strain out the paint blobs that floated on top.

So much paint had boiled away that what had once been an aqua baptistry was now mottled with unsightly gray and brown patches. Fortunately, from pew-level, the damage couldn't be seen. And a final straining with a piece of netting before people arrived that evening made the water the best it was going to be.

"At least the bottom won't be slippery," Bob intoned, "and if tiny blue flecks stick to the baptism robes, or to Doris's pretty hair after she comes out of the water, most people won't see it. I'd say we're in business!"

~ THE BAPTISM ~

Andy was among the first to arrive that evening, and he commended the efforts of the work crew.

"This should work," he said.

He did think, however, that the plastic covers on the pews looked odd. They gave the impression that painters were to arrive at any moment to wield their brushes. But, of course, the covers couldn't be helped. It was important to protect the clothing of those who gathered to observe and celebrate the baptisms.

Andy wondered how much of the usual church service setup would work, and he began to arrange things.

He held his breath as he plugged in the microphone for the song leader to use. He prayed it wouldn't short out. It had been set on a block of wood to keep it off the damp carpet. After an initial SNAP, the mic seemed to be fine, but once it was turned on, Andy left it alone.

Sadly, there would be no instruments. Even if they had dried out, the piano and organ would be woefully out of tune. The hymns would have to be sung without accompaniment. The congregation would understand.

Time was growing short. Andy saw the deacons and deaconesses greet the Archers and Doris, when they arrived, and whisk the three of them downstairs to the dressing rooms. Andy knew it was time for him to dress, too.

He hurried to don his baptism robe and waders. In a few minutes, Marilyn would start the congregational singing.

———————

Andy drew back the baptistry privacy curtains as soon as he had descended the four steps into the pool. Now he could see the crowd that had gathered.

In addition to the regular church members and a pew full of Doris's family in the front row, there were faces Andy had never seen before. He learned afterward that some were from the Episcopalian and Methodist churches, who had heard about the "boiling baptistry" from the radio and had been intrigued. Others had heard the story from their First Baptist neighbors. The reporter from the *Cherish Observer* hovered at the edges of the room with his photographer, and the fire chief sat near the back. The chief was hoping, like the rest of them, to learn just what the Baptists did with so much hot water.

So, it was that in front of a varied assortment of sprinklers, pourers, and immersers, plus the reporter from the *Cherish Observer* and his photographer, Andy dunked Bud, Doris, and Jeff—one at a time—in the Name of the Father, the Son, and the Holy Spirit, in tepid water that was speckled with tiny flecks of aqua paint.

Doris's family was impressed, but her brother couldn't resist a comment. "It sure is a lot of bother to immerse," he told Andy, afterward. "We Lutherans use only a couple quarts of water at most, and we're just as baptized."

Andy patted him on the back. "Baptists never do anything halfway," he said. "If you're going to take the plunge, you take the plunge!"

Doris added, "We had no idea our baptism would be this newsworthy. Nobody's going to forget it!"

When the last of the crowd had left, Lester Wiley looked over the shambles of the sanctuary and shook his head. It certainly wasn't what he had expected when he had first turned on the gas jets yesterday morning and had set out for Harmony. Lester still wasn't sure how things had gone so wrong.

He sighed and headed downstairs to pull the plug on the baptistry drain. Tomorrow he would pick up supplies, including some brushes and a can of aqua paint. Danny Hart and Bob Parks had promised to help him get everything back to normal.

It was going to take some time.

CHAPTER TWENTY-ONE

JEFF'S MISSION

By late October, the baptism incident was all but forgotten. The baptistry and the sanctuary walls had been repainted, the pews had been revarnished, and the piano and organ had been restored and tuned (the hardest part had been getting the moisture out of the organ pipes). Even the aisle carpet had been replaced. Everything looked as it had before the baptism, and the refurbished sanctuary provided a perfect backdrop for the Archer wedding.

It wasn't a large wedding, but it was one of Andy's favorites. That's because the focus was on the intended and the Lord, without a lot of extraneous pomp and circumstance. At some weddings, the sacred covenant was nearly crowded out by all of the activities and performances packed into the service.

Today, Doris looked lovely in white. It was her first marriage, and she was radiant. Only one friend stood up for each of the Archers: Doris's sister held her flowers, and Jeff guarded the rings.

There was no vocalist, just the strains of *O Promise Me* on the like-new old organ, and there was a brief fanfare at the end. Several members of the church attended, and there were many tearful relatives from Doris's family. Bud had little family left, but an uncle and aunt smiled as Bud kissed his bride.

Everything in the service was just right, Andy thought. Simple and sure, with God's blessing over all.

———————

A couple of weeks later, as Andy scanned the congregation he noticed that Jeff was missing. Jeff's newly married father and step-mother were there, but no one stood next to them. It was unusual. Ever since his conversion and recovery from drug addiction, Jeff Archer had faithfully attended church and Sunday school. He had been a sponge, soaking up all he could about Jesus and the Bible. Jeff had even begun to help Chelsea with the teens.

"I want to be useful," Jeff had said, "and I want to let people know what the Lord has done for me."

He radiated a contagious vitality, and the youth loved him.

After church, Andy waited for Bud and Doris at the exit line.

"Where's Jeff?" he asked.

"He's gone to Florida," Bud said. "Jeff heard about a Christian group that does beach ministry, and he contacted them a few weeks ago. When they invited him down, Jeff started packing and left immediately. I'm surprised he didn't tell you."

Andy recalled, then, that Jeff had left a message with Opal late last week, and Andy had not yet called him back. Andy had completely forgotten!

"Have you heard from Jeff since he got to Florida?" Andy asked.

"Yes. Jeff called yesterday," Bud said, "and he was excited. He said a 'Pastor Mike' is letting him stay at his house, and Jeff has already led two people to the Lord! He said the kids on the beach listened when he told his story of getting off drugs. One of the guys he talked to is now getting help to kick his habit."

Andy was amazed. Jeff had once been afraid that turning to God would mean God would make him a preacher. Now he was

Debby L. Johnston

joyfully running to the ministry call. It was a blessing to know that God was using Jeff's experience and testimony to reach others for Christ.

"Thanks, Bud. If you talk to Jeff, again, please tell him he's in our prayers and that I'd love to hear from him."

CHAPTER TWENTY-TWO

A DIFFERENT THANKSGIVING

On the Wednesday before Thanksgiving, Andy tried to ignore the tantalizing aromas floating through the parsonage. It was hard to dismiss the smell of baking pies you knew you couldn't eat until tomorrow.

Abbey set the hot pastries on the counter to cool and knew that it took every ounce of Andy's self-control to keep from pinching off a finger-full of crust. She glowered at him with a look that said: "Don't you dare!"

In response, Andy shrugged and smiled innocently. He hummed "Here We Stand, Like Birds in the Wilderness" and sauntered into the television room. Tomorrow they would eat like royalty at Molly and Paul's, but unfortunately, today the pies were off limits.

This year, Paul's dad would join his son and daughter-in-law, and Andy and Abbey, at the farmhouse. Mac and Rachel would not be coming because they had barely recovered from a nasty flu and weren't up to the trip. Rachel assured Andy and Molly that she was well enough to get a turkey going for the two of them and Grannie. Mac would fetch Grannie on Thursday morning so that she wouldn't be alone for the holiday.

It was good that everybody would have turkey, Andy thought, and he day-dreamed again about Molly's dinner table. He was primed for turkey, dressing, and pies. It was just a shame that tomorrow was so far away.

Supper was the hardest for him to endure. While Andy would have found homemade soup and sandwiches satisfying on any other day, tonight the satisfaction of his appetite was tarnished by anticipation of tomorrow. His cravings remained unsated, and when bedtime finally came, he crawled under the covers with bologna on his breath and turkey on his mind.

Once he did get to sleep, Andy was busy. As a mighty caped Superman, he fought heroically against the forces of evil. In his dream, Andy swelled to know that Abbey thought him a hero. He heard her calling him, and he strained to hear her words. But she seemed to be moving away... Or maybe it was him who was moving away...

Suddenly he remembered that he was asleep. In the conscious world, Abbey was patting and calling him.

He groaned and peeked half-eyed at the alarm clock that had not yet gone off. It confirmed that he had another fifteen minutes to dream. Normally, it was Winston who woke him early. Why wasn't Abbey letting him sleep?

She patted him again and called out, "Honey, look!"

Andy finally managed a muffled "Hmmm?" but he didn't open his eyes.

"Look at the snow!" Abbey insisted.

"Is it pretty?" he managed to croak. He wished Abbey would leave him alone until the alarm went off.

"Y-e-s," she said hesitantly, "but it's also DEEP! Andy, it must have snowed all night, and it's still snowing."

Andy knew it was useless to try to sleep longer. He yawned and rubbed his eyes. With a sigh and a slow deliberation, he rolled out of the covers. Once he stood up, Andy stumbled across the room to look out the window. Winston jumped at every step to get his master's attention.

Abbey held back the curtain as Andy dutifully leaned in to peer out. He expected to see a little snow, but instead, Andy whistled in astonishment.

"Wow!" he exclaimed. "I had no idea this was supposed to happen. I don't think we can get out of our driveway."

"I know," Abbey said.

Andy turned on the radio. The local announcer was in the middle of coverage of the freak snowstorm that was to have passed through but had, instead, unexpectedly lingered over this part of the state and dropped several feet of snow.

As they listened, the announcer reported, "Holiday travelers are stranded all across our area. Sadly, many will be celebrating Thanksgiving at a truck stop instead of with their families. The storm is making it impossible for thousands to get to their holiday destinations. If you're just waking up, don't go out. Plan, instead, on huddling in for the long haul. Yes, folks! This is the snowstorm of the decade!"

In frustration, Andy plopped into a kitchen chair. No turkey!

"I guess we'll have to call Molly and Paul," he sighed. "I can't believe this."

"At least we aren't stuck somewhere on the way to your folks' place, or mine," Abbey said. Then she added, "Don't worry, honey. I'll find something good for our Thanksgiving dinner. It just won't be turkey."

Andy sulked. When Winston insisted he had to go out, Andy heaved himself from the chair and led the pup through the garage. Andy unlocked the outside door and crossly gave it a shove. Usually, the door would have swung wide, but this morning it didn't budge. Andy pushed again, but again the door remained fast.

Andy rubbed a warm fist over the frosted window pane to see outside. Through the little clear spot, he blinked at what he saw. This door was never going to open. A giant snowdrift had curled snugly around the back of the house and was piled as high as the door knob.

Winston looked up expectantly, and Andy looked down. Andy told the confused dog they were going to have to go out the front door.

Andy's boots had been in the garage and were cold when he pulled them on. His coat from the closet was warmer, and Andy threw it over his pajamas. A hefty steel snow shovel completed the ensemble, and Winston trailed him through the living room to the front door.

White also blanketed the front porch, but nothing like the massive drift by the back door. Andy's weight against the front door prevailed, and he quickly lifted snow off the steps in a skinny strip to a three-foot patch at the bottom. Winston got the idea. The now-desperate dog made haste with his business and scampered back up the steps to go inside.

As Andy surveyed the neighborhood from the porch, he marveled at the pristine panorama before him. As far as Andy could see, not a single foot- or tire-track marred the snowy expanse. No one had ventured out. Everything was level and white. And it was so deep that it completely buried the bushes in front of the house across the street. It was as if they didn't exist.

Andy finally came inside, pulled the door closed, and ducked under Abbey's scowl as he tracked back through the house in his wet boots. Before Abbey could say anything, the telephone rang. Andy scooted faster into the garage while she answered the phone.

Andy could hear her decrying the snow with someone, but he had no idea who was on the other end of the line. Then he heard, "That's a fabulous idea, Betty! Sure, we'll bring the pies over around noon."

When Abbey hung up, she sang out, "The Darrell's have turkey!"

Andy cheered. "Hooray! Turkey and pies!"

"And," said Abbey, "cranberry salad and corn casserole. That's what the Harts are contributing."

"You don't say!" exclaimed Andy. "It's almost like this was planned."

But then, Andy remembered Molly and Paul. As if on cue, the phone rang again and this time it was Molly.

Molly was concerned for them. "Even if you made it out to the highway, you'd never make it down our lane. Don't come!"

Then Molly suggested, "We'll just postpone everything until the roads are cleared. I can refrigerate the turkey, and we can heat it up once everyone can get here."

Andy told her about the neighborhood potluck, and Molly sounded relieved. "I'm glad you two can have Thanksgiving dinner with friends. Paul and I knew you didn't have any turkey and only had pies. We felt bad for you. You go ahead and eat your Thanksgiving meal. Of course, we'll miss you, but we can always get together on Sunday like we usually do."

Then Molly added, "And we don't have to worry about Paul's dad—he spent the night here. The only one who's had to brave the elements is Paul. Thankfully his snowshoes were in the back hallway instead of out in the barn!"

It sounded like everyone was taken care of. Andy smiled. This year's holiday was going to be different and memorable (and still tasty!) for everyone. Andy wished Molly and Paul a happy Thanksgiving before they hung up, and then he and Abbey enjoyed a leisurely breakfast—a mere precursor to the feast that was to come.

Forging a trail through the thigh- to waist-high snow proved coldly challenging, even though the destination was in sight. It was a heavy snow, and wet, and it clung to Andy and Abbey's clothes and added more weight with each step. Andy persevered in the lead, stomping and blazing an uneven trail for Abbey and the pies.

When Andy and Abbey finally caught up to the track the Harts had beaten earlier, Andy was glad because he was getting tired. It was easier to make headway on an already trampled path.

How wonderfully warm and delicious-smelling the Darrell's house was when they got inside. Candles had been lit, and Betty and Erica had finished setting out plates and napkins. Extra leaves had extended the table past the dining area and into the living room, and four folding chairs now supplemented the six that matched the dining set. Filled bowls and piled platters steamed in the center of the table. Children and men hovered impatiently underfoot.

When at last it was time to offer grace, Stu called for bowed heads.

"Dear God, thank you for allowing us to gather here as friends with a bounty we hadn't expected," he prayed. "Guard and keep safe all of the travelers who are stranded. Help them to get home, soon. Bless them and bless our families who are having Thanksgiving dinner without us. We offer our thanks, Heavenly Father, for everything You have blessed us with throughout the year, and we thank you again for this meal we are about to enjoy. In Jesus' Name, we pray. Amen."

Plates were raised to receive slices of turkey, and in no time the heaping bowls on the table were emptied. Every bite was savored, and there was no leaving room for pies. Dessert would have to come later.

As they ate, a few snowflakes fell upon the world outside, but nothing accumulated. Even if it had, those inside wouldn't have cared. They were all warm, thankful, and well-fed. This Thanksgiving, the snow had made it hard to gather with family, but it had not conquered love. The people gathered here were a family of the heart.

———————

After the meal, the overstuffed men and boys stumbled in agony into the living room to fall, Daliesque, over the sofa and chairs. The women stoically took up dish cloths and towels and set about taming a counter full of dirty dishes, pots, and pans. When they finished, the women joined the overfed nappers in the living room.

It was a bother when the telephone rang. Stu could hardly pull himself up in his chair. "I ate way too much!" he complained. With considerable effort, he stretched to pick up the receiver on the end table next to him.

Stu listened for a moment and then handed the phone to Andy. "It's for you," he said.

Andy asked in surprise, "Who knows I'm here?"

"Your mom said Molly told her," said Stu.

It was hard not to listen when Andy took the receiver and pronounced a rousing, "Hi, Happy Thanksgiving!"

But his greeting apparently fell flat. Andy's smile faded, and Abbey's eyes inquired. She grew alarmed when Andy whispered, "Oh, no!"

As Abbey flew to Andy's side, her heart pounded. Was it Andy's father, she wondered. It didn't sound encouraging.

"We'll get together with Molly and Paul and try to get out of here as soon as the roads allow," Andy said into the phone, solemnly.

Abbey's mind raced. It must be Andy's dad, she thought. Was Mac hurt—or worse? Since Rachel had tracked Andy down, it must be bad, whatever it was. Abbey's mind began to process things they needed to pack for the trip north.

"We'll call before we leave," Andy said into the receiver. "It should be tomorrow or Saturday. All right, Mom. Yes. Goodbye."

Expectantly, everyone waited as Andy returned the phone to its cradle and lowered himself into his chair. He closed his eyes.

"It's Grannie," Andy said tonelessly.

Everyone drew in a breath, and Abbey cried, "Not Grannie!"

In a near whisper, Andy explained. "Dad went over to pick her up, this morning. But when he got there, he learned that last night Grannie had tried to walk from her apartment to the Ben Franklin. And she fell..."

Andy's voice broke. "...and nobody saw her..."

He sobbed. "...and she died!"

Everyone was stunned. The living room of people rose as one and surrounded Andy with whispers and hugs. It didn't seem possible that the vibrant woman who had visited Cherish just a few weeks ago was now gone—and in such a tragic way. No one knew what to say. Even the boys were silent; grief was new to them.

Betty hurried to the kitchen and began wrapping leftovers. She knew Andy and Abbey wouldn't stay. Stu gathered the Garrett's coats and boots, and Betty loaded the empty pie basket. She told Abbey, "You won't have to cook tonight, dear, or even for lunch tomorrow. There's a little of everything here for you two."

Betty added, "Whenever you leave to head north, just bring Winston over. We'll take good care of him until you get back."

Andy could not hold back the tears. "I'm sorry that today turned out this way. Thank you, friends."

Stu pulled on his boots and carried the food basket ahead of the Garretts to the parsonage. The path was easier now than it had been at Noon.

Once at the parsonage, Stu set the basket on the kitchen counter and repeated, "Remember, if you need anything, just call."

Abbey and Andy nodded and voiced their thanks. Then Abbey walked Stu to the door, and she watched as he set off for home across the yards.

Andy sat at the kitchen table with his head bowed. Winston looked up but did not press for attention. Like dogs often do, Winston knew something was wrong, and his twisted little ears hung.

Andy finally managed to say, "I know Grannie's with Jesus, but I hate how it happened! We didn't even get a chance to say good-bye."

Abbey held her husband close. Her heart was breaking, and she knew that his was shattered.

She prayed softly in his ear, "Heavenly Father, tell Grannie good-bye from us, okay? And let her know she will be terribly missed. But, God, thank you so much that Grannie's with You! And thank you for the promise that we will see her, again—one day."

Together, Andy and Abbey cried.

CHAPTER TWENTY-THREE

TO MY FATHER'S HOUSE

Andy telephoned his parents around midday on Friday to tell them that the snow still was not cleared. Plows had not reached the parsonage cul-de-sac. And Molly had reported that the farm entrance was still impassable, too. She said that Paul planned to tackle part of the lane before nightfall.

Abbey listened as Andy and his parents talked. At one point, when Andy closed his eyes, Abbey knew he was struggling to maintain control. Andy told her, afterward, that was the moment his Mom had asked him to do the funeral.

He sighed. "I know God made me a minister for this kind of thing, but I wasn't expecting it to include Grannie."

He sucked in a ragged breath, and Abbey hugged him. "God will help you," she whispered.

<hr/>

With no way to get out and onto the roads, Andy had time to grieve privately and to begin preparing for the funeral. Abbey let him work without interruption, and Winston curled up next to him on the sofa. Abbey knew her husband was struggling, and she prayed that God would give him the emotional strength to minister to his family. Abbey was grateful that they were still snowed in and that Andy had no church demands.

The sounds of a muffled scrape on the parsonage street came in the wee hours of Saturday morning. Abbey was glad their suitcases sat ready, and she and Andy slept peacefully until around seven. After breakfast, Molly called to confirm that the farm lane was clear. There was no excuse, now, not to load the car and begin the journey.

Andy had shoveled the drive yesterday afternoon, but now he had to remove the snowplow mess at the driveway entrance. Even so, it didn't take long to get ready.

"Lord, keep us safe as we travel," Andy prayed before backing the car out of the drive. "And help us to share Your promise with Mom and Dad as we mourn our loss, together."

Stop number one was the Darrell's. Stu carried in Winston's bed and bag of food, and Betty and the boys held Winston in the picture window so the Garretts could see him wave his paw. Andy and Abbey were grateful that Winston could play with Roxy and the boys while they were gone.

Now the Garretts made their way through town to pick up the highway to Harmony.

Everything they passed was plowed so high that it was hard to see all but the tallest landmarks from the car. The roads were walls—a white maze—and it seemed as if there was no town behind and beneath the snow. And yet there were signs of business.

Although shops were closed and virtually unseen, a thin lane for parking had been carved in front of the courthouse. Andy surmised that the hardware store across the square might be open, too, because he saw a few hardy souls heading that direction. Nothing could keep farmers down.

And coffee could be had. A row of sideways "Yes, We're Open" directional signs flagged the snow banks to guide customers to the Star Diner. If they had had time, it would have been fun to stop and share snow tales with other diners. But their mission urged them on.

Once beyond the square, Andy and Abbey's course straightened. Usually from the car, you could see across the fields for miles, but today it was like shooting through an open-topped tunnel. The drive was quiet, and the scenery was cut off.

After a mile or so, Andy spoke.

"Don't you wonder what wondrous things Grannie is seeing in Heaven? I like to picture her dancing with joy!" he said.

Abbey smiled. "No doubt in one of her hand-made evening gowns?"

That brought a chuckle. Then Andy said, "I miss her laugh, too. But I know I'll get to hear it again."

The two of them imagined Grannie's last visit. It was hard to picture her without at least a smile. Her laughter had been contagious, and it filled their memories.

Abbey then speculated, "As beautiful as laughter is on Earth, can you imagine how much more beautiful it will be in Heaven?"

Andy liked that. He agreed that everything in Heaven must be happier and sweeter and brighter than anything on Earth. And then Andy wondered: was red lipstick redder in Heaven, too?

Andy pictured Grannie, sporting her favorite hat and with her lips newly rouged, walking with Jesus just inside the heavenly gates. How Andy wished he could overhear the stories Grannie might be sharing as she and Jesus walked!

———•———

"It doesn't seem possible she's gone," Molly cried when she saw her brother. "Grannie seemed timeless."

Molly and Andy consoled one another.

"Grannie is timeless," Andy said. "We'll never forget her."

Molly agreed and hugged him.

"I know," she said, "and when we get to Heaven, Grannie will already be there."

"And wouldn't it be something," Andy asked, "if the first smell we have of Heaven is Grannie's fried chicken?"

Molly laughed.

Of course, Andy doubted such a thing. After all, Heaven was filled with the fruit of the Tree of Life. He wondered what that fruit must taste like, and he decided that it must taste pretty wonderful to outshine Grannie's chicken!

The four of them decided to take Paul's car. It was bigger than the Garrett's car, and it would be more comfortable to spread out in the Doaks' sedan. Andy especially appreciated that Paul would drive. It would let Andy relax a little longer.

"Who's taking care of your animals?" Abbey asked Paul, once they were underway. "Is your dad coming to the farm?"

"No, Dad won't have to come," Paul said. "We have great neighbors. The Bennetts live the closest, and when we need help, they always come to the rescue. Molly and I help the Bennetts sometimes, too. They've agreed to take care of things until we get back."

Abbey nodded. "Good neighbors are wonderful," she said.

Abbey could think of nothing more to say to carry the conversation forward, so it grew quiet for several miles. There was little to look at and, therefore, little for comment.

After a while, Andy noticed that a frown had formed on Molly's face, and he asked, "You're not looking forward to spending the night at Mom's and Dad's are you?"

Molly confessed, "You're right. For years I dreamed of getting away from Mom's and Dad's craziness, and now we're going back to that house. Who knows what they're going to be like for the funeral?"

Andy agreed. "There's no way to predict what they're going to be like over the next couple of days. And because it's their own home..."

Paul interrupted and announced firmly, "Well, I can tell you this: if your parents start fighting, we're going to a motel."

Nobody contradicted him. It certainly was a possibility.

"At least we'll all be there, together," said Andy.

CHAPTER TWENTY-FOUR

GOOD-BYE, GRANNIE

At the door, Rachel seized her children in compulsive hugs and an outpouring of tears.

"Thank goodness; you're here!" she sobbed. "I can't believe Mama's gone."

Andy and Molly returned the impassioned grief embraces their mother had saved up for their arrival. Their tears mingled freely with hers.

Their father stood apart.

Rachel continued to cling and cry, and it became uncomfortable to linger half in the doorway in the grip of her emotion. Andy finally asked, "Where do you want us to put our things, Mom?"

Rachel collected herself enough to point to the stairs. "Molly and Paul get the back bedroom, and you and Abbey can have the front."

But once more Rachel clutched her daughter before letting the four of them into the house.

The men led the way up the stairs with the suitcases, and the women followed so they could hang up their good clothes. They all hurried to freshen up so they could rejoin Mac and Rachel.

A small buffet of sandwiches and salad had been laid out, and when they came back down, Rachel commanded Mac to turn off the television. She continued to blow her nose and wipe away stray tears.

"Now, Andy, say grace," Rachel said.

Surprised at the request, Andy bowed his head. It was the first time he'd prayed in his parents' home, and it was likely the first time that grace had been spoken within these walls.

Andy was still wondering at the request and had just begun praying, when his mother suddenly intoned, "I just wish Mama could have…"

Rachel crushed a handkerchief into her face and sobbed. Andy stopped in mid-prayer.

"For Pete's sake, Rachel, get 'hold of yourself!" Mac snarled. "You can't cry the whole time they're here."

Those around the table cringed.

Andy couldn't bear it. He could feel the tightness forming in his chest, and he gritted his teeth. It was the old smothering feeling from his childhood. But then Andy shocked them all.

"Well," Andy announced with energy, "if Grannie were here, we wouldn't be standing here with frowns on our faces. She'd have us all in stitches about something!"

Blinking, his mother turned.

Molly took up the effort. "Andy's right. Grannie would be making Paul take another sandwich, whether he wanted it or not, and she'd be complaining that the coffee wasn't hot enough, even though it scalded your throat all the way down."

Paul chuckled and said, "And Grannie would be making us all hurry to eat and clean up stuff so we could watch some TV program or other with her."

"Well, it's too late, tonight, to watch those crazy soap operas!" Mac boomed with a scowl.

At that, everyone laughed. It was a release of tension, and it surprised Mac—who finally smiled, too.

"Grannie sure did love her shows, didn't she?" agreed Abbey.

With the mood lightened, they all ate and were free to celebrate the fun of Grannie. They told story after story—but the pleasantness didn't last.

Somewhere in the middle of someone's happy memory, Mac suddenly expelled vehemently, "It's just an all-fired shame!"

As if hurling charges, he continued fiercely, "It should never have happened. She was an old woman, and she had no business going out that late alone, and down that alley..."

"Dad," Andy tried to interrupt him.

Mac clamped his jaw and heaved his chest in anger to finish with, "If I had gone a day earlier to get her, maybe none of this would have happened."

Rachel sobbed, "I just can't believe that no one found her!"

Rachel keened and swayed in her grief.

Surrounded by those frozen from years of hurtful drama, Abbey was the one who rose to comfort Rachel. It was obvious that the woman's children could not do it, and Abbey knew that Mac's attentions were toxic.

As Abbey held her mother-in-law, Molly asked, "When do we go to the funeral home?"

Mac contributed the facts. "The family's private time is tomorrow at ten. Public viewing is at one. The funeral is at four." Mac then crossed his arms over his chest as if to strangle further conversation.

Molly sighed and rose to remove the dishes from the table. Mac shoved back his chair and retreated to the living room. Andy and Paul shook their heads and resolutely made their way to the sofa; Andy turned on the television. Abbey directed Rachel to the kitchen to begin the cleanup.

There was no more conversation of Grannie, or virtually anything else, for the rest of the evening.

Entering the room where Grannie lay was surreal. Surely the person lying there was not the exuberant woman who had howled at Andy's childish jokes and had smothered him and Molly with her love and kisses. It could not be the Grannie who could put Rachel in her place with a look or who could cause Mac to step back a bit when he crossed a line. Surely, any minute, Grannie would rise up and howl at what a spoof it was for them to see her here, at a funeral home, of all places.

But of course, it was not a charade. The stranger lying so very still and commanding whispers in her presence was evidence that Grannie had left them.

Andy paused at her casket and gazed at the eyes that would never open again. Then, even in his sadness, he managed a smile. Whoever had been responsible for her makeup had at least allowed Grannie the dignity to have the reddest lips the dime store could make possible. Andy resisted the urge to bend down and kiss them, knowing they would not be warm.

<hr />

Grannie's friends did not travel anymore, so visitation and service attendance was limited to a few of Mac and Rachel's acquaintances, a couple of Andy and Abbey's Barton College friends, and a handful of relatives Andy and Molly hadn't seen in years.

"We have a lot more relatives," Andy whispered to Abbey, "but my parents aren't on speaking terms with most of them."

As the clock struck four, the funeral director bent to confer with Rachel and then disappeared. Andy stood and walked to the lectern.

Andy composed his notes and took a deep breath. His greeting then encompassed all who had gathered to remember Estelle Marie Dow, affectionately known to the family as "Grannie."

Andy read Grannie's obituary, which seemed far too short, and he said, "Grannie was so much more than these few words on a page."

Molly nodded.

"Grannie's life was LIVED to the fullest in everything she did," Andy continued. "She inspired life. Everywhere she went the fun followed. Grannie was the one that Molly and I wanted at our birthday parties and weddings. Grannie made Christmas sparkle in Mom and Dad's living room, and she told the best stories. But you also need to know that Grannie was the guilty party who started Molly and me down a dubious path at an early age. We weren't even in school, yet, when she introduced us to Friday night professional wrestling!"

Andy saw his mother lift her chin from her handkerchief with a faint smile.

"It's true!" Andy continued, and Rachel now gave a half-nod in affirmation. "Molly and I would put on our pajamas and lie on the floor with goblets of grape juice and heaping bowls of popcorn, way past our bedtime. Then we'd yell at the refs with Grannie and boo at anyone she took a dislike to—and how Grannie loved Gorgeous George!"

Mac looked up, now, and almost smiled.

"It seems odd not to have Grannie standing here and saying something practical and wise about funerals and helping us remember happier moments. She was a very practical woman, you know. Grannie never believed that man made it to the moon (silly nonsense, she called it), but she rescued me as a youngster from measles that hadn't broken out, and she knew some wicked remedies for colds that could make your toenails fly off!"

Some of Mac and Rachel's upper crust acquaintances weren't sure what all of that meant, but they smiled politely.

"Grannie also took no sass from us, but Molly and I always knew her corrections with willow switches would be followed by teary hugs and ruby kisses.

"Personally, I most appreciated Grannie as my greatest cheerleader after I told her I was going to seminary. I often overheard her tell friends that her grandson was going to be 'a man of the cloth.' I'm convinced it was partly because of her many prayers that I made it through school.

"Grannie finally got to hear me preach at my first church several weeks ago, and I know, without a doubt, she is proud, today, that I'm the one 'speaking the words over her.' It certainly is my privilege and honor."

Andy paused and swallowed to relax his throat, which had tightened with emotion. Then he braced himself more solidly on the lectern and began, again.

"That doesn't mean I find this to be easy. But my task, today, is not just a sad one. It is also a joyful one because we know Grannie is with the Lord. We cannot imagine her last minutes on Earth—how she must have been in pain from her fall, and how cold and fearful she must have felt. Thankfully, such sufferings are only the tiniest of pinpoints in the timeline of eternity. Grannie is now in the timeless comfort of Heaven! One minute, she was cold and alone in a frozen alley, and the next minute she was with the risen Lord and basking in the glow of His glory! Grannie's first breath in Paradise was richer than any experience she'd ever had on Earth.

"And that leads me to share that not all of Grannie's experiences on Earth were easy. As a youth, she outlived most of her relatives, who died in the great 1918 pandemic: whole households dying in one day! Then she married a Kentucky sharecropper, only to have him die of tuberculosis. With a young daughter to care for, Grannie began to clean houses and take in laundry. Hoping to find better pay and a better life, she and her daughter boarded a bus to Chicago; but things, there, were even harder. Grannie worked cleaning public restrooms for months before someone pointed out an ad for a live-in domestic. She applied, and her cooking is what got her the job. One taste of Grannie's fried chicken and there was no question; she was hired."

Rachel affirmed the truth of the story with a nod.

"Grannie worked for that family until her daughter married, and then she went to work for Steward's Craft Supply Company, where she made finished display models from the products they sold. She was a multi-gifted woman, who sewed, embroidered, crocheted, and knitted with ease.

"I'm sure many of you have at least one thing Grannie created using her talents; you probably received it as a Christmas present. I have a sweater..."

Andy dramatically produced a boy's sweater with the Superman "S" embroidered on the chest and a cape stitched to the back.

"From that Christmas forward, I flew everywhere!" Andy said. The crowd laughed as he demonstrated his flying technique, patterned after George Reeves in the old black-and-white *Superman* television series.

"Just like Superman, Grannie seemed invincible and all-knowing when I was growing up. Now she has taken a great leap—the biggest leap of all—and God has made sure she didn't make the leap alone. Grannie knew the Lord, and the Bible tells us that angels were assigned to bear her to Heaven, just as they did the poor man in Luke 16:22. Jesus said that when the poor man died, the angels carried him to Abraham's side.

"Furthermore, Acts 7:55-56 leads us to believe that when Grannie arrived, Jesus, Himself, was there to receive her. Imagine! Grannie seeing the Risen Lord and gazing into the very face of God!"

Andy paused, and Abbey smiled.

"Our tears today are not for Grannie. She is healed and restored, and she is in the presence of her Lord in Paradise. She has gone away from us. She has gone ahead of us. We are the ones experiencing the sting of death because we miss her, but Grannie is alive! We are the ones awaiting the day of our eternal leap.

"No, our tears today are not for Grannie. She is healed and restored and in Heaven. Our tears are for us, who are left behind. We grieve our loss of her. We miss her unique friendship and fun; we miss her solid faith in God's providence—even during trying times, and we miss her wealth of homespun advice and wisdom."

Andy now looked steadily at his mother and father, and he nodded to Abbey and Molly before he said, "Grannie was a good mother, a good mother-in-law, and a good grandmother, and we are all grateful to God for allowing her to be a part of our family. Our hope is in God's promise that we may all see her again. We can be sure of it—when we answer Christ's call on our lives."

Andy did not take his eyes away from his parents.

"It is our acceptance of Jesus in our lives that opens the door to Heaven."

Mac broke eye contact first, and he stiffly looked past Andy. Rachel appeared wistful and lowered her eyes. Only Molly smiled eye-to-eye at the triumph of the Promise.

Andy and Abbey were stunned. Abbey saw the hurt on her husband's face when they got back to his parents' home.

Andy and Abbey had stopped for a cup of coffee with a college friend who had come to the funeral service. Now, they had walked into the Garrett kitchen to overhear Mac angrily spitting, "Who does he think he is, preaching to us like that? It's one thing to talk about the stuff she believed, but I don't buy it. The old woman's dead and that's all there is to it. There's no heaven and no hell. It's a bunch of nonsense. Some minister! He made us all look like fools."

Paul made a noise to let Mac and Rachel know that Andy and Abbey were home. Rachel put on a cheerful voice and face.

"There you are! What time do you children have to leave in the morning?" she asked.

There was silence.

"Early, I think," Andy finally said.

Then he turned, and without another word, walked up the stairs.

———⋙•⋘———

Alone with Abbey in the bedroom, Andy's bitterness poured out. His father's words had stung, just as his words had always stung since childhood. Andy fought his anger.

"I expected too much," he told Abbey in a harsh whisper. "I guess I was stupid to think they might be touched by the message and that they would respect me as a minister. I'm disappointed that they got nothing out of the message except that I was 'preaching to them.'"

Then he said, "I guess I was preaching to them. But it was because I thought the funeral would help them understand what God's grace meant to Grannie and what Christ means to me. I thought they might at least respect it as a message of hope."

Abbey quietly answered, "You don't know, honey. It may have had more of an impact than you think. Just the fact that your father felt compelled to talk about it means it's gotten under his skin."

Andy sighed, "I just get tired of being ridiculed and bad-mouthed as if I'm still their great disappointment—as if I've done nothing worthwhile with my life and don't have a worthwhile profession. I just wanted them to understand God's peace and everlasting life. Grannie knew Jesus well; and He's the One who changed me. But Mom and Dad are still what they've always been—the most negative and unhappy people I know."

Andy tossed his suit jacket and tie onto the bed. Then he plopped heavily next to the clothes. He shook his head in resignation.

Abbey comforted him. "Honey," she ventured gently, "your parents have gone a long time without God in their lives. It may take a long time for God to work in their hearts. Plus, it isn't up to us to convince them. That's God's job. We just have to live our lives as Christ has taught us, and we need to keep praying for them. That's our job."

"I know," Andy admitted. He was sorry he had let his old hurts take over.

He sat for a moment and then prayed, "Lord Jesus, I lift up my parents to You. I trust You to do Your job. I'll do my job and pray for them. And Lord, please keep working on me."

The ride back to Cherish was quieter than the trip to Herndon had been. Molly made a single mention of their parents' unhappiness, but Andy did not follow up.

The mood in the car remained gray until Molly remembered that she had something to give Andy. She pulled out two small packages their mother had given her as she'd said good-bye.

Molly handed one to Andy.

"Mom said these were for you and me."

Andy wondered what the parcels might contain. Each package was small and thickly wrapped in newspaper. He carefully tore his open, but Molly saw hers, first.

"Oh, look!" Molly cried. Then Andy exclaimed, too. Each treasure was one of Grannie's grape-juice goblets, perfect for a night of popcorn and wrestling.

In an instant, time melted away. Brother and sister flew back to childhood. In their pajamas on the living room floor, they were caught in the flicker of the old Sylvania. It was ringside on Friday night. They heard the clang of their goblets, smelled the butter on the popcorn, and rallied to Grannie's angry-fisted challenge of a questionable call by a beleaguered referee.

The memory lived! The goblets wove their Grannie magic one more time. Their mother could not have given them a better gift.

PART THREE
OPENING THE DOOR

CHAPTER TWENTY-FIVE

NEWS (FEBRUARY 1980)

"I'm pregnant!"

Molly trumpeted the words into the phone the minute her brother picked up. "We're going to have a baby!"

Andy's whoop startled Opal in the outer office. And in his exuberance, Andy also spilled the coffee on his desk.

"That's fantastic news!" he said. "How far along are you?"

"Put a mark on September 6 on your calendar," Molly said. "We didn't want to say anything until the doctor confirmed there were no worries. You're the first person we've told."

Andy whooped again. "A baby! I can't wait!"

Molly laughed and then she said, "I know all about morning sickness. I just hope I'm not going to be sick for my whole pregnancy."

She also told Andy that she and Paul had started to pull things out of the spare bedroom and tuck them away in the attic. She and Paul had picked out a crib, a rocker, and other furnishings from the Sears catalog and were waiting for delivery.

"I think we're going to paint the room a pastel orange," Molly said. "Not too bright, and neutral enough for a boy or a girl."

"Yes, a boy or a girl would be perfect," Andy said without thinking. "I can't wait to tell Abbey!"

⟶·◈·⟵

Andy tried to imagine Molly pregnant. What must it feel like to be pregnant, he wondered? How must it feel to know a new life is growing inside of you? Women amazed him. They managed pregnancy with such aplomb. He was sure that if he were pregnant, he would be a nervous wreck.

"Thank goodness you're not a woman and never will be," Abbey chuckled at his musings.

Andy grinned and said, "But I'm glad you're a woman." He wrapped her in a hug.

Then he said quietly, "I need to tell you that Molly was worried how you would feel to know she's pregnant and we can't have children."

"Oh! Poor Molly!" Abbey cried.

It made her sad to think that Molly would worry about this in the middle of her joy. Both Andy and Abbey had moved past that disappointment long ago.

Abbey said. "Doesn't Molly know how lucky you and I are? We get to be Aunt and Uncle! I can't wait!"

Andy lifted her chin and kissed her. "I told Molly that very thing, but she may need to hear it from you. It will settle her worries."

Then Andy exclaimed, "And you're absolutely right. I'm going to be an uncle!"

He struck a pose and announced, "I intend to be the best uncle any child could ever have."

Abbey had no doubt. What child wouldn't want an uncle who, himself, was a child at heart?

———◆———

It was hard for Andy to keep his mind on his work. In the middle of his sermon preparation for Sunday, he found himself daydreaming about his new niece or nephew, and he reflected on how the farm would be an ideal place for her or him to grow up. Andy's thoughts oscillated between dream and reality—between an imagined child's barnyard pleas to "See this, Uncle Andy! See what I can do!" and the sermon and the bulletin outline before him. Andy kept pulling his thoughts back to the task of coordinating a very busy worship service.

Most Sunday's were simple, with announcements, hymns, prayer, anthem, and sermon. But this Sunday he also had to squeeze in a mission award presentation, recognition of new Eagle Scout, Ronnie Strong, and a children's choir number with a little speaking part for Andy. Andy would have liked to have spread these out over several Sundays, but it could not be helped. He would just have to pay attention and keep things rolling.

"All I need is one more thing," he muttered with good-natured sarcasm.

And then on Sunday morning, one more thing happened. A raspy-voiced Luther Sharp telephoned the parsonage during breakfast. He croaked, "I hate to ask, but as you can hear, I'm sick. And I was wondering if you or Abbey could teach the adult Sunday school class this morning."

Andy had so much to do today and didn't want to have to juggle anything else. Nevertheless, he assured Luther that the class would be taken care of.

When Luther hung up, Andy nervously approached Abbey.

"Luther is sick," he began. "Luther was wondering if one of us could teach his Sunday school class this morning."

Abbey read the stress in her husband's eyes, and she knew it was an appeal for her to take the job. "Sure," Abbey said, trying not to sound grudging about it. Fortunately, she had read her lesson, so at least she knew the topic. Abbey just wished she'd had time to prepare to teach it. The adult class could ask the most difficult questions.

As it turned out, the adult class went smoothly. Sadly, it was because several of the most vocal members were out with whatever sickness Luther had.

Then, because teaching always made Abbey late for choir, she raced to throw on her robe and slip into the choir loft without creating too much disturbance. When Abbey got there, everyone else had just stood for the first hymn. Good timing, she thought! It was good cover for her to sneak into her place.

The introductory measures for the hymn began—but oddly, they were not from the organ. Without even looking, Abbey knew that Lena Thorndike was at the piano.

Poor Marilyn! Theresa Jackson must be sick.

Abbey could only guess how stressed the music director was at the last-minute substitution—and with good cause. It didn't take long for trouble to start.

Lena had assumed that the congregation would be singing all four verses of "There Shall Be Showers of Blessing," even though Marilyn had just announced they would sing verses one and four. Lena had never bothered to look up to catch Marilyn's cues.

Abbey admired that while Marilyn could have had the congregation sing the two verses and sit down—leaving Lena to play the other two verses alone, Marilyn instead punted. Marilyn began verses two and three after verse four so that all four verses were eventually sung. The congregation gamely followed her lead. Relieved, Marilyn then sat until it was time for the choir number.

The extra business of this morning's service delayed the choir anthem and only added to Marilyn's anxiety. Since Lena hadn't practiced with the choir on Wednesday, no one knew what tempo Lena was going to decide to take when it was time for them to sing. Abbey smiled encouragingly at Marilyn during the mission presentation, the Eagle Scout recognition, and the children's song (sung *a cappella* and led by Chelsea). Finally, the chancel choir stood.

The entire choir saw Marilyn anxiously beseech Heaven for a miracle. Then, the beleaguered director raised her hands to cue the first measure. Thankfully, Lena looked up, and everyone started together on the downbeat. Then, unfortunately, the two minds led off in separate directions. Half of the choir followed Marilyn's direction, and the other half followed Lena's non-stop, steady-on, full-speed-ahead pace, which ignored all fermatas and rallentandos. Marilyn's hair seemed to frazzle before everyone's eyes.

When the two factions of the singers ended and the choir members took their seats, Andy said, "Uh, thank you, choir," and Marilyn hid her face in her hands.

CHAPTER TWENTY-SIX

RACHEL'S NEWS

Spring passed, and then part of the summer. In addition to the noticeable changes in her body, Molly's hormones now fluctuated wildly, too. Her emotions vacillated from highs to lows without rhyme or reason. And Paul patiently responded with more hugs, kisses, and whispers of love in her ear.

Then on top of her discomfort and all of her emotional ups and downs, a phone call came that nearly drove Molly over the edge. It happened so fast and so unexpectedly that Molly could hardly believe it was real. But it was.

It was a blind-side alert from her mother who said she was flying in to help her daughter get ready for the baby. Dad would not be coming.

Immediately, Molly called Andy and cried into the phone, "I don't know if I can do this, Andy! I don't want her to come, especially not now. I can't handle Mom when I'm in good shape, and now I'm an emotional wreck. Besides, Paul and I have already moved everything out of the guest room, and we don't have a place for her to sleep. Oh, Andy! Why does she have to come?"

Abbey heard Andy say, "I'm sorry, Sis. I wish for you that it wasn't happening, but I don't think we can tell Mom not to come. It would only make things worse."

Then he said, "I'm sure she just wants to do what mothers do when their daughters have babies. I guess we shouldn't be surprised. But don't worry; we'll keep Mom at our place. And hopefully, she won't stay long."

Abbey's eyes widened. She wasn't sure Andy's mom was ready to return to the scene of her last disastrous visit.

Andy continued to console his sister, and when he hung up, he turned to reassure his wife. "Don't worry, Abbs. Remember, when Mom and Dad aren't together, there's nobody to fight with. It'll be fine." (Under his breath, Andy hoped he was right.)

Once the initial shock wore off, Abbey decided it might be fine. Hosting just one of Andy's parents had to be simpler and less unnerving than having them both. Abbey would also have to act as if nothing had happened to her wonderful lamp. She couldn't let her mother-in-law feel guilty forever.

Most important, Abbey knew that she and Andy had to do it. It was the least the two of them could do for Molly. Molly didn't need the extra stress of twenty-four hours a day with her mother.

The typically scorching days of late July held off, and the drive to Decatur was sunny but pleasant. Rachel was waiting at the airport.

"Hello, children!" she cried, and she wrapped Andy and Abbey in a big, showy hug.

"Thank you for keeping me. I just had to come and be with Molly while she's expecting. Maybe I can help, some."

Abbey sensed no awkwardness in her mother-in-law's greeting, which made her glad. She hoped it would be the same once Rachel got to the parsonage. Abbey had left the new lamp glowing in the window before she and Andy had left for the airport.

"Won't it be wonderful to have a baby in the family, again?" Mom asked with enthusiasm on the drive home. "I've always loved babies."

Andy wondered. He tried to imagine his mom in a pleasant setting with him and Molly as little ones. Perhaps it had been less turbulent, once, in the Garrett home. Or was his mother only painting a fictional picture of what she wished had been true?

Abbey's hosting worries did not materialize. It was, indeed, easier to host her mother-in-law than both of Andy's parents. Plus, Rachel was only at the parsonage part of the time. Rachel spent the better part of her day at Molly and Paul's. Paul would pick her up from the parsonage after finishing his morning chores, and Abbey and Andy would pick her up from the farm in the evening.

Abbey had told Molly to call, anytime, if she got overwhelmed. If things got bad, Abbey said she would drive over and collect Rachel.

Abbey wasn't sure what she would do with her mother-in-law for a whole day, but she knew she had to offer. No doubt, the phone would ring before long. But it did not.

Unexpectedly, Rachel was not Rachel.

Molly had braced herself against parental interference. She was determined to hold her own on how she wanted the baby's room set and with what colors she wanted it decorated. Molly was ready to put her foot down against any unwanted advice, especially any suggestion that she and Paul weren't going about things the right way. But for all of Molly's emotional exercising, nothing happened.

Rachel never once dictated to her daughter how to arrange things or what colors to use. She pleasantly took her cues from Molly on every decision regarding baby preparation, and unlike Mac, who was tighter than Scrooge with his purse strings, Rachel bought all kinds of infant necessities.

She even took everyone to dinner from time to time before Andy and Abbey drove her back to Cherish.

"It's almost nice to have her here," Molly confided in surprise. "I wouldn't have thought it possible."

Molly had tentatively even begun to look forward to her mother's hugs and warm whispers of, "I love you, honey, and I love that little baby."

"I love you, too, Mom, and I'm grateful for your help," Molly was truthfully able to say.

The entire visit was so nearly normal that Molly couldn't help but wonder if she were dreaming. Surely this wasn't the mother of her childhood.

Andy and Abbey marveled, too, at how Rachel glowed with her reports of all she and Molly had done each day.

Amazingly, in her excitement, Rachel laughed.

Andy couldn't recall the last time he'd heard his mother laugh—truly laugh without an undertone of snobbishness or derision. Her genuine laughter, now, caught him off guard. Andy didn't know if he could trust what he was hearing.

If all of this was put on, his mother was a remarkable actress, Andy thought. And if it was put on, he wondered how much longer she could keep it up.

———◦●◦———

As the week wore on, things began to change.

Like a wound up doll, Rachel had danced earlier in the week, but now her pirouettes had become sluggish, and although she still helped at the farm, she slumped. The laughter faded. It was hard to tell from Rachel's expression what had caused the rapid decline, and Andy became apprehensive.

Maybe his mother was just sad that her visit was drawing to a close. After all, in a normal person, that might be a reasonable reaction; but this was his mother, and Andy wondered.

He cast about for anything that might shed light on her change of disposition: some little aggravation or unintended slight. Andy was keenly aware of how his parents could twist the most innocent things into ugly, painful accusations. He wondered what his mother might be harboring and sharpening for the right moment. Perhaps she disapproved of something Molly and Paul were doing, or maybe she didn't like something that he and Abbey had done while she was at their place.

Andy didn't want to hear any of it. He wished she would leave her negativity at home. Why couldn't things end pleasantly? There were only a couple more days to go.

On the last night of Rachel's visit at the parsonage, Andy's chest grew tight. His mother had asked him and Abbey to come and sit in the living room with her for a minute. It was as if she had requested a formal meeting. Andy gritted his teeth. He did not want to hear a single negative word about Molly and Paul or himself and Abbey.

Andy perched warily on the edge of the sofa, ready to rise in protest if things turned sour. When his mother spoke, however, Andy turned sharply to make sure he had heard correctly. Her news wasn't about him and Abbey, or Molly and Paul. It was about herself.

Rachel had cleared her throat and stated quietly, "I think I'm sick."

Because it wasn't what he had been expecting, Andy had to hear it again before the words sank in. Rachel repeated it. "I think I have something very wrong with me," she said.

Her matter-of-fact statement left Andy and Abbey unprepared with a response before she went on.

"I've guessed as much for a while," she said calmly. "I've tried to ignore it, but now I'm going to a doctor when I get home."

Rachel rested her hand on her abdomen. "There's something wrong, here," she said.

Abbey found her voice before Andy did.

"Mom, do you suppose it's just an upset of some kind—perhaps an ulcer?" Abbey asked.

Andy quickly followed up, "Have you told Dad?"

"No, I'll tell your father when I get back," Rachel said, answering the last question, first.

Then she answered Abbey's question: "I've had ulcers before, and this is entirely different. I think I have something far more seriously wrong."

The discussion felt surreal. Over the years, Andy had watched his mother drag the family through a gambit of hysterical ailments. When he was younger, she had spent a lot of time in the hospital recovering after the most horrific of his parents' fights. Then, as he had grown up, Andy had wondered if some of her illnesses had been fake—a way to punish his dad (for what, Andy didn't know).

Andy's impulse, now, was to question whether it was for real, this time—or was his mother trying to grab Molly's spotlight? His mind fluctuated between shame for thinking such a thing and anger that he would even have to.

And yet somehow, something in his mother's manner, tonight, arrested him. This was not how she had behaved before. In the past, Rachel had hysterically and dramatically commanded attention. This evening, there were no theatrics, and there was no drama. This was not his mother's usual performance. Was it possible that this time she truly had a serious illness—perhaps cancer? She seemed tired.

Rachel continued in the same calm voice: "Before I check with the doctor and possibly end up in the hospital, I wanted to come and help Molly get ready for the baby. I am so happy for her and so proud of her."

Andy thought he was going to faint. His mother had just complimented Molly.

But then she continued, "And I also wanted to talk to you."

Aha! Here it comes, thought Andy—the backhand of the compliment. Or perhaps this was going to be a criticism against him and Abbey for something. Andy braced himself.

His mother's next words, however, caused his heart to leap: "I wanted you to know I've been thinking a lot about God."

Andy sucked in a breath and held it.

Rachel continued, "I remember the things you said at Mama's funeral and how you talked about the things she believed. I'm scared. And I think it's time I started to think about what you said. I want to know I'll go to Heaven when I die."

Rachel's eyes filled, but they did not spill over. For a typically emotional woman, she was maintaining considerable control. Andy thought it made her look more vulnerable; she now seemed smaller and sunken into the cushions on the sofa.

Gently Andy asked, "Mom, do you know that God loves you?"

Rachel laughed quietly, twisting the tissue she held in her hand. "Well, if He does, honey, He has a funny way of showing it."

Andy prayed as he searched for what to say. He knew Abbey was praying, too.

"The Bible says that God loves the whole world so much that He sent His Son to show us. He showed us His love by dying for us, to save us from ourselves," Andy said.

His mother sighed. "I've heard my mom say all of that a long time ago, but I didn't pay any attention to it. Now I wonder if it's too late for me."

Andy had a sudden thought. He fumbled for the wallet in his back pocket, and he pulled out a card the size of a credit card. Andy handed it to his mother.

"Mom, do you remember this picture? It's like the one Grannie had hanging in her hallway—the one with the bright gold frame. I bought this card years ago at a bookstore because I recognized it as the one I had seen at Grannie's house."

His mom smiled in surprise. "Yes, that's the picture of Jesus she liked so well! I always wondered whose door He was knocking at."

Andy said, "William Holman Hunt painted this picture as an illustration of a verse in Revelation, chapter three. That's where Jesus says that He's standing at the door and knocking, and if anyone hears His voice and opens the door, He will come in and dine with him. What that means is that Jesus continually stands at the door of our heart, knocking and knocking until we let Him in."

His mother nodded her head slightly as she listened.

"There's one more thing about this picture you might not have noticed," Andy said. "There is no latch or doorknob on the outside. See, Mom? There is no way for Jesus to let Himself in; the door has to be opened from the inside.

"The verse in Revelation 3:20 says specifically, *'If anyone hears my voice AND OPENS THE DOOR, I will come in.'*"

Andy paused because he saw his mother examine the picture and notice for the first time that he was right; there was no door knob or latch. Rachel put her finger where the doorknob should have been.

"He's been waiting a long time," she said quietly. "I guess I just didn't hear Him knocking."

"He's still there," said Andy. "And He's still knocking."

It was quiet for a moment. Andy wondered if his mother understood.

Then Rachel said, "Son, I want to open that door. How... how do I do that?"

Andy softly said, "I think you're doing it right now, Mom. Just talk to Jesus and tell Him you want Him in your heart. The Bible verse depicted in the painting says that when you hear Him knocking, and you finally open the door, He comes in! It's that simple."

Rachel stared at the picture again, and then she said very quietly, "Okay, Jesus. If You're still there, I'm opening the door..."

Andy's heart beat wildly. Then he saw a smile, a tentative smile, slowly and spontaneously make its way across his mother's face.

"I think He came in," she softly exclaimed. "I almost thought I heard my Mama laughing! If I become a Christian, I'll see her again, won't I?"

"Yes," Andy assured her. "When Christians die, we all go to Heaven. Grannie is there, and Jesus will be there, too."

"That's what I needed to know," his mother said.

Andy tried not to be too emotional, but he could barely say, "Abbey and I have been praying for you and Dad for a long time."

"I can't believe I waited so long," Rachel whispered. "This is the first time I've felt Jesus is real." Andy hugged her.

His mother said, "I wish your dad could do this, too. He needs to know there's a door. But I'm afraid he's going to need much more. I think that even when he knows the door is there and that Jesus is knocking, he'll have a hard time opening it."

Andy wondered why everything was always so hard for his father.

"Pray for your dad," his mother said.

Andy took her hand. "We will, Mom. But let's pray, right now, for you. Let's ask God to help you find out what's wrong inside of you, and let's pray He'll help you with whatever it is."

When they finished praying, Rachel announced steadily, "I don't think God is going to make me well, Son. But…"

Andy was going to protest, but something stopped him.

"But," she continued, "I'm not afraid, now. I'm just not afraid."

———————

Molly was speechless. Andy and Abbey had stopped at the farm on the way back from the airport. Andy had told her about their mother's possible illness.

"I don't think she's faking it, Sis," Andy said. "I believe her. I believe Mom truly is sick, and I know she's been frightened about it."

"I'm surprised she didn't tell me," Molly said.

Andy suggested, "I think it's because she didn't want to spoil all the plans for the baby. Mom wanted her time with you to be a happy time."

That thought caught Molly off guard.

"Everything is different," she said.

"And," said Andy, "there's something else."

Molly stiffened slightly. Andy knew she was expecting the bad news, now—something negative from her parents about her and Paul or about Andy and Abbey.

Instead, Andy said, "Mom asked Jesus into her heart, last night."

Molly cried out. It was the last thing she would have imagined him to say.

"It's true, Sis," Andy said. "I could see the change in her. I know you'll recognize it, too."

Like her brother, Molly was in awe about their mother's acceptance of Christ. She tried to imagine it. She also tried to imagine her mother seriously ill. These new things were going to take a lot of getting used to.

Molly couldn't help wondering, however, why this good thing couldn't have happened sooner, without the threat of sickness? Everything related to their parents always seemed to be difficult—even this. Molly wondered why her parents could never have peace.

Andy interrupted his sister's thoughts. "We need to pray about Mom's visit to the doctor. And we need to pray for Dad to find God's peace, especially if it turns out that Mom is sicker than we hope."

"I know," said Molly. "Dad will be awful about it."

———

Over the next few days, Andy was preoccupied with the changes in his family. He felt pulled back into his parents' world. If his mother was as sick as he suspected, things were going to be more difficult than ever— even though his mom had become a Christian.

"God, where are You taking all of us?" Andy prayed. "I'm more concerned for my parents, now, than ever before. Bring Your healing and love to their wounds, Lord. And especially help my dad."

CHAPTER TWENTY-SEVEN

CHANGES

When Andy walked into the church office on Tuesday, he gasped.

"What did you do?" he croaked at Opal.

"You don't like it?" Opal asked, startled.

All of the dark strands of her spiky, to-the-four-winds tangle of a hairdo were now remarkably blond! The pencil poised precariously behind her ear fell out as she turned to face Andy.

Quickly realizing how much his appraisal counted, Andy stammered his recovery.

"It-it's very nice," he said. "I just wasn't expecting it."

"Well," Opal said, "we're all blonds, now—my sisters and I, I mean. We were shopping in Ft. Marshall, and we saw these three teenage girls sitting at the cosmetics counter getting free facials. So we decided to do that. The demonstrator kept saying she thought Pearl was a closet blond because of her coloring. It tickled Pearl so much that we stopped at the mall and bought some blond hair coloring, just for fun. Then Pearl said, 'You know, we've always had the same color of hair since we were kids. It'll seem funny for me to be blond and the rest of you to be brunettes.' That prompted Ruby to pick up a box of coloring, and then, of course, I had to get one, too, and... Well, now, we're all blonds."

"You know, I'm getting used to the idea," Andy said. "It looks pretty good! I had just never imagined you as a blond."

"You worried me," Opal said. "You're the first person to see it, and I was afraid it might be a bit much. But if you think it's okay..."

Andy walked around her as if contemplating her new look from all angles. "Ye-e-s," he said. "It's quite nice. It gives you a spark!"

Opal looked pleased. "Good!" she said, and her fingers raked through her spikes one more time.

—————⋙●⋘—————

On Sunday, Andy had preached from Acts 12, and he knew that the sermon was the inspiration for Opal's newest poem. As usual, she portrayed the story with her unique touch of humor and truth.

SILLY RHODA
By Opal Reese

"Rhoda, discourage
Whoever's outside.
Just tell them we're busy
And can't be annoyed.

"Now, let's all get back
To our prayers for Peter.
He hasn't much time, now,
So we haven't, either.

"Tomorrow he'll die
If it's as the king says,
Unless the Lord changes
His circumstances.

"Now, don't bother us, Rhoda!
We're too busy, please.
Just ask that poor stranger,
If he would, please leave.

"Now, Rhoda, it's no time
For hysterical visions;
You know very well
That Peter's in prison.

"Well, if it IS Peter
(I doubt if it's him),
Why don't you simply
Just usher him in?

"You mean it IS you?!
The Lord heard our prayers?
Rhoda! How could you
Have left him out there?"

Andy turned to the blond sitting at Opal's desk and laughed. He thought to himself how nice it was that some things—like Opal's talent and humor—did not change.

Rachel's doctor's report was not encouraging. The doctor said her cancer was quite advanced, and he said it was beyond meaningful treatment or surgery. As kindly but as truthfully as he could, the doctor predicted that Rachel very likely had only a short time to live.

"Some palliative chemotherapy treatments will keep your pain under control for a while," he offered. "And there's always hospice."

When given her choices, Rachel elected the chemotherapy but she insisted on staying at home.

Andy was heartbroken that there was no hope. He wondered for the second time in his life how something as deadly as cancer could live and grow inside of you undetected and steal your future. He despised cancer. The only marvel was the calmness exhibited by his mother.

On the telephone, Rachel had said, "It's your dad I'm worried about. He's trying to bully the doctors to 'do something,' but of course, they can't. Your father can't buy me health, this time. This time, no one can help. And I choose to be home."

Andy then told her that he and Molly were coming to Herndon.

"We've talked," Andy said before his mom could object, "and Molly and I think you and Dad are going to need someone there. Instead of hiring a stranger, we'll come. Molly and Paul will come first, next week, and then Abbey and I will come a few days after that. We don't want you two to be alone through all of this."

Surprisingly, his mother didn't oppose the plan. Instead, she seemed relieved. "That would be helpful," she said. "I'm terribly tired."

"I'm sure Molly will call you soon," Andy said, "so you'll know when she and Paul will be arriving."

———◦◦◦———

Phillip Doaks waved to his son and daughter-in-law as they pulled out of the farmyard and into the lane. He felt in high spirits to be back at the farm, if only for a short while. Phillip had respectfully stayed out of Paul's way once he had turned the farm over to him. And although Phillip's body had said it was time to retire, his heart had still missed farming. He was pleased, now, to have been asked to watch things as the younger Doaks made their trip to Herndon.

Paul had arranged for his dad to do only the milking and the light chores while he and Molly were gone. Neighbors (the Bennetts) would come to help with the heavier work, and they would feed his dad.

Phillip looked forward to meals with Ron and Sheryl Bennett. Sheryl was a superb cook. It would be worth a few days of arthritic pains just to slather some real old-fashioned farm butter on her homemade pancakes in the morning.

Paul glanced again through the rearview mirror. As his dad had waved goodbye, Paul had noticed that, in his worn bibs and Pioneer Seed cap, the man looked younger. There had also been a satisfaction in his father's eyes to have been asked for help. Perhaps he and Molly should invite Dad to help at the farm more often. In fact, Paul would make sure of it once they returned home.

In addition to making all the farm arrangements, Paul had done all he could to ensure that Molly would be comfortable in the car on the trip. He reached over, now, and took his wife's hand. "You're getting prettier all the time," he murmured. Paul wanted Molly to know how deeply he loved her through every gain and glow.

Paul announced, too, that when they got to Herndon, it would be his job, not Molly's, to do all of the housework. It would be just like they'd begun to do at home. As Molly had grown larger with her pregnancy, he had told her, "You cook and do the dusting, and I'll run the sweeper." Now in the car, he added, "And I'll lend my expertise to cleaning your parent's tubs and sinks."

"Thank you, dear." Molly smiled. "We'll make a great team."

Paul had been anxious about the trip, and he hoped that Molly would bear up well. Molly had been determined to go, but Paul knew it would take a physical and emotional toll on her. He knew that Mac would likely become fierce as Rachel's health declined, and Paul wished that his Molly wouldn't have to contend with her dad's anger and conflict at this stage of her pregnancy. But they had not chosen the timing of this family difficulty; God had.

Paul could only pray that things would not get too bumpy, on the road and in Herndon.

⸻

When the Doaks arrived at the big house on the Herndon bluffs, one glance told Molly a great deal about how things had been going.

The center of the room bore a few vacuum tracks, and Molly was impressed. She had never known her father to vacuum or dust. (She knew it had to be her dad's work because none of the tracks ventured under and around the furniture or along the walls).

Molly also saw dishes drying in a drainer by the sink, and she assumed that her father had done those, too. She doubted, however, that he'd been cooking. Discarded containers from a deli confirmed her suspicions. To her knowledge, her dad had attempted cooking only once. It had been when she and Andy were children, and it had ended with a bang. The pressure cooker he'd abused had exploded and sent a steaming spray of chicken-and-noodle-paste across the ceiling. Molly knew her dad would not try cooking again.

A laundry basket of folded clothes lay next to her mother's chair. Since Mom was too weak to navigate the basement steps, Dad must have brought them up for her to fold.

Seeing all of this, Molly was glad that she and Paul had come. They were here to put Dad out of a job, and Mac seemed relieved to have them there. The furrows in Mac's forehead had deepened since Molly and Paul had seen him, last. The dark circles under his eyes made Molly wonder if he had been sleeping.

Mac still cursed with nearly every utterance, but it was usually under his breath instead of the full-throated roar he had always maintained. Molly and Paul also watched in wonder to see Mac treating Rachel as if she were made of china.

His tender actions to his wife reminded Molly of when, as a child, she had seen her father protectively lead Mom out to the car during one of her illnesses. Just hours before that, the two of them had been yelling so hatefully at each other that this gentle scene had seemed incongruous. Molly had never been able to resolve the opposing images in her mind. As she saw her dad's devotion, now, she was just as confused.

Paul suggested that Mac's softened response was because there were no combative buttons he could push in good conscience. He was floundering without the counterbalance of Rachel's barbs to his jabs and growls; Mac couldn't figure out exactly how to act when off the battlefield.

The hardest part for Molly was that her parents didn't talk. They not only didn't fight but whole conversations of unspoken words hung in the air—words that might have helped them work through and face Rachel's illness as a couple. Instead, the two of them (and especially her dad) seemed determined to avoid discussing the inevitable. It was as if not speaking of death would keep it from happening. The result was that the house reverberated with the tension of an unexploded bomb.

Molly leaned on Paul. Without him, she would have run screaming into the street at least once a day. Paul would anticipate his wife's need for rescue and show up at just the right moment to offer a quick walk around the block. Or Paul would find an excuse to take Molly to the store.

Paul also began to separate Mac from Rachel. He would take Mac on errands and leave Molly and Rachel alone. With Mac gone, Paul hoped Rachel would share with her daughter. Mac, too, sometimes shared his fears with Paul.

Paul informed Molly, one day, "Your dad's asked me if your mom is sharing with us anything she hasn't told him. He's terribly worried about losing her."

Molly marveled. "The two of them have fought for so long," she said, "it's hard to imagine them caring what happens to each other. The sad part is that I don't think they know how to live apart, even though life together has always been a battle. I don't understand it, but I believe that it's true."

She quietly added, "What in the world will Dad do when Mom dies?"

———◆———

As lunchtime neared, Molly was glad the pork chops had finished browning. Without the sizzling, she could hear as Mom and Dad talked in the other room. In the relative quiet, Rachel was telling Mac the reason she wasn't afraid to die.

"I talked with Andy," Rachel said. "And he helped me open the door of my heart to let Jesus in."

Molly didn't move. A creak of the floor boards would give away that she was listening. In the quiet, she closed her eyes, afraid to hear what might come next. But her dad said nothing.

"And do you know something else?" her mother continued. "Now I understand what changed Andy so much. You remember what he used to be like…"

The growl came, now, in a terse reply, "That may be all right for you, but you know that won't work for me!"

Molly waited. Her mother did not follow up. The sound of the television grew louder, and Molly knew her father had turned up the volume.

With a sigh, Molly went back to whipping the potatoes. It was nearly time to call Paul downstairs to eat.

CHAPTER TWENTY-EIGHT

CRISIS

With the permission of the deacons and church board, Andy contacted the Baptist Area Minister, Vaughn Wood, to fill the First Baptist pulpit while he and Abbey went to Herndon. Andy also asked Reverend Wood to pray for his parents. Andy explained that his mother had let Christ into her heart but that his dad was still in battle with God.

"Let's pray, right now," Rev. Wood said over the phone, and the words of his petition expressed the deepest desires of Andy's heart. Andy was grateful for the prayer, and he knew his minister-friend would continue to pray while they were away.

———⊷●⊶———

When Andy and Abbey arrived at the senior Garretts' home, Andy was shocked at the decline in his mother. He wondered if his father might also be ill. Both parents had dark circles under their eyes, and a weariness had settled over their movements. Andy almost didn't recognize them as the same people he had wanted to escape from, years ago.

Mom sat propped up on the sofa, and Andy and Abbey gathered in the living room so Rachel could receive their fragile hugs. Dad never moved from his recliner, so they came to him with their greetings, too.

"Glad you came," was all Mac said. His words were clipped, and Andy saw anger surging under the sullenness—an anger that seemed unsure where to strike.

Abbey noticed that Mom's hair and nails had been done and she told Rachel how nice she looked.

"Molly did it," Rachel said with a weak smile. And Rachel pointed out her new robe and gown. "Molly bought them," she said. "Aren't they pretty?"

Abbey recognized these personal touches as expressions of love from Molly for a mother with whom she had just begun to have a real relationship. Abbey was glad there had been time for Molly to offer her gifts, just as Rachel had been able to give so generously in preparing for the baby. Although it was stressful for Molly to witness her mother's inevitable decline and her father's anger and denial, Abbey also knew that this visit had not been wasted. Molly would have no regret. She had done what she could.

———◦◦◦———

In the kitchen, Molly showed Andy and Abbey the groceries she'd stocked and what leftovers could still be eaten.

Molly also declared, "They don't talk. Especially Dad."

Andy recognized the tension in her voice. Stress was one thing he and his sister had shared over the years. Molly didn't have to tell Andy how being here had strained her well-being. He was here to relieve her—to take the pressure on himself, now. That's what a brother did.

"They just sit in silence," Molly said. "And Dad uses the television as a barrier to conversation."

Andy could see it. He wondered how Molly and Paul had been able to manage, and Molly shared that she could not have done it without Paul.

"Paul would take Dad to the grocery store, the pharmacy, or the coffee shop—even though Dad growled about it," Molly said. "And on those occasions, Mom might say a few words. Otherwise, she says nothing. She's pretty weak."

Paul said that Mac would open up a little whenever he and Dad were away from the house. "He's definitely hurting," Paul said.

Overall, Andy was impressed with how wisely Molly and Paul had managed his parents. Andy wondered how he would fare, now. As a pastor, Andy had lots of experience in counseling other people's families. To other people he was a voice of wisdom; they readily welcomed his counsel and freely confided in him. But Andy knew that, to his dad, his counseling credentials were invalid. He had no idea how to help his father open up and work through the fear and pain of Mom's impending death—especially with a son he sometimes still referred to as "that idiot son of mine." Andy recalled all too vividly his father's accusation after Grannie's funeral. Despite all of his seminary knowledge and training, Andy felt powerless to help. He knew he had no weapons in his arsenal capable of winning this battle. He hung his head.

But even as he let that thought form, Andy stopped short.

It wasn't true! He wasn't powerless.

That was a lie of the Deceiver; Satan had been whispering defeat! But Andy Garrett, a child of The King, wasn't without resources. The Great Counselor was never empty-handed. Andy remembered that he had all the power of Heaven behind him.

Andy squared his shoulders and gave his sister a hug. "We have to keep praying, Molly. With God, we can do anything. This is His battle, too."

Andy and Abbey knew that Molly and Paul were grateful to be relieved of their posts. It had been only a few days, but it had been hard. Molly was glad that she and Paul had come, but she had also wearied quickly and was glad to be returning home tomorrow. She told Andy that she missed the sanity and peace of the farm.

In the living room after supper, Andy made several attempts to make the last evening for the six of them a pleasant one, but he did not succeed. No matter what anyone shared, it was swallowed up in the fog of his parents' oppression. Finally, Mac abruptly turned on the television and levered back his recliner.

Nothing that flickered on the screen held meaning, so bedtime came early. Everyone retired, and the house grew silent.

Andy crawled into bed and gathered Abbey into his arms. He kissed her softly before they rolled apart to go to sleep. Andy was grateful to have Abbey here with him, and he hoped Molly and Paul could rest more comfortably tonight.

With that thought, he reached over and turned off the light.

Immediately a cry rang out and the light came back on. It was Rachel.

The second-floor occupants tore out of bed and raced down the stairs. Rachel was tossing violently. Although she'd had her pain medications, it was obvious they were no longer effective. Mac stood dumbly in the corner, not sure how to help his stricken wife.

"Let's get her to the emergency room," Andy commanded, without waiting for a consensus.

While the others scrambled to their rooms to get out of their pajamas and into their clothes, Andy picked up the phone to call for an ambulance.

"No," his dad interrupted. "Take my car."

Mac handed Andy the keys. "It'll take too long to get an ambulance here. It'll be faster if we take her. Rachel can lie down in the back."

Knowing it was true, Andy drove his parents to the hospital. The others followed in Paul's car.

Fortunately, the emergency room wasn't too crowded, and when the technicians saw Rachel writhing and crying out in pain, they rushed her through to a bay for evaluation. It felt like it took forever for an injection to arrive with something strong enough to bring her relief.

Then another eon passed before the doctors admitted her and the transport staff wheeled Rachel's bed into the elevator and up to a sixth-floor room. Rachel remained connected to several machines and an IV drip. She hardly roused, now, which was good. It meant she wasn't suffering.

In her room, Mac collapsed into the chair beside the bed and covered his face with his hands. Andy drew up another chair and put his hand on his dad's shoulder. Abbey, Molly, and Paul sat on the end of the empty bed in the room.

As time passed, they decided to take turns staying with Rachel. Mac insisted on being first, and Paul sat with him. The other three moved to that floor's lounge, where they prayed and curled up in uncomfortable chairs to sleep.

———◆———

In his dreams on the sofa in the lounge, Andy kept trying to fly, but nothing was working. Andy had always flown in his dreams, and he knew the euphoric feeling of lift-off. But tonight, Andy could not make the feeling come. No matter what he did, his airs were restricted. Andy was heavily rooted to mere inches above the ground.

When he awakened, it was three o'clock. Abbey and Molly were sleeping soundly. Andy pulled Abbey's coat over her shoulders, and he left her and his sister in the quiet.

In his mother's room, Andy saw that his father had nodded off to sleep. Andy took over Paul's watch, so his brother-in-law could retreat to the lounge. As he sat now, Andy watched his parents breathe. "God," he whispered, "help them. Help me to help them."

Every once in a while, his mother would moan and change position, and the rearrangement of the IV tubing would cause the drip bags to shudder. Whenever she moved, Mac would rouse, too. At one point Mac realized that Andy had taken the chair next to him, and he rubbed his eyes.

"Dad, why don't you go out for a while and sleep on the sofa in the lounge?" Andy suggested. "Mom's sleeping well, now."

To his surprise, his dad nodded and left the room.

Alone with his mother, Andy found his mind slipping back to scenes from his childhood. He forced his daydreams to select only the pleasant memories.

At first, those memories came with difficulty; they were so few and far between. But soon, a few kind moments began to weave their way through his reverie. He remembered his mom pointing out the elephants on his wallpaper—elephants his baby tongue had called "hahnas." He remembered soup and grilled-cheese-sandwich lunches, and there had been cookies and milk in the middle of afternoon play. He recalled the feeling of cool antiseptic spray and kisses on scuffed knees, and he heard his mother's laugh when Grannie came to visit. He even remembered a time when his dad had taken him to a car show.

Then, just as Andy was starting to fall asleep, a dark dream crept in, and it flooded him with all of the terror he had felt as a child. He had feared his father, and now he heard his dad shouting again: "the kid's an idiot and a disgrace!"

Andy awakened with a start, unwilling to lend those memories life. He felt chilled, and he pulled his jacket closer. He saw that

Abbey had slipped into the room and was watching him. Her hand on his shoulder felt warm. How he loved her!

———❖———

At six o'clock Andy felt another hand on his shoulder. This time, it was Molly.

"Why don't you go and sleep in the lounge for a bit, now? Then, maybe around eight, we can get some breakfast."

He smiled, gave his sister a hug, and relinquished his chair. With Abbey and Molly on guard, he quietly wandered out to the lounge to sleep.

———❖———

At eight, in the cafeteria, rumpled and only partially rested, four of them downed plates of scrambled eggs and pancakes. Mac had insisted he wasn't hungry, so they had left him by Rachel's bedside. They made some tall to-go coffees and took a sack of breakfast for Mac, in case he changed his mind.

When they arrived at Rachel's room, they were astonished.

The nurses had been able to awaken her, and she was sitting up. Rachel was yellow and thin, and she looked very tiny in the bed, but thankfully, she wasn't in pain. She smiled when she saw them.

"How did I get here?" she asked. Andy told her, and his mother nodded as if vaguely recalling the events of the night.

There was a light knock on the door, and the doctor entered.

He seemed surprised that Rachel was awake, but he said nothing. They all knew she was on a lot of painkillers. The doctor's kind smile, however, told them he wasn't hopeful about her condition. This rally was only temporary. He listened to Rachel's heart and breathing, checked her drips and chart, and then said, "You probably already know you're in serious condition, my dear. We can keep you fairly pain-free, but there's not much more we can do."

Mac immediately demanded, "How much time does she have?"

The doctor reluctantly replied, "Not much longer."

Mac bristled. "Can't you talk plainly and say if it's a day, or a week, or…"

The doctor now bluntly answered, "Mr. Garrett, your wife could go in a few minutes. But then again, she might be with us for a day or two. I'm sorry, but this is not something I can predict that precisely."

The anguish of helplessness contorted Mac's face.

The doctor softened as he spoke to Rachel, "It is good you have your family here, it is good you are without pain, and it is good you are all able to talk together. Many people don't get this kind of time. It is a gift, a blessing. I hope you can enjoy it."

With that, he lightly squeezed her hand, turned, and left.

CHAPTER TWENTY-NINE

STANDING WATCH

During the day they all sat, and the hours dripped slowly, as though time had turned from water to heavy oil. Their thinking grew numb. Except for Rachel's request for Andy to read her the Twenty-third Psalm and repeat the verse and the story of the painting of Jesus Knocking (Mac said nothing), most of their talk stopped. Nurses slipped in and out.

One nurse had just left when Andy asked his mother, "Mom, do you remember when Grannie was in the hospital—the only time she was ever in the hospital?"

His mother lifted a weak smile.

Molly said, "That's the time Dad insisted she get a full checkup, even though she wasn't a bit sick."

Mac retorted, "Well, she had just turned seventy, and I had the money to make sure she was healthy!"

"Yeah, Dad, but they kicked her out a little early, as I remember," grinned Andy.

It surprised them when Rachel took up the story. "I remember that Mama made Andy bring her a big flower pot, some potting soil, and a trowel from the dime store. She wanted to repot that poor root-bound little ivy someone had sent her. When the nurses wouldn't let her out of bed, she transplanted it right there on the sheets!"

Rachel giggled weakly. They could all picture the horrified nurses who had seen all of that dirt. The head nurse had shown up only minutes later to tersely announce that the rest of Grannie's tests would occur as an outpatient.

Rachel's jaundiced eyes sparkled at the memory.

In response, Andy and Molly shared more stories for Rachel's benefit, and most of them were about Grannie—about her cooking, her sewing, and her love of dime stores. Rachel added her remembrances to theirs.

"She'd turn the gas burner on high," remembered Rachel, "and she'd fill the skillet with bacon grease. Then she'd stand there turning the chicken with her three-tined fork, and it always turned out perfectly."

"And," laughed Molly, "her iced-tea pitcher always had about an inch of undissolved sugar in the bottom."

"And," Andy added, "she lived to be eighty-four! The doctors don't know everything..."

His comment brought them back to the reality of the hospital room, and Andy was sorry he'd said it.

But Rachel moved them forward again. "I remember just before her seventy-fifth birthday when Mama decided to paint her apartment orange."

Andy jumped in: "Yes! And she stood on the counters to paint the upper part of the kitchen."

"She could do anything," Molly laughed.

The stories made the time pass without heaviness, and as evening drew on, they were pleased to have Rachel still with them, even though, now, she slept a great deal.

Andy and Abbey took first watch in the hospital room that night. To help them stay awake, Abbey turned on the television without the sound, and Andy engaged in a quest to find a vending machine with a couple of candy bars.

The hallway was quiet. When Andy passed the lounge, he noticed that his father was missing. Andy assumed that Mac was in the restroom. But then, before he reached the vending machines, Andy heard him—of all places—in the hospital chapel. The door had not shut all the way. It was just a small room, set with dim lighting, an altar, a kneeling bench, and a couple of chairs. His father did not see him. Surprised as Andy was to find his dad there, he was not surprised at the vehemence in his voice.

"You're supposed to be good, God," Andy heard his father say, "but I see the real You! Rachel didn't do anything wrong; I did. Take ME, not her! I know You hate me, but don't make her suffer for it."

His dad wept bitterly and beat his chest.

Shaken, Andy backed away from the door. Andy knew that God heard Mac's anguish and that Mac was crying out in the only way he knew how. Andy hurt for his father, and he wondered if he should go in, but almost immediately Andy felt a barrier. He was not to interfere. This exchange was a private thing between his dad and God.

Instead, Andy prayed for the Holy Spirit to open his father's understanding. Sadly, he sensed that the awakening might take a long time.

Rachel died the next afternoon, with everyone there. She merely stopped breathing. And Mac stopped talking.

Andy and Molly cried in their loss. They tried to include their father in their grief tears, but he remained stiffly aloof. Mac did not shed a single tear—which only made their sorrow deeper.

Andy mourned that he had just begun to know his mother in a new way, and he mourned that his father had not been able to share that spiritual relationship with her. Now she was gone. Andy knew that his mother was in Heaven, and he prayed even more diligently for his father.

The days that followed passed in a blur.

Friends of the Garretts brought food, and Andy and Molly made preparations with the funeral home. Mac refused to go.

It was Molly who made the calls to relatives, while Mac sat dumbly in the recliner.

It was Andy who wrote the obituary, while Mac refused to think about the past or the present.

Mac refused to go to the funeral home, except for the service itself, so Andy and Molly valiantly received condolences and made excuses for their father's absence.

Mac never once looked at his wife as she lay in peace.

During the service, Mac sat stiffly looking at the closed casket and the spray of flowers across the top, and Andy wasn't sure his dad even heard the words he and Molly spoke during the service.

Afterward, still without a tear, Mac shook hands woodenly with those departing. He refused to go to the cemetery, so Paul went to the house with him until the interment was over.

"He hasn't moved from the recliner since we got home," Paul whispered.

And that is how Mac remained. He moved only to eat.

So, it was natural that they worried about him.

CHAPTER THIRTY

EMILY RACHEL

On September 9, Emily Rachel was born.

Like a mini Molly, with wisps of curly blond hair and blue eyes, Emily also had Paul's smile. Andy held his niece and posed for a photo.

"I intend to spoil her to the bone," Andy announced, "and I want her to see this picture, so she'll know I started the day after she was born!"

Then, whispering in the baby's ear just loudly enough for Molly to hear, he said, "When you're a little older, I'm going to let you stay up to watch wrestling, and we'll eat popcorn and drink grape juice in goblets."

It made Molly cry. "Grannie would have loved to have done that," she said. "I only wish Emily could have known her."

"I wish Mom could have known Emily, too," said Andy, gently swaying with the little one in his arms. "Mom would be proud to know you named the baby after her."

Molly agreed.

Then, inexplicably, as babies do, Emily began a protest. She kicked her tiny feet and contorted her little mouth into a wee cry. Papa Paul stepped in to take the unhappy bundle into his arms. He took pride in being the only one, besides Molly, who could calm his baby girl when she cried.

"She knows my voice," Paul declared.

And it was true. Emily did know his voice because in the evenings before she was born, Paul had laid his head on Molly's belly and cooed and talked. He had even sung to his baby-to-be. Now, it was his crooning that settled her.

Emily's favorite song seemed to be "You Are My Sunshine." The minute Paul's mellow tenor voice took up the melody, Emily's eyes locked on his face, and she stopped crying. She was totally captivated by her daddy.

Molly and Paul were lucky parents. Emily was a sweet baby who didn't get her days and nights mixed up, nor did she cry all day with colic. She was an easy child.

Abbey came to the farm and helped Molly with the cooking and cleaning in her first week at home, but Molly was soon up and doing for herself. Abbey and Andy still made many visits. Andy loved being an uncle, even if it meant a diaper change once in a while.

"There's hardly enough poo, here, to bother with," he exclaimed at the changing table, one day.

"You just wait," Molly countered. "That'll change soon enough."

Andy and Abbey were glad that even after Molly had resumed housekeeping, Paul continued to do her farm chores. Paul insisted that Molly was to spend her time with the baby. Molly didn't object; she loved being a pampered mother.

With so much attention on the baby, weeks passed without a visit to Emily's grandfather. Andy and Molly telephoned Mac from time to time to report on Emily's progress, and although they sensed that he was lonely, their father's monosyllables revealed little about how he was doing.

Molly pictured him still in the recliner just as they had left him after the funeral, and she worried. Was he going out at all? Was he eating? There was no way to know.

Molly's concern prompted her to ask Paul what he thought of possibly asking her father to come and stay with them. As Molly had expected, Paul looked surprised. After all, Paul knew how distant his wife's father had been when Molly and Andy had been small. Not only would Molly's dad be tougher to manage than the baby, but there was no way to know how he would react around Emily, especially if she started crying.

Even so, Paul did not hesitate. He agreed to the idea, wholeheartedly.

"Your dad needs somebody," Paul said, "and it's either Andy and Abbey or you and me. I'd like to think it was you and me. We have more space than they do in the parsonage. I could start to clean out my old room in the attic for him, and until that room is ready, we could keep Emily with us and set a cot in Emily's room. Plus we have a whole farm for Mac to wander. Maybe he could help with chores. It might give your dad some purpose."

Then Paul surprised Molly when he added, "I think this is an offer we need to make in person. Let's go and see how he's doing, Moll."

CHAPTER THIRTY-ONE

DAD SAYS NO

"I appreciate the offer, but no."

Mac's answer was final. He refused to move in with his children.

"I'm just fine," he declared.

Molly could tell, however, that her father was not fine. He was thin and gaunt, and he moved slowly. Her father looked old—too old. It was apparent to her that he wasn't taking care of himself.

He wasn't taking care of the house, either. The only part of the house that had been touched was the vacuumed circle in the middle of the living room floor. Dust lay thick over everything else. The bathrooms were far from sparkling, and the bedsheets had not been changed in a long time—maybe since Mom had died? There was nothing in the refrigerator—her dad said he ate out a lot. He didn't even make coffee.

Mac seemed to live in the recliner and the car.

"Just come for a month or so," Molly suggested, but Mac wouldn't answer. His mind was made up, and Molly could not change it.

<hr>

Molly and Paul tried to persuade Mac again, a few weeks later. Over the phone, they invited him to come for Thanksgiving. At first, he said he didn't think so, but the more Molly talked about the meal she was planning, the less adamant Mac was about not coming.

"Turkey with all the trimmings, right?" he asked.

"That's the plan," said Molly, "and homemade pecan rolls for Thanksgiving breakfast."

Molly could practically hear her father's stomach growling. In the end, Mac said he'd come—just for the holiday, mind you.

———

Molly and Paul were shocked at how much thinner Mac had become. He walked and moved like a ninety-year-old man. The circles under his eyes accentuated a haunted look that never went away.

He said virtually nothing. His responses were grunts. He obviously hadn't come to talk. And he hadn't been in the farmhouse for ten minutes when he staked out the recliner and sat, just as they remembered seeing him at home.

Molly was determined to get him out of that chair. He was not going to sit and deteriorate at her house. Her plan was already formed, and she began to carry it out the next morning.

At the smell of homemade bread, fresh from the oven, Mac left the living room and established himself on a stool in the kitchen. He waited impatiently for the bread to cool enough to cut, and he watched Mollie work. She finally poured him a mug of coffee and opened some of her apple butter. The sliced bread didn't last long. He ate half the loaf and asked for more.

"Don't spoil your lunch," Molly teased.

That afternoon, Paul drew Mac outside to lounge in the porch swing and then to ride with him while he did chores. As they bounced along in the truck, Mac expressed surprise at all there was to do on the farm.

Molly served a hearty supper when they returned, and Mac and Paul retired after the evening news.

The routine was repeated, with variations, the next day. As Mac moved, his color began to return, and his stiffness diminished.

Back from chores that night, Mac watched Molly care for the baby. Emily seemed to know that her grandfather needed a smile; every time Mac's face came into her view, she grinned and gave a happy kick.

"She likes you," Molly told him.

He replied, "And she looks like you."

Even so, Mac swore he would not hold Emily.

"I'm not good at that," he would growl whenever Molly offered her to his arms.

Overall, Mac's disposition, like his health, improved hourly. Outside of a few curse words (bad habits die hard) his belligerence hadn't reared its ugly head, once.

Molly hoped that when Andy and Abbey came tomorrow for Thanksgiving, her father might even find some occasion to smile.

Then unexpectedly, around one o-clock in the morning, yells riddled the night.

The outburst shattered the peace of the farmhouse. Molly shivered, and Paul leaped from their bed. In a bound, Paul was at the baby's crib only a few feet away. Paul's sleep-muddled mind struggled to identify the threat, but he could find none. Emily was crying, but it was not her screams they had heard. The yells continued, and Paul shot through the door and down the hall.

Adrenaline flushed through his veins. Paul threw open the nursery door, ready to fight—he didn't know what.

Why was Mac screaming? It unnerved Paul that he couldn't see anything of danger by the stark sliver of light from the hallway. Paul fought the disorientation of being jarred awake so alarmingly.

There was no overhead light in the baby's room, and only one of Emily's tiny lamps remained on the dresser. (The other had accompanied Emily to Paul and Molly's bedroom.) As Paul fumbled to find the lamp, he could just make out Mac's form in the middle of the cot. He saw that Mac was clutching his hair as he screamed, "Save the baby! Save the baby!"

Paul strained to see what Mac was staring at in his terror.

"Not the baby! Not the baby!" Mac screamed at the top of his lungs. "Oh, God, save the baby!" Tears streamed down his cheeks as he bellowed.

Paul's sleep-thick fingers finally managed to switch on the lamp. Its low-watt glow was practically worthless. Paul ran to the cot, anyway, for whatever understanding he could gain of what was going on.

Suddenly it became clear that Mac was not seeing what Paul was seeing. Mac was caught up in a scene somewhere in his mind—a powerful dream. Even though his eyes were open, Paul could tell that his father-in-law was not awake.

Paul put a knee on the cot and gently laid his hand on the screaming man's shoulder. Mac flinched, but he did not move.

"It's okay, Mac," Paul soothed. "It's okay. It's just a dream. It's okay."

Mac seemed aware of Paul's attempts to comfort him, but he continued to yell.

Paul kept his voice low and calm.

After a few minutes, Paul felt Mac's tension ease, ever so slightly. Mac's screams melted into convulsive sobs. "Not the baby!" Mac keened. "Not the baby!"

In a trembling heap, Mac slumped. He rocked in his agony, with hands stifling his moans.

Paul let him cry. And he rubbed his father-in-law's back and soothed him with more reassuring words.

"It's okay," Paul repeated again and again.

Finally, Mac lay down, still weeping. He curled into a ball, and his sobs faded into whimpers. When the crying eventually stopped, Mac's eyes closed but his brows remained twisted. Mac seemed to have moved past the nightmare and into a less terrified state of sleep.

Paul stayed for a few more minutes and watched his father-in-law's breathing settle. Once Paul was sure Mac was all right, he went back to the master bedroom.

There, Molly sat with Emily in her arms. The baby had gone to sleep, but Molly remained wide-eyed. Paul kissed his wife on the forehead and laid his baby in her crib.

"It was a bad dream," Paul explained. "Your dad seemed to be terrified. I don't know what he was seeing, but it was powerful enough to make him scream."

"It was awful!" Molly whispered. "His cries about 'the baby' scared the wits out of me. I was sure something had happened to Emily, and I nearly died!"

Paul held her close. "Emily's fine," he soothed.

But Molly still trembled. "When the yells kept coming," she whispered, "I could hear Mom and Dad screaming at each other in the old house on Sharon Avenue. Andy and I were hiding like we used to in the closet in the dark, and I just wanted their yelling to stop! It was so real I could almost feel the walls shake from the things Mom and Dad threw at each other. I haven't felt like that since I was in grade school. And I never want to feel that way again!"

Molly shuddered and clung to her husband. Paul's strength was solid, not like the shifting uncertainties of her childhood. Molly drew from his calm.

Finally, her nightmares faded— just as her father's had, only a few minutes ago. Paul settled his wife under the covers and turned off the little lamp on the dresser, to sleep.

———➤●◄———

The next morning was Thursday. Acutely aware that it would be a bigger job than normal with Mac and the baby, Abbey had come prepared to help Molly. From the look of things, it was good that she and Andy had arrived early. Molly looked exhausted.

"We didn't sleep well, last night," Molly confided. "Dad had a screaming nightmare and had us all up for about an hour, and then I couldn't get back to sleep. I knew morning was going to come quickly, but I couldn't sleep! I did get breakfast done, and I managed to get the turkey into the oven by seven, so we could eat on time. But I'm worn out."

Abbey reassured her sister-in-law, "Why don't you go and rest? I'll get the other things going. I can put together the salad and peel potatoes. I can also make an attempt at dinner rolls— yours are always so much better than mine."

Molly would have protested, but she was exhausted, and she knew it would be better for everyone, including Emily, if she could get a little more sleep. She thanked Abbey and padded upstairs to bed.

Paul kissed Abbey's forehead. "Thanks, sis," he said.

"Don't thank me, yet!" Abbey jested. "I'm no Molly in the kitchen."

Paul replied with a grin, "You'll do. You'll do."

Abbey laughed.

Paul rounded up Mac and Andy to go with him to the barn. He had already done the milking, but with breakfast over, it was time to do other chores. Andy grabbed the last sausage from the counter and shoved a pecan roll into a napkin. Andy then kissed Abbey and hurried out the door, after the others.

In the quiet that followed the men's departure, Emily cooed. Her carrier was propped on the floor, right where Abbey could keep an eye on her. What a good baby!

As Abbey let the dough rise for the rolls, she put together a cranberry salad and then wielded the potato peeler. The morning sun streamed through the curtains above the sink and gave the old farm kitchen a cozy glow.

How delightfully homey, Abbey said to herself. No wonder Molly and Paul loved it here.

———————

When Molly heard the men tramping up the porch steps a little later, she came downstairs. The crisp air and chores had energized the guys. They were laughing as they traipsed into the kitchen. Even her father was laughing. What a miracle, thought Molly.

Molly's nap had refreshed her, and she was grateful for the work Abbey had done. Now she checked Emily's diaper and fed her, and Abbey laid out the plates and silverware. The aromas had made everyone eager for the meal to begin. Finally, the turkey was carved and the potatoes were whipped, and no one had to be called to the table. Andy quickly said grace.

The turkey and dressing, mashed potatoes and gravy, beans and scalloped corn, cranberry salad, and homemade jam on yeast rolls lived up to every description Molly had given her father when she was enticing him to come to Harmony. Mac's plate overflowed, and he ate without restraint.

"Why don't we do this more often?" asked Andy, with his mouth full.

"Because we'd weigh five hundred pounds!" Paul replied. Paul patted his stomach. Mac nodded in agreement but was too busy spooning out more gravy to bother with conversation.

"Don't worry about leaving room for pie," suggested Molly. "We'll have that, later."

"Yes!" cried Andy. "The feast goes on!"

———

After the meal, Molly was flabbergasted when the men offered to help with the dishes.

"Of course!" she said quickly before they could change their minds. Even her father grabbed a dish towel.

While the fellows filled and refilled the sink with dirty dishes, Molly and Abbey picked the bones of the turkey carcass and stored the leftovers.

———

Within an hour, swelled bodies were splayed, unmoving, across various sofas and chairs in peaceful naps. Only the ticking of the mantel clock marked the muted tread of time through the lazy afternoon.

Perhaps because, earlier in the day, Molly had been granted a couple of hours to catch up on her sleep, she awakened first. Silently, she brushed Andy's shoulder until he, too, roused. Molly put a finger to her lips, and Andy followed her into the kitchen.

"Come upstairs while I change Emily's diaper," Molly whispered, and Andy followed her.

While Molly powdered and pinned, Andy listened to the story of last night's nightmare.

"Dad seems to be reliving something," Molly said. "He talked in his sleep about 'saving the baby.' I wonder if he's remembering the crib death of their first child. Maybe putting Dad's cot in Emily's room was a bad idea."

As children, Molly and Andy had inadvertently learned that their parents had had a baby boy before either of them had been born. They had also overheard that the child had died of crib death. Andy had suffered in terror for weeks after learning that. With no idea of what crib death was, Andy had feared he might die of it, too.

Molly now put Emily on her shoulder, and Andy got the baby to smile.

"I wish Grannie were alive," said Molly. "She'd know what this was all about, I'm sure."

"But," said Andy, "even when I asked Grannie things like this she wouldn't tell me."

Molly knew it was true. What a strange family they had. Molly wondered if she and Andy would ever know the why of it all.

Molly and Andy could now hear voices downstairs. Nap time was over and the ballgame would begin. Molly would make another pot of coffee.

———————

When the sun went down, Paul lit a fire in the fireplace, and Molly and Abbey served the pies.

As the evening settled, Mac became quieter. Perhaps it was because of memories, Andy guessed. This Thanksgiving was Dad's first without his wife. Molly imagined the same thing.

Not wanting the day to be lost to sadness, Mac's children and Paul made it a point to put their focus on Emily and the future.

"You know, Mac," said Paul, at one point, "I find myself daydreaming about how pretty Emily's going to be."

"And do you imagine some pimply kid coming to date her?" Mac spouted, almost immediately.

"Is that what you thought of me?" protested Paul, in surprise.

Molly snickered, and Mac finally grinned.

The exchange, light-hearted as it was, did make Paul think. Paul decided that being the father of a daughter wasn't necessarily easy. Paul sympathized for the first time with what Mac may have felt when Paul had come into Molly's life and stolen her away from home.

Paul realized that, for all his bluster, Mac had cared.

CHAPTER THIRTY-TWO

THE SECRET

After Thanksgiving, Mac did not leave for home as he had vowed he would.

Instead, he awoke on Friday morning and joined Paul for the early chores. At breakfast, Mac ate as if he'd never eaten before. Then he lingered in the doorway to watch Molly change and dress Emily. After that, Mac went to town with Paul.

On Saturday, when Abbey and Andy came for lunch, they smiled to see Mac still there. They understood that Paul and Molly's plan was working. Mac was acclimating to their routine and becoming comfortable in their home. Everyone hoped he would stay. If Mac stayed, it would solve their worry about him, and it would eliminate the need for trips to check on him.

Although Mac sank into the recliner as the men waited for lunch, it was clear that he had not become one with it, as he had at home.

After lunch, Molly pulled out a deck of cards, and everyone engaged in a four-handed game of Pinochle. Mac played every hand, and Molly and Abbey took turns to sit out and care for Emily. In an attempt to combat Mac's cut-throat strategy that guaranteed his wins, the game was marked by laughter and a friendly cheat of outlandish table talk.

Half-way through four rounds, Molly called a time-out for refreshments, and she reported quietly to Andy in the kitchen: "No nightmare last night."

"His color is better, too," Andy observed. "I know he likes your cooking."

"I hope he'll stay," said Molly. "I wake up every morning half-expecting him to be gone. He and Mom used to do that all the time—just pick up and leave with no notice. I'm always relieved when he shows up for breakfast. I can't imagine him languishing back in Herndon the way he was."

Andy and Molly didn't say it, but they knew that tomorrow would be the test. Would Dad be there when they got back from church? Once he was alone (they were certain he wouldn't go with them), would their dad pack up and leave?

Only tomorrow would tell.

As expected, Mac didn't go to church—but he didn't leave, either.

It was a relief to find him watching television when they returned. It signaled that he had decided to stay. Perhaps Mac realized he was better off here.

No one mentioned it. A tiny gleam in Mac's eye made Andy wonder if his father knew what they'd all been expecting. And Andy thought Mac seemed a little pleased with himself.

Perhaps it was Andy's imagination. Nevertheless, they were all glad he was staying.

Midday on Monday, Andy and Abbey arrived at the farm to find Mac and Paul gone. Molly explained that they were out checking on a fence break and corralling some loose cows.

"It happens once in a while," Molly shrugged. "It's usually not too serious."

Andy didn't mind that the men were gone. It meant there was less competition for Emily's attention. Andy immediately goo-gooed before the baby's myopic little eyes, and he was rewarded with a grin and an energetic kick. Next, he examined Emily's tiny hands and kissed her baby cheeks.

"What is it that makes babies so soft?" Andy asked. He bent over and lifted Emily overhead. When she stared into his face, Andy mimicked the purse of her perfect little lips.

"She's yours, now," Molly laughed. "In fact, why don't you entertain Emily for a few minutes while Abbey and I go through some of Mother's clothes that Dad brought with him?"

At the prospect of being left alone with his niece, Andy threw a hand at the ceiling as if to say, "Do what you like—I've got the best job in the world, right here."

Molly led Abbey upstairs.

"I've meant to go through these, ever since Dad got here," Molly said. "But it's been too busy, and I haven't had a chance."

Three large cardboard boxes waited for them in the back of Molly's closet. It took only a minute to pull them out.

With the first one on the bed in front of her, Molly hesitated for a moment. (It must be bittersweet to go through your mother's things, thought Abbey.)

"I can't believe that Dad was able to go through Mom's stuff already," Molly said. "I was surprised when he showed up with these. He didn't say much, just that he wanted to bring a few things because he was coming down to see us."

Molly finally opened the box. It was filled with shoes. The styles were beautiful, and they were all from pricey leather. But Molly shook her head.

"I don't think so," she said loudly.

Abbey knew that Rachel's feet had been exquisitely tiny and that none of her shoes were going fit them. She smiled at Molly, and they put the box back on the floor.

The next box was more promising. It contained sweaters and cardigans of various styles. Dad had left the clothes on their hangers and had just laid them into the box.

Molly decided that the things in the boxes must have been whatever Mom had had in her closet. Dad had just reached in and cleared it out.

Molly pulled out a sweater and handed it to Abbey.

"This one looks like you," she said. Abbey protested until Molly insisted, "I can't wear all of these! I'd love for you to have some."

Abbey did finally take two. She thanked Molly for sharing.

"Mom would be happy to know you have something of hers," Molly said.

"And I feel proud to have them," replied Abbey.

With two more sweaters under her chin at the mirror, Molly pulled them both to her face. She drew in a breath.

"Can you smell it?" she asked. She sniffed again and drew in the scent of her mother's perfume.

Abbey could smell it. It was like a breath of Rachel in the room. Molly smiled.

"My memories of Mom have changed in the last month," Molly said. "I never used to imagine her happy. But I imagine that she is, now. Knowing that she was at peace with the Lord when she died has helped me, and I treasure the week we had together getting baby things ready. I would have hated to go through these clothes or smell her perfume if relationships had stayed as they were. I'm more grateful than I can say that God let her spend precious time with me and that He drew her to Himself!"

Abbey said, "I'm glad for her and you!" and they hugged.

When the box was empty, Molly tipped it off the bed. As she did so, she caught a glimpse of something left inside.

When she realized what it was, Molly flung it out onto the bed with a cry: "Why was this on the bottom?"

Crushed from the weight of everything else, was her mother's fur stole.

"Dad knew better than this!" she exclaimed in frustration.

Molly quickly hung the stole on a hanger, but despite her attempts to re-fluff it, the once expensive fur remained flat and pathetic looking. Molly pursed her lips in disgust.

"At least it won't go to Goodwill," she announced. "I remember when Mom bought this at Buckners, the most expensive dress shop in town. Mom and Dad fought for days over how much it cost. Now it'll never be worn again!"

Abbey commiserated with her. What had been a beautiful stole had become a pitiable wrinkle of fur, crushed in the bottom of a cardboard box.

Molly said, "Maybe Dad ruined it on purpose so he wouldn't have to see it again."

She sighed and wished things had been different in her childhood.

Molly crossly slid the box across the room and pulled the last box onto the bed. This box was larger. As if afraid of what she might find, Molly slowly pulled back the flaps. But then she smiled.

Inside was a wide assortment of outfits that were more practical and less connected to quarrels between her mother and father. Molly pulled out some blouses and slacks and offered some to Abbey to try on.

When the box had been emptied, Molly tentatively searched the corners. Sure enough, there was something buried in this box, too. She pulled out her mother's jewelry case.

The case brought another flood of memories. Ensconced in the little satin trays were pins, earrings, and necklaces that Molly had seen her mother wear to dinner parties and country club events, scores of times.

As she lifted out the various pieces, Molly assumed that everything here was costume jewelry (surely her dad had locked the rest away in safety boxes, but she couldn't be sure). In any event, Molly saw that most of the items were far too ostentatious for the farm or Cherish. Only the pearls would be practical, and she and Abbey selected a couple of strands.

"I'll keep the rest, just to look at," Molly said. "Or in case Paul and I receive an invitation to the White House!"

Molly now turned to the mirror with an affected air and a string of rather rich-looking gold and diamond-like stones around her neck.

"How do you do, Mr. Thayer?" Molly postured, in a feigned cultured tone. "No, I'm not going to a dinner party. I've just decided to wear these little jewels with my blue jeans to buy chicken feed."

Abbey laughed at her performance.

"I'm afraid we just don't run in the right circles for some of this," Molly grinned, and Abbey agreed. Cherish and Harmony were a far cry from Herndon and Chicago.

With no more clothes to go through, Molly and Abbey put everything away. They packed Abbey's selections for her to take home, and they put Molly's items into the closet and her chest of drawers.

Molly had decided to keep the jewelry case on her dresser, but as she lifted it up, she accidentally snagged the box lining on the dresser corner. It tore more of the seam away.

"Oh, dear!" Molly cried out in disappointment.

Where the loose brocade had caught, a piece of yellowed paper now peeked out. Curious to see if it was anything special, Molly unfolded it.

A look of shock crossed her face, and it startled Abbey. Molly shook her head as if trying to clear it.

"What is it?" Abbey cried when she saw Molly clutch her heart.

"Oh, my!" Molly exclaimed.

Molly shook her head, again. It was clear to Abbey that Molly was stunned by whatever the piece of paper held.

"Abbey, call Andy up here!" Molly now commanded.

Abbey had no idea what was going on, but she ran and called down to Andy. At the urgency in her voice, Andy hurried up the stairs with Emily on his shoulder.

"What's up?" he asked, not sure what was wrong.

Molly took Emily from him and passed him the paper. Abbey could see now that it was an old, brittle newspaper clipping. She was glad that Andy read it out loud: "*MacAndrew Garrett Acquitted in Death of Infant Son.*"

"What?" Andy cried. He gripped the clipping tighter and read further:

"*Late this afternoon, the jury in the State of Illinois versus MacAndrew Douglas Garrett of Herndon found the defendant not guilty in the death of his infant son. The jury determined that abuse was not a contributing factor in the child's bruising and death. They believed the defendant's testimony regarding his attempts to revive the child he had found dead in its crib. The Garretts were not available for comment following the verdict.*"

Unsure that she'd heard correctly, Abbey asked, "Does that mean they thought Mac might have killed the baby?"

"I guess so," Andy said.

The three of them scarcely breathed as the impact of what they'd found began to register.

Abbey quietly said, "How awful!" Molly hugged Emily closer and rocked her. And Andy still gripped the paper in his hands. They were all too dumbfounded to say more.

The afternoon light filtering through the thin curtains at the window could not overcome the shadow that had suddenly filled the room.

"We were always told the baby had simply died," Molly whispered. As a child, she and Andy had come to grips with the term "crib death"—but only after years of not knowing for certain what those words meant. As adults, that expression had finally lost its power over their imaginations. But now, here were new words—"murder trial" and "acquittal"—that cast new shadows and conjured new scenarios. What had happened?

At the least, a trial would have tortured the young couple already mourning the loss of their first baby. At the most, the accusations must have had some basis for a criminal case to be initiated. What was the truth? Why had it been covered up for all these years?

No wonder their parents weren't entirely normal.

But it had happened so long ago.

Molly mused, "Why didn't Mom and Dad tell us?"

Andy replied, "Because I don't think it's over. I think this still haunts. This has to be the experience Dad's been reliving in his nightmares: you said he kept crying, 'Save the baby!'"

The thought now chilled Molly. She pulled little Emily tighter to her breast.

"This must have twisted their minds," Andy said. He added, "And maybe this explains some of their bizarre behavior."

Molly shivered and said with a flash of insight, "No wonder Dad never spanked us! He didn't dare leave a mark on us for fear..."

The thought startled Andy.

Suddenly Molly snatched the paper from her brother and stuffed the jewel case into a drawer.

"Let's put this stuff away and go downstairs. I don't want to look at this anymore," Molly said, and she charged through the doorway.

Being downstairs, however, did not cancel out the chilling revelation. It was impossible to put aside what the siblings now knew. A few words on a yellowed piece of paper had changed everything—and it was rewriting their past.

Every event from their childhood now replayed in their minds, unbidden, in light of the knowledge they now possessed. Things they remembered from years ago had not always been what they had seemed.

Molly found herself caught in the memories of her mother's many sicknesses. So many of them had seemed contrived at the time, but Molly now believed they all had psychological roots in this awful event.

Andy's mind processed the labyrinth of his father's responses to—everything. No wonder his dad always lashed out so bitterly! Andy recalled how Mac had never had a good word to say about the past. His father had always pushed forward, leaving the past behind him as quickly as he could. Surely this was in some part why he had worked so hard and had clawed his way to respectability and social acceptance.

Andy's thoughts whirled until Molly asked, "What do we do when Dad and Paul come back? Do we tell Dad what we know?"

After considering for a moment, Andy said, "Yes. I think we should tell him."

He added, "What harm can it do, now? If anything, it might bring Dad a little peace to know the secret is out. Now that Mom's gone, he's left carrying this all by himself."

CHAPTER THIRTY-THREE

TELLING MAC

About a half hour later, Mac and Paul returned. They were full of the story of the cows on the road and the break in the fence.

"Your dad's a pretty good cattle driver," Paul declared. "He teased 'em with a switch and kept yelling 'roll 'em, roll 'em, roll 'em!'—and those fool cows went right back into the field where they belonged!"

Mac laughed at the recounting of his achievement. "Nobody was more surprised than I was!" he said.

His eyes sparkled. It had been a great afternoon out-of-doors with his unexpected cow-herding success.

Those listening to their tale put on the proper smiles and remarked on the event, but none of the three carried the banter forward. For them, the moment was pregnant and awkward. The ebullient cow-herders barely noticed, and Paul and Mac chattered on.

It was Molly who reigned them in. "Okay, you two," she said. "Go in and get washed up and we'll have some coffee in the kitchen."

Andy and Abbey helped her set out the mugs and spoons and a pitcher of cream. Molly was right to gather everyone around the table for The Discussion.

Paul and Mac were still clapping each other on the back as they slipped into their chairs and Molly filled their mugs.

Molly then got their attention.

"With everybody here, there's something we need to talk about," she began.

"Sure, Hon. What's up?" Paul asked. He assumed it was about her father staying with them longer.

Molly didn't answer him. Instead, she pulled out the clipping and slowly unfolded it.

It wasn't until Molly had slid it across the tablecloth that her father realized what it was. In an instant, horror contorted his face. Mac gripped his head with his fingers.

"Oh, no!" he cried out.

Paul didn't know what was going on. He shot Molly a look of surprise and confusion, but Molly was just as shocked at the intensity of her father's response as Paul was. Abbey picked up the clipping and handed it to Paul. As Paul read, he let out a long breath.

Molly said, "Dad, we accidentally found the clipping hidden in the jewelry box you brought from home."

She didn't say more but waited for her father to regain his composure. When he did, it was with a look that was half-defiant, half-defeated. Mac stated dully, "I'm sorry you had to learn about this. It was a long time ago."

"Dad," protested Molly. "What's to be sorry about? We should have known about this long before now."

Mac closed his eyes, and then he said, "I guess so."

"You weren't guilty, Dad," Molly forged ahead. "We're adults. It's okay for us to know."

But instead of responding with relief that the secret was out, or with anger about all that had happened, Mac dropped his head once again into his hands, and this time, he nearly wailed.

⇒•⇐

Stunned by Mac's reaction, no one knew what to do. They were at a loss as to how to comfort him. Paul made an attempt.

"Dad," he said, "It's over, you know? It's true your baby died, but you have two grown children who didn't die. They're here, and all grown up, and you can be proud of them for what they've become."

Mac just shook his head. "You don't know," he blubbered. "You just don't know."

Finally, Andy leaned across the table. "Okay, Dad, we don't know. So why don't you tell us? We're all here. Tell us about it."

In response, Mac's sobs grew deeper. It was several minutes before he quieted, but even then he did not raise his head. Instead, he spoke bitterly through his fingers: "What you don't know... what you don't know... is that I did kill that baby!"

Shocked, Molly cried out, "What do you mean?"

Andy calmed her. "Wait," he said. "Wait until we hear the whole story."

Andy turned to his father, "Dad, you have to tell us what happened."

Paul held a fist to his mouth, unsure of where this was leading.

———————

Mac was like a stone. Then after a long and tortured silence, he tried to speak. But it was no good; he couldn't get beyond his emotions. Mac's head remained bowed, and he shook it in a vain attempt to banish the demons raging through his thoughts. The tears would not stop. Molly grabbed a box of tissues and tossed it into the center of the table. Paul passed it to Mac, who nearly emptied it with blowing his nose and wiping his eyes.

When the emotion was spent, Mac cleared his throat. He closed his eyes as if deciding where to start. Finally, he began, and except for Emily, there was silence around the table.

"Your mother got pregnant on our honeymoon," Mac said. Molly and Andy already knew this part of the story, but they had never heard the details.

Mac said, "We were excited. We didn't have two dimes to rub together, but it didn't matter. I was cleaning boilers and coal furnaces whenever I could get the work. I would go from house-to-house and neighborhood-to-neighborhood offering my services and taking orders. We lived in an old drafty two-story apartment. When the baby came, he was the joy of our lives, and we loved him so much!"

Mac sighed and gathered another tissue. Molly and Andy tried to imagine those days.

"Your mother had had a difficult time with the delivery, and as hard as she tried, she wasn't strong enough to take care of the baby without help. So Grannie came. Rachel could stay in bed and recover while her mother was there. Grannie bathed and fed and diapered Little Mac—that's what we called him. After a couple of weeks, I had learned how to do all of that, too. I was so careful when I bathed him, to make sure he was safe..."

Mac's voice broke, and he blew into the tissue. His listeners waited until he could continue.

"I changed his diapers and warmed his bottle," Mac said. Then as if to affirm that he knew what he was doing, he added, "I tested it inside my elbow to make sure it wasn't too hot. I did everything perfectly. Even Grannie said so."

Mac sighed. "Rachel was doing better, and we decided that Grannie could go back home. We were eager to take care of Little Mac all by ourselves."

Mac blew his nose again. He looked at Emily. "Mac looked like her," he said, "All happy and sweet."

He set the tissue down and grimaced as if steeling himself for what came next.

"After Grannie left," Mac said, "Rachel still tired easily. I would have to get up in the middle of the night when Mac cried; I would get his bottle and rock him. Then, one night I was exhausted from work, more than usual…"

Mac snorted in derision at himself. "I was so tired," he spat.

"I was so tired that after I had rocked him with his bottle, I put him on his back in his crib, and I put the bottle on a rolled-up diaper next to him so he could keep feeding. I watched him and watched him, but then I dozed off.

"He never cried. He never made a sound… and when I woke a little later, I thought he was asleep. I took the bottle to the kitchen and came back to pull the cover over him…"

Now Mac cried out, "But he was so cold!"

Molly got up and hugged her father's shoulder. Her tears matched the anguish twisting his face.

Mac cried out again, "He wasn't breathing! I picked him up, and I knew that in the hospital when babies are born the doctor gives them a slap, and they start breathing. So I slapped him, and I slapped him, and I slapped him—but he didn't breathe! He didn't breathe! And I screamed. I just screamed 'NOOOOOOO!!!' And I hugged him, and I wanted to die with him."

Mac rocked and sobbed. And everyone cried with him.

Paul hovered over Molly as she tried to comfort her father. Andy put his hands on his dad's shoulders, too, and Abbey hugged her husband.

"So you see," Mac cried, "I killed him! I killed him!"

He rocked in his pain.

"And then," Mac cried, "Rachel came down the stairs. I'll never forget the sound of her screams. And a neighbor came and saw that the baby was dead, and she called the ambulance. But it was too late!"

Mac gritted his teeth and sat with his eyes closed, breathing in half sobs. His sobs and his rocking were the only movements around the table. Everyone relived the pain with him.

Finally, Mac stopped rocking. His breathing was still uneven, but he was gaining some control. There were only facts to relate, now. Facts didn't have emotions.

"The coroner was called," Mac said, "because the baby was bruised from my slaps. And I was charged. We went to court, and I couldn't cry. I couldn't show any emotion at all."

Mac sat motionless, now, as he must have sat then. In a hollow voice, he said, "I hated myself. I despised myself. If I could've died right then, I would have. But then they found me not guilty..."

He registered the unbelief he must have felt then, and he repeated, "They found me not guilty; but I think I would have handled it better if they had hanged me. At least then the pain would have been over."

Mac closed his eyes. But then he opened them, again, and looked at the ceiling. He seemed to see there the events after the trial.

Without expression, he said, "And Rachel—Rachel hated me. She hated the sight of me. I let her hit me and hit me, and I didn't even feel it."

Then Mac tensed and spoke more rapidly. "Then, somehow I got angry," he said. "I got angry at everything that had happened. I was angry that Rachel was weak. I was angry that Grannie wasn't there. I was angry that I had been working so much that I was beyond tired that night. And I was angry that God hadn't stopped it all from happening!"

He slowed a little. "And Rachel began to realize that part of it was her fault, too, for not helping that night when I was so tired. So, we held each other responsible in our guilt and our anger.

"After the trial had ended, we co-existed," he said, "but we never talked. We avoided each other. If one was in a room, the other moved to another room. We didn't sleep together. We didn't eat together. We didn't sit together. It was like we were dead to one another…"

He paused before going on.

"Then one day, little by little, we started to try again to be something to each other. It took a long time: over a year."

"But then," Mac cried, "it started all over again! Rachel said she was pregnant. I was scared, and I was angry with her. Didn't she know I never wanted to have another baby, again? I couldn't do it, again—I just couldn't! I started working more and staying away from home. I didn't want to be there. I couldn't be there. Rachel was on her own with this one."

Looking at Molly with a plea in his eyes, Mac confessed, "In my fear, I never held you when you were born. I never fed you. I never changed your diapers. I never wanted you. I'm sorry!"

He closed his eyes. "But you lived. And when you were finally walking and feeding yourself, and I realized you were going to live, I tried to let go of my fears. I decided we could make it as a family of three."

"But," he said bitterly, "I didn't know that your mother was hiding another pregnancy from me! When I realized it, I went to pieces again. I couldn't take care of a child and Rachel, both. I became nearly paralyzed with fear."

Mac went on. "Thankfully, Grannie came. She took care of you and your mom, and I stayed away. I worked almost nonstop, just so I wouldn't have to be home, and I was so mad at Rachel."

"We were never intimate after that," he said. "I'm ashamed to say it, but I hung out in bars and spent time with other women, just so I could forget."

"But I always came back," he said. "Rachel knew what I was doing, and it made her anger only hotter against me."

Before Mac could go on, Molly blurted out, "Why didn't you two get a divorce?" It was what everyone had been thinking.

"A divorce? A divorce?" Mac laughed bitterly. "I had a wife and two kids to support. And a divorce wouldn't have made the nightmares go away. At least Rachel and I understood each other's nightmares. As much as we hurt each other, we hurt more when we were alone. So we stayed. We stayed, and we fought. And I know it doesn't sound logical, but it was the fighting that kept us going."

Molly could hear the fights, like the first night she'd heard her father's screams at the farmhouse. Paul saw her anguish and put his arm around her.

"Then, just like when Molly came, I stayed away until you were about two years old," Mac said to Andy. "That's when I could finally look at you and not see Little Mac's tiny blue body. I never held you or took care of you until you were old enough to do things for yourself. Rachel spoiled you and called you her boy."

Mac tried to smile.

"Rachel knew I still had my flings,' he went on, "and it infuriated her. Sometimes she'd lapse into such anguish that she'd end up in the psychiatric ward at the hospital. I hated that. I knew it was my fault, but I couldn't change. I did love your mother, I really did, but our relationship was so messed up by the past. We even pledged never to talk about it again or to tell you children. We made Grannie promise, too. We didn't want it to hang over you—isn't that a laugh!"

Andy didn't laugh. He knew now why Grannie had not told him the story when he had asked. And he doubted their father had any idea what he and their mother had done to him and Molly. Their parents had been too busy with their own nightmares.

"I just wish I could forget," Mac groaned. "I wish it would all wash away and I could wake up as if it had never happened."

"You cried out in your sleep the other night," Molly told him. "You were screaming something like 'Save the baby!' You scared us, and we wondered what it was about."

Mac breathed, "That's the dream. That's the one I always have. In my dream, I wake up and... it starts all over again."

Only Emily moved and gurgled. Everyone else sat in silence, even though the story had ended.

Finally, Andy said, "The difference now, Dad, is that we all know. You're not alone, now. You're not alone in this, anymore."

Mac just cried.

———————

Dad refused to go to a counselor. Andy had gently suggested it, but Mac had said no.

And yet Mac stayed; he did not retreat to Herndon. The family believed he didn't want to be alone with his nightmares any longer. They sensed his need to lean on them; to be surrounded by those who knew the truth.

Mac also seemed obsessed with little Emily. He watched as Molly cared for her, and his countenance would soften, but he still would not hold her. "I love that you gave her Rachel's name," he said one day, but he never answered Emily's little arms whenever she reached out to be held.

The days passed and everyone wrestled with their own piece of what they had learned. Their knowledge changed them, in small and large ways. The story that now belonged to all of them wove through their present and their future, as well as their past. Some of it brought healing, and some of it still hurt.

The catharsis—the expelling of the story—did not heal Mac. But it seemed to relieve some of his pain. It did not leave him devoid of the memories, but it did diminish their power to haunt. The dreams still occurred, but not with the same intensity. Mac's cries in the night were not as desperate, and when Paul comforted him, Mac went back to sleep with less difficulty.

"It's like a physical wound," Andy suggested to Molly, one day. "It's trying to become a scar. The scar will never be gone, but the pain of it will hopefully go away."

"I've tried to talk with Dad," said Molly, "and I know you have, too. But I think the only one he talks to is Paul."

Molly added, "I think they talk while they're out doing chores."

That seemed logical to Andy, because Paul was not a character in the story of Mac's past—and Paul, the steady one who had rescued Molly, was a good listener.

CHAPTER THIRTY-FOUR

SMOKE

Clouds on the horizon threatened rain, not snow, and although it was warmer than usual, it was time to think about the approach of Christmas. Mac helped Paul retrieve the Christmas decorations from the loft as Molly had requested. Then the men headed back to the barn to fork clean hay into the already mucked stalls.

Molly expressed frustration.

"Don't forget that you promised to take me into town," she yelled from the back door.

Paul called back, "Oh, yeah. Give us a minute." He and Mac abandoned their task, cleaned up quickly, and snagged the car keys from the kitchen hook. They pulled the sedan around to the back door.

"I appreciate your help," Molly said. "I need you two to watch Emily while I'm shopping."

Once they were in town, Mac and Paul learned that Molly meant for them to entertain Emily in the car. The men were not to follow Molly into the stores. "Don't ask," was all she would say. "Christmas is coming, you know."

Mac and Paul were only allowed to help with the grocery shopping. Then at home, before the groceries could be unloaded, Molly whisked an armful of mysterious packages upstairs.

"No peeking," she ordered.

A little while later, the men heard the crinkle of wrapping paper and the snap of tape. When Molly came back down and Paul went up to change into his work clothes, he had to pretend that he didn't see the gifts under the bed.

———⟫●⟪———

Paul and Mac hurried now to finish spreading clean hay into the stalls before the afternoon milking. They also managed to load hay into the open truck bed to take to the bull tomorrow in the field. Then Paul pulled in and parked inside the barn.

"Dry hay will be easier to offload," he explained to Mac, who hadn't yet thought that far ahead. It did look like it might rain.

As Paul cut the engine and let the keys dangle in the ignition (they were seldom removed), Mac asked why Paul didn't get a new truck.

"This thing's missing a window and looks pretty beat up," Mac pointed out.

"Don't need anything fancy," Paul replied. "I just haul hay and odd equipment in it. Don't want to put any money into something I don't have to. It's got a lot of life in it, yet. I imagine I'll keep it until it doesn't run anymore."

Mac shrugged. The broken window bothered him. Mac didn't like things that didn't work. But it wasn't his truck.

The cows were coming in, now, and claiming their stalls, so Paul took his milking stool off its peg and went to attend to them.

Mac left the truck and looked out to where his car sat. He'd been careful to park it away from the trees. The perfectly detailed Lincoln looked out of place, here, but Mac admired it. Nothing broken on the Lincoln would ever remain unfixed.

———⟫●⟪———

After a late supper, Molly set a kettle of water on low on the back burner. She'd make herself a cup of decaffeinated tea after tending to Emily. It was time, now, to diaper and feed the baby.

Downstairs, Mac read the paper and Paul worked on some bills. As he licked the envelope on the last payment, Paul stretched and asked if Mac wanted to come with him to make sure the chicken coop was secure for the night. Mac agreed, and the two men grabbed their jackets.

Molly heard them leave. She finished feeding Emily, who then promptly fell asleep in her arms.

By the dim glow of the one whimsical little elephant lamp that had temporarily come from Emily's room to their dresser, Molly followed the twitch of her baby's eyelids. She wondered what dreams played through her infant's thoughts. How wonderful it must be to have no bad memories and to sleep so peacefully.

Molly tried to let the tranquility of the evening blanket her, too, and she was grateful for the calm.

In the near darkness and the quiet of the bedroom, Molly felt the start of a dream, and she let her eyelids fall. As she did, the rocker stopped.

———>●<———

From his spot near the chicken coop at the far end of the barnyard, Mac observed that it was "raining, over yonder." Lightning forked the night sky, and a strong breeze turned up Mac's jacket collar. It was time to get inside.

Paul nodded as he worked. "You're right. I'd better hurry," he said.

The men had checked the henhouse and had confirmed that in spite of the hole in the fence, the roost was full. The chickens had sensed the coming storm and had wisely chosen to seek the shelter they knew best. With pliers in hand, Paul was still weaving and twisting a wire over the fence breach to keep the hens from escaping, tomorrow.

"Okay," Paul said when he finished, "let's get these pliers and my work gloves back into the barn before we get wet."

The breeze stirred and sent dust and loose straw into their faces. They shielded their eyes with their sleeves as they hurried across the yard.

As they ran, Mac and Paul didn't see that the same breeze that was bothering them had pushed open the kitchen door; it hadn't latched properly. The impish wind invaded the house and swirled leaves across the floor. Then it lifted the stamped bills Paul had left on the table and sent one of them down to the scrubbed linoleum. Capriciously, the breeze skipped a wadded paper towel across the counter and onto the stove. There, the paper encountered the teakettle that simmered and waited for Molly.

The little gas flames of the burner licked lazily at the paper's edges. Then the flames took hold and flared. The blackened paper hugged the kettle and might have burned out except that another tease of breeze blew off a glowing corner and sent it swirling into the air. The paper flew around and around until it landed on the curtain. There its flame burned a tiny hole in the fabric. That little black hole grew, and as it got larger, it flared upward and caught a frilled edge of the curtain pullback.

The fire became more eager, now. Fueled by the breeze, a row of flaming tongues ate across the top of the curtain to the other edge. The flowers on the wallpaper browned along the way, and it was all quiet—oh, so quiet!

The indifferent breeze continued to flutter the curtains, and it fanned the flames. More wallpaper caught fire. Now the hundred-year-old wood of the window frame burned, and fire shot up the wall.

The breeze was relentless and spread the flames across the ceiling to another wall, then more wallpaper, and then the oak cabinets. Then the fire crossed the room to the hallway and the living room doorway—and it wasn't quiet anymore. Black smoke poured into the living room and up the stairs.

The men in the barn smelled it at the same time Molly did. Startled from her nap, Molly jumped from the rocking chair and ran down the hall. Emily cried as she ran. Already, the stairs were red with flames that were forcing smoke up to the bedrooms.

Paul stared in disbelief. It couldn't be a fire. Not the farmhouse! Surely this wasn't happening! He felt like he was running in slow motion. Paul raced in a panic to the porch and screamed for Molly to get out of the house.

"Get out, now!" he bawled into the burning kitchen.

But Molly had nowhere to go.

"I can't get down the stairs!" she shouted back, frantically.

Paul could barely hear her over the noise of the fire. He raced for the hose beside the porch and turned it on. Mac, who was at his heels, grabbed the hose from his hands and told Paul to go around to the back to see if he could get Molly and the baby.

Paul ran, trying to think of how to save the house and his family. When he rounded the corner, Paul saw Molly open the upstairs window and look desperately for some way to get down.

"Throw me the baby, Molly," Paul cried, just before he tripped in the dark on something hard. Paul realized too late that it was the old lawn mower he had carelessly abandoned there. Paul had struck it with such force when he tripped that he knew he'd broken his ankle, and when he crashed to the ground, he'd also fractured his arm. Paul couldn't put pressure on his arm or get ahold of anything to get himself upright.

"Wait, Molly! Wait!" he called again. "I can't catch her!"

Paul shouted for Mac to come. He wasn't sure his father-in-law could hear, but suddenly Mac came wild-eyed and charging through the dark. Somehow Mac missed the lawn mower.

Paul shouted, "Mac, I've broken something, and I can't catch the baby. Please get her!"

Then Paul hollered, "Molly, toss Emily to your dad!"

Molly could barely see the men below, and she hugged Emily tightly, afraid to send her precious bundle down.

"Oh, God!" she cried. "Please help us!"

Mac stood with arms raised and called out to her. "I'm here, Molly! I can see you and Emily."

Molly and the baby were both in light colors that gave enough contrast for him to make them out in the dark.

Molly could hear the fire roaring behind her, even though she had shut the bedroom door. The light had gone out, no doubt because the electric wiring had been compromised. There was a threatening glow under the door, and smoke curled upwards into the room. It was all happening so quickly.

Finally, wrapping Emily more tightly in the blanket and bending as low as she possibly could from the window, Molly strained to make out where her father was waiting below. She closed her eyes and choked out a desperate prayer. When she opened her eyes, Molly let her baby go. As she did, she screamed a cry to Heaven.

Mac saw the whiteness of the little bundle dropping down, and he heard Molly's scream. It tore at his heart and pulled him into a mighty focus on his task. Mac didn't even realize he was shouting, but Molly heard him entreat, "Oh, God, please let me catch her!"

Mac stood and sobbed when he felt the little bundle in his arms. He clutched her so tightly he was afraid she might smother, and he made himself cradle Emily more softly.

"Did you get her?" cried Molly, desperate to know if her baby was safe.

"Yes! Yes, I got her!" Mac called out.

"Give her to me, Mac," yelled Paul, "and help Molly."

Mac hurried the bundled baby over to where Paul still lay on the ground. Mac nearly stumbled over the lawn mower, and Paul told him to move it away from below the window. With a mighty heave, Mac pushed it away. Paul took the baby in his good arm and dragged himself away, too, as best he could, so the ground below the window would be clear.

"Don't you have a ladder?" cried Mac. "Can I get a ladder from somewhere?"

"It's broken," said Paul. "It doesn't extend, and it won't work."

Mac cursed.

The men could barely see Molly, now, in the dark.

"I can hear the fire behind the door," Molly cried.

"Molly, you've got to jump!" yelled Paul.

"I'll try!" Molly yelled back, but she couldn't see through the dark, and she was terrified.

All of sudden Mac yelled out, "Wait! Wait, if you can, Molly!"

Mac yelled, "I'm going to bring the truck around. There's still some hay in the back, and it won't be as far to fall."

Before Paul could object to the time it might take to get the truck, Mac tore off in the dark.

Then the rain came.

It was the lightning that gave Mac his bearings.

He remembered the keys were already in the truck's ignition, and he quickly slid into the seat. The engine started the minute he pressed the accelerator and clutch and twisted the key. In seconds Mac was careening across the yard to the back of the house.

Mac edged the vehicle as close to the house as he could, and then he stood in the truck bed, ready to break Molly's fall.

The light from the headlights and the intermittent flashes of lightning helped Molly to gauge her jump. It also stoked her courage to see the dimly lit figures of Paul and Emily.

Finally, a flame shooting under the door of the room forced her to action. Molly climbed out of the window and clung for a moment to the ledge. With a prayer, she pushed off and aimed for the truck.

She hated the sensation of falling.

As he had promised, Mac managed to break her fall. But even though he and Molly landed in the hay, Molly's right leg caught the truck's side rail. They heard it crack.

It hurt, but it didn't hurt.

Molly decided it must be shock—she must be in shock. What bothered her more was the rain. It was cold! It made the straw slippery, and it made her clothes heavy.

She felt her father's arms cradling her and rocking her, and she heard him sobbing over and over, "Oh, Molly! Molly!"

Paul could see and hear Mac's sobs, and he began to be afraid.

Paul feared how close to overload Mac might be. The tormented man was already an emotional mess. Mac couldn't fall apart, now. They needed him.

Paul was helpless and could do nothing; only Mac could help them, now.

Paul knew he had to keep the tortured, sobbing man on task. In desperation, Paul raised his voice to cut through the rain.

"MAC! MOVE THE TRUCK, MAC," he commanded as loudly and calmly as possible. "NOW!"

It was the voice Paul's colonel had used in Korea to focus the troops in the middle of chaos.

Flames now shot from the window where Molly had just been, and sparks were flying everywhere.

Mac heard the command, and just as the troops had during the war, he responded.

Mac released Molly to the hay in the vehicle bed, and he let himself down to the ground. He took Emily from Paul and put her on the seat of the truck. Then he went back and carefully lifted Molly inside the cab. Mac placed Emily into Molly's arms, and Molly cried as she relived the terror of dropping her baby into the dark, only moments ago.

Finally, Mac retrieved Paul. Because there was no more room in the cab, Paul commanded Mac to lift him into the truck bed. With superhuman strength, the once wasted old man didn't hesitate. Mac pulled his son-in-law from the ground and set him into the truck.

"Now," instructed Paul, through the pain of his broken ankle and arm, "drive the truck back into the barn entrance."

Mac climbed into the cab and punched the accelerator. With a roar and a spin of tires, he circled the house and pulled the old truck into the barn.

———————

It was a relief to have the barn block out the rain. Even so, it was cold.

Molly shivered and suggested they move to one of the cars, across the yard, but Paul reminded her that the keys were in the kitchen—a kitchen now totally in flames. They would have to take the truck to the neighbors' house for help.

"But, wait! We can't," Paul backtracked. "The Bennetts are out of town and won't be back until tomorrow afternoon..."

"Then we'd better just get you to the hospital," Mac broke in. Mac was taking command, now, and his voice was his old voice of authority. Molly recognized the tone. It was his no-nonsense, do-what-I-say voice. It used to frighten her, but now it was reassuring.

Paul was relieved to hear it.

"Let's get you all dried off and covered as much as we can," Mac directed, "and I'll drive you there in the truck."

Paul pointed Mac to the pegs along the wall that held his rain poncho and rain hat, and he told Mac where to find the calving blankets. They dried themselves with some of the blankets and kept the others dry to wrap around Molly and Emily on the trip.

Mac arranged Paul with the rain poncho in the back of the truck, to shield and keep Paul as warm as possible for the ride. Then Mac piled the rest of the blankets around Molly and Emily. Molly huddled as far from the cab's broken window as she could.

"Now, tell me where I'm going," demanded Mac. "Where do I go?" Mac climbed into the driver's seat and twisted the key, as before.

In a splattery trail of mud, the truck lurched down the lane toward the hard road.

Behind them, the house continued to burn, and the rain seemed to have no effect. The orange of the fire could be seen in the clouds as they drove away.

Emily fussed in dislike of the wet clothes and diaper, and Molly hugged her closer and warmed her with kisses.

Mac couldn't tell how Paul was faring. He hoped Paul was all right with all of the bouncing.

Then Molly heard Paul call, "Tell Dad to take the corn road. It'll be faster."

At the dark intersection, Molly made her father slow down. She told Mac to turn, and they were soon hurtling along the dark, narrow back road to town.

CHAPTER THIRTY-FIVE

WAITING ROOM

Even though it was raining and pitch black, as fast as Mac had driven the trip took them about twenty minutes. It had seemed like an eternity before they pulled up to the Harmony Hospital emergency entrance.

Mac raced inside. Within seconds, hospital staff poured out of the doors to help. The workers wasted no time in whisking Paul and Molly into the sanity of dryness and light.

The injured were a sight!

Paul, covered in mud and with a huge gash on one leg, lay helpless with a useless arm and a severely displaced ankle. Paul's drenched overalls, slippery and cumbersome from the rain, had to be cut off. And although he was in shock and great pain, Paul never stopped rattling off his farm's location and begging someone to call for a fire crew. Because Paul would not settle until the call was made, one of the nurses took down the information and handed it to someone else. Paul urged them to call the Hayes, too, so the next nearest neighbor could help with chores until the Bennetts came home. The Hayes knew Paul's dad, and they would report that Paul and Molly were okay. Dad Doaks would know to come and check things out and milk the cows, tomorrow.

In a separate emergency bay, pieces of straw poked out of Molly's hair and sleeves. Her smoke-gray face contorted in pain when the hospital staff examined her swollen right leg.

Emily, without her wet blanket and with a dry diaper, was in the best shape of them all. After her quick checkup, she was returned in a portable crib to Molly's bedside. Molly thanked God that her baby was safe.

Once Mac was certain that everyone was being cared for, he searched out a restroom where he could relieve himself. In the mirror, Mac frowned at the old man he had become and at the scrapes he hadn't realized covered his face and arms. Because it had been wet, his hair was matted and had collected into a ridiculous pompadour to one side. His shirt buttons at the bottom were gone, and his shoes and socks were filthy with mud. Mac nearly depleted the bathroom's paper toweling in an attempt to clean off his shoes, and he tried to straighten his clothes. He tucked in his shirt where the buttons were gone. Without a comb, he couldn't do much about the hair; he just wet it again under the faucet and ran his fingers through it. It wouldn't matter. Who was going to see?

Mac was surprised at how busy the emergency room was. He felt sorry for the staff who had to work these late hours. Mac also wondered what time it was. He'd lost all track of the hour; his watch was missing. He just knew he was exhausted and needed sleep.

As he tried to find a comfortable way to doze off in the only empty waiting-room chair, Mac remembered that no one had called Andy.

Mac heaved himself upright, again, and rubbed his eyes. He headed for the pay phone he'd seen outside the building, but when Mac got to the door, he remembered he needed money. He checked his pockets and found a nickel and two pennies. Mac hoped the hospital staff would help.

"No problem, sir. You can use this phone," a serious-looking desk clerk told him. Mac pulled out the combined Cherish/Harmony phone book and looked up Andy's number.

"Son," was all he was able to get out before Andy said, "Dad, what's wrong?" Mac could see the clock, now, and he realized it was after midnight.

"It's okay, Andy," Mac said. "We're all okay."

"Okay from what, Dad? What's going on?"

Mac could hear Andy yelling to Abbey that something was wrong at Molly's.

"We're at the Harmony Hospital. Molly and Paul's house just burned down, and we got a little busted up getting out of there. But, seriously, we're okay," Mac insisted.

"You're all at the hospital?" Andy asked.

Mac told him about the broken bones and emphasized that he and Emily were just fine.

"We're coming over," Andy said. "We'll be there as soon as we can get dressed. We'll hurry."

Andy and Abbey had a sack of burgers and fries with them when they came. After hugs and reassurances, they followed Mac to the emergency bays.

Mac was completely exhausted and could hardly stand, so they excused him to return to his chair in the waiting room to sleep. Then a tired Paul told Andy and Abbey the story of how fast the house had gone up in flames.

"I can't imagine what started it," Paul said. "We didn't even have the fireplace going." Although knowing the cause of the blaze wouldn't undo anything, Paul continued to wrack his brain for a reason.

Abbey shuddered when Paul told how Molly had dropped Emily into Mac's arms and then had jumped. Abbey couldn't imagine Molly's terror. It was one thing to jump when you could see clearly, but it was quite another thing to drop your baby two stories into the dark! Abbey's heart pounded at the thought.

Paul also told about the rain and the crazy ride in the dark.

"And when we got here," Paul said, "I had somebody from the hospital put a call through to the fire responders. But I doubt there's anything left."

Paul teared up, now. His chin quivered as he said, "I don't care about the house—well, of course, I care—but I was terrified that I was going to lose Molly and the baby."

Andy patted Paul's arm. "They're both okay," Andy assured him.

Paul cried again when Abbey lifted Emily so he could kiss his baby's face. Abbey had taken charge of Emily because Molly had suggested she take the baby to the parsonage.

Suddenly, Paul remembered Mac.

He said, "I hope Mac's okay. Have you talked to him? We sure had a lot of excitement tonight. With Mac's state of mind already messed up, I hope this won't throw him into something else."

Paul recalled how close Mac had come to a breakdown after Molly had jumped into his arms.

"Dad just looks tired," Andy said. "We'll take him home and let him rest."

Paul nodded. He was tired, too—too tired to talk anymore tonight.

Andy and Abbey stayed until Molly and Paul were formally admitted. Then they kissed and hugged the patients goodbye. They would visit them, again, tomorrow.

A groggy Mac followed Andy and Abbey to the car, and then he melted into the back seat and slept. He didn't even rouse when

Andy stopped at a 24-hour K-Mart, and Abbey bought bottles, formula, sleep outfits, and a package of diapers.

At the parsonage, Mac slept in his clothes, too tired to change.

The next day, the Garretts returned to the hospital. Molly and Paul had been assigned to the same room, which made visiting easier. Molly hungrily reached for her little girl and kissed her.

"She looks great," Molly told Abbey, and Abbey assured her that Emily had slept well.

The terror of last night was gone from Molly and Paul's faces, and it was good to see them free from pain.

"We slept well, too," Paul said. "What a night!"

Then Paul told them his father had just left. Phillip had come to the hospital after taking care of the early chores and had reassured his son that the only thing lost was the house. The barn was untouched by the fire.

"Dad said the cows were a little jumpy when he came over to milk them, but when they heard his voice they calmed right down. It tickled Dad that they still remembered him."

Then Paul added, "This afternoon, Dad's going to ask the Bennetts if he can bunk at their place; it'll be easier to keep up with the milking."

Mac had been silent until now, but now he offered, "If your dad needs some extra help, I could come over, too."

Andy was surprised, but Paul smiled. "I do think you've started to get the hang of farming, Mac," Paul said. "You never know, my dad might give you a call."

It was quiet for a moment, and then Paul motioned for Mac to come closer. Mac approached the bed, and Paul grabbed his hand and shook it.

"Mac," Paul said solemnly, "I want to thank you! We couldn't have made it to the hospital without you."

Mac was touched but waved off the praise with his usual gruffness. Then he retreated into the background and out of the spotlight.

Now Molly and Abbey talked. Molly helped Abbey make a comprehensive list of things the baby would need, and Molly outlined Emily's schedule. Abbey marveled at the amount of time and supplies a baby required.

Then Abbey shared her hope to borrow a crib and a changing table from June Green. The parsonage's matronly neighborhood babysitter used to keep her grandsons during the week, and Abbey thought June still had several pieces of baby furniture stored away.

As the women talked, Emily gripped her toy giraffe (a gift from Abbey) and murmured. Despite the circumstances, she was content and kicked her little feet and sucked on her pacifier. From Emily's sweet disposition, today, one would never have known that she had been through so much excitement the night before. Abbey admired the gift of infants to be innocent and protected. Emily had been no trouble last night at the parsonage, and Abbey didn't anticipate any problems tonight. Emily was easy to care for.

They all talked awhile longer but Andy and Abbey kept an eye on the clock. It was important for Molly and Paul to get their rest. It wouldn't do to overtire them. Plus, the patients had procedures scheduled, and they would be leaving the room, soon.

Abbey finally collected Emily's blanket and reached out to take the little one from Molly. But, unlike last night, Molly stopped her.

"Wait," Molly said.

Abbey left Emily in her mother's arms. It seemed that Molly just wanted to fuss with her a little longer before letting her go. Abbey smiled as Molly kissed her baby girl and straightened one of Emily's frilly sleeves.

But then Molly turned to Mac.

"Dad," Molly said, and her father looked up. She beckoned him to her bedside, and he came with a question on his brow.

Molly then lifted Emily up—and Emily reached out her little arms.

"Dad," said Molly, "here's your granddaughter."

Mac froze. A conflicted look crossed his face, and a long moment passed.

But then...

Mac reached out for Emily. When he felt her in his arms, Mac sobbed. He pulled the infant to his chest, and he rocked her back and forth.

Molly simply said, "I trust you, Dad."

CHAPTER THIRTY-SIX

PICKING UP THE PIECES

The crib and changing table from June Green made baby care easier for Abbey. Abbey no longer had to sleep on the living room sofa with Emily in the dip of the pulled-out recliner and Winston locked in the bedroom. For two nights before the furniture delivery, Abbey had barely slept. She had tuned one ear to Emily's breathing and had checked on her often. Then last night, Abbey had awakened to find Mac in the recliner with Emily in his arms. Mac had shushed Abbey and smiled. Abbey had never seen her father-in-law more contented than at that moment. The haunted look was gone from his eyes, and the furrows were absent from his brows. He was at peace.

Abbey also realized that since Mac and Emily had come to the parsonage, Mac had not awakened, even once, in the night. Perhaps God had used the drama of the fire and the baby's rescue to burn away the horror of the past and finally strip it of its power to torment.

The four of them (Mac, Andy, Abbey, and Emily) went every day to Harmony so Molly could hold her baby. Molly missed her little girl, and she couldn't wait to leave the hospital and return to mothering Emily again. The more Molly improved, the more impatient she became.

"I wish things were normal, again," Molly whispered often. But there was no way to go back. There was no farmhouse to return to.

Paul could sense his wife's need to get a grip on their future, and he began to include her in his ideas.

Finally, one day, Molly said, "Paul and I have been talking about what we are going to do when we leave the hospital."

Before Molly could voice their plans, however, Mac interrupted.

"I've been thinking, too," Mac said. "And here's what we're going to do: I go stay at that little motel on the highway, and Andy and Abbey keep the three of you in their guest room."

Mac stated it as if it were a command.

Surprised, Andy nodded. "Yeah, we could do that."

Molly and Paul protested that it was too much to ask of Andy and Abbey, but Andy and Abbey assured them they would love to have them at the parsonage.

"It will work," Abbey insisted, and Molly and Paul reluctantly agreed to the solution.

"But," Paul said, "it'll only be temporary. What we need is to figure out what we're going to do about a house at the farm. Unfortunately, it's going to be quite a while before I can manage the chores, let alone build a house. But my dad could stay with us and do what he's doing now, for a while longer."

Once again, Mac interrupted. "Let's set a mobile home out there, for now. Then you can take your time on what to do about a house."

Molly smiled at her dad. Her take-charge father had thought this through. "We had the same thought," she said, "and we thought that if we get a large enough mobile, we could have you and Paul's dad stay with us and help with the farm until Paul's able to manage. What do you think?"

Mac nodded as if that had been his idea, and he said, "I'll get some brochures and start looking. It shouldn't take long to set the mobile in place."

Paul laughed. "Well, I guess we have that all figured out. The only problem is that we need to wait on the insurance money."

"No, you don't," Mac interrupted, again. All eyes turned to him. "I'll go and get the mobile, now. I'll put the money down, and you can keep the insurance money for building the new house."

Andy gasped. His dad had never offered such a thing in his life.

Molly was also stunned. "Why, Dad," she said. "That would certainly simplify things. We could get back to normal—or whatever is going to be the new normal—much sooner. I don't know what to say!"

"Then don't say anything," said her father, with feigned gruffness. To cut off further discussion, Mac lifted Emily from Molly's arms and headed out the door for a walk down the hallway.

Mac had thought through some other plans, too.

Because his Lincoln had escaped the fire, Mac had a car but no keys. He groused about having to do it, but Mac finally confided in a man from his coffee circle about how to find his spare house key. Back in Herndon, Henry Dedman searched in the flower box as directed, entered the home, and retrieved Mac's spare house and car keys from a hook in the kitchen cabinet. The keys took only two days to arrive by mail.

Mac then recruited Andy to take him to the farm to pick up his car. The Lincoln had been parked beside the barn and had been untouched by the fire. On the way back into town, Andy followed his father to the Travel Stay by the highway outside of Cherish. It was the only motel within twenty miles.

"It's fine," Mac said, as he carried in his suitcase and plopped it onto the bed without even looking around. "After all, I'm only going to sleep here—as long as you'll feed me, that is."

Andy smiled. "Sure, Dad."

"Every meal, Dad," Andy said. "You're welcome for every meal, and in between."

After Mac was settled at the motel, Abbey rearranged things at the parsonage. She pushed back much of the furniture to widen the pathway through the living room. And she put new sheets on the guest bed for her and Andy. Molly and Paul would stay in the master bedroom with Emily. Emma Peters had loaned a riser with arms for the commode, and Stu Darrell had delivered a second recliner for the living room.

Abbey looked around and was satisfied.

She told Andy, "I think we're ready to bring the Doaks to their temporary home."

CHAPTER THIRTY-SEVEN

ORNAMENTS

Paul and Molly were thankful to be out of the hospital. They were still recuperating but no longer needed everything done for them.

"It's nice to be able to sink into real furniture and eat in a real kitchen," Paul said when he was wheeled into the house. And Molly was ecstatic to be with her baby. Except for physical therapy in Harmony, the Doaks could spend their days with family while they rested and grew stronger.

⸻ ❧ ⸻

Shortly after the Doaks had settled into the parsonage, the weather gave way to a shivery wintry blast. December, at last, became December. Cold weather and snow draped the countryside in a festive glitter that guaranteed the upcoming Christmas would be white.

Abbey stenciled snowflakes on the parsonage windows, put up a crèche, and strung lights on a small artificial tree she had set on the antique table. (Mac and Rachel's lamp was stowed away until after the holidays.) A gloriously red poinsettia that had come with Molly from the hospital sat on another small table.

After all the bad things that had happened, it felt good to have something good to anticipate. Emily sensed the cheery mood and her little voice cooed. She loved the tree lights. Winston loved the company. And Mac loved keeping the secrets. Mac had been pressed into service by Molly and Paul to buy presents since everything Molly had bought earlier had gone up in flames.

Other things were falling into place, too.

When Dad Doaks came for dinner at the end of the week, he satisfied his son with news of all that was happening at the farm. The cows were back to full milk production, the pigs and bull were doing fine under the Bennett's care, and no chickens had escaped from their pen.

"You're putting on weight, too, I see," teased Paul. He knew his dad was eating well at the Bennett's.

After dinner, Phillip and Mac took turns reporting on the delivery and placement of the mobile home. The two men had joined forces and were collaborating on plans for the utility hookup that would happen next week, and they agreed that the mobile would be ready to move into in no time. It was gratifying to see how much the two fathers thought alike and how the project had forged a good friendship and working relationship.

Paul was proud of how his dad had taken Mac into his confidence, and Andy and Molly were pleased that Mac had curbed his dictatorial tendencies to work with Phillip.

Mac offered, again, to help with the chores. And this time, Phillip told him to be at the farm in the morning—at five-thirty.

Mac didn't even blink. He said he'd be there.

"Great!" said Phillip. "If I can sweet-talk Sheryl Bennett into it, I'll bring you some of her breakfast sausages and rolls."

———————

From that time, forward, Mac helped every day with the chores. Sheryl supplied an extra portion for his breakfast, and she also fed Mac, Phillip, and her husband lunch each day. At night,

Phillip went to the Bennett's for supper and bed, and Mac went to the parsonage for his supper. Then Mac retired to his motel room.

Mac liked the routine. It kept him busy. He liked being useful, and he loved the time spent with his family.

Due to the avalanche of health and farm concerns, no one had talked about the fire since the Doaks had come to the parsonage.

The fire seemed long ago.

But one night, Molly reminisced. "I can't believe how quickly our lives changed!" she said. "Thankfully, God was looking out for us. One minute I was putting Emily to sleep, and the next minute half the house was on fire and there was no way I could get down the stairs. I heard Paul yelling beneath the window, but it was too dark to see anything!"

Paul shook his head. "And then I tripped over that stupid lawn mower. If Mac hadn't been there…"

As they recalled the awful events, Mac remained silent. It was hard to read his face.

"Bringing the truck under the window was great, Dad," said Molly. "It gave me the courage to jump." She was going to describe her fall, but Mac interrupted so swiftly it caught them all by surprise.

"If God was looking out for you," he blurted, "why did you have to break your leg?"

The force of Mac's challenge hung in the air. Mac had not used that tone since before the fire. Molly's chest constricted.

"And," Mac continued with vehemence, "if God was there, why did the fire have to happen in the first place? Why did Paul have to break his leg? Why was Molly hurt so much she couldn't keep the baby with her in the hospital?"

And then, as if it just welled up and spewed out, Mac spat his usual epithets and cried, "And why did Little Mac and Rachel have to die?"

No one spoke. Mac's eruption had caught them off guard. Paul cleared his throat and stared at the refrigerator, Molly hiked Emily onto her shoulder, and Abbey sighed.

Andy finally replied.

His response, though delayed, was more emotional than he had intended. His words spilled out with an earnestness that Andy hadn't exposed before in his father's presence.

"We all know the world isn't a nice place, Dad," Andy declared. "It's obvious that life is twisted and hurtful and desperately in need of a big God."

"Yeah!" Mac interrupted scornfully. He shook his head. "People say 'God is love, God blesses us, God answers prayer,' but I've never seen it in my life!"

Andy's response, now, was rapid. It made the others blink when he countered with, "But, Dad, you have!"

Mac's mouth formed into a straight line.

Andy continued, with feeling. "God gave you Molly, and He gave you me, and He gave you little Emily. And He blessed you with your business and making money. (Yes, you have had to work hard, but you were not left in poverty.) You've just chosen to throw the blessings back in God's face because you couldn't turn back the clock about Little Mac."

Andy continued with barely a breath; he couldn't stop. The dam had broken; things he had stored up over the years now crashed through, unimpeded by the reserve of fear or the concern of offense. Everything poured out in a fervent flood.

"Dad, we live in a world where nobody is immune from problems. We all have things we wish we could change, but that doesn't mean God is absent or doesn't care. God's right here, in the middle of the troubles with us. God even came to Earth in the person of Jesus and lived an unbroken life in the midst of our broken world—and He suffered for it. God knows what it feels like to be poor, libeled, misunderstood, beaten, stripped, and put to death for crimes He never committed. In the person of Jesus, God lived all those things, just like we do. And He died an awful death. Yes! God even knows how death feels."

Andy continued without pause. "And when He died, Jesus did something special. Jesus broke through! He came back to life and broke a hole into Heaven, just for us. We were too messed up to be able to do it for ourselves. In the same way that you love little Emily and reached out to save her, God loves us. He loves you, Dad, and Jesus is holding out His arms to save you; but you've got to make the jump. You've got to trust. You've got to believe."

"Doesn't anything ever get made right?" Mac rallied, his voice still charged with anger.

Andy was calmer, now. "There are a lot of ways to answer that, Dad. One way is to say that everything is made right in Heaven when we die. Another way is to say that God will go a step further and eventually make a whole new Heaven and a new Earth—and the new Earth will be better than this old one ever was, even before Adam and Eve messed up.

"And," concluded Andy, "there's one more way to say it. It has to do with your response. What I mean is this: when you reach out to Jesus, He heals you of your brokenness and sin. When you let Him, He opens your heart to see Him at work in everything around you—even in the broken things, here and now. You might say that God makes US right!"

Mac heaved a mighty sigh. He sat with his eyes cast down.

Andy was silent. He waited. Was God working in His dad's heart?

When Mac spoke again, it was to ask quietly, "Is it too late for me? I'm old and set in my ways, and I've cursed God all my life."

Andy didn't look at his wife or sister. Instead, he silently prayed.

"No, Dad," Andy said. "It's never too late. God's arms never get tired; they're still there, waiting for you."

In the pause, Mac looked at little Emily. Andy knew his father was back at the farmhouse catching Emily as she dropped from the window. Mac's brows drew together tightly, and the emotion of that terrible night twisted his face.

No one spoke. The only sound was Emily gurgling around the finger she had in her mouth.

"I think I finally understand," Mac said at last.

His voice was tight. "You're saying that God has always been trying to show me His love, but I just couldn't accept it. I've felt too guilty, and my guilt has made me mad at Him."

Mac paused. "I do see how He gave me things for which I should be grateful. I do love you and Molly—but I've always thought it was too late for me, that I was just a loser and that I had to make my own way. I've scratched and clawed and fought, all my life! But nothing I've grasped for has ever been enough. Nothing I've ever done has really fixed anything."

He continued. "It nearly killed me when I lost your mother. And then I almost lost Molly and the baby..."

Mac whispered hoarsely. "I need something," he said. "I need something I can hold onto to."

Andy quietly answered: "That's why Jesus came, Dad. You can hold onto Him. He's forever."

In the moment that followed, Molly added softly, "We all know Jesus, Dad. We reached out to Him a long time ago. Even Mom finally reached out to Him, before she died. Now, it's you."

Mac inhaled deeply and let it out slowly.

"I don't know how," he said. "I don't know how to reach Him. Help me to pray, Andy. Help me pray!"

Now it was Paul who said, "You don't need Andy's words, Mac. God wants your words. Just ask Him, and He'll catch you."

CHAPTER THIRTY-EIGHT

SETTING THE PIECES IN PLACE

The next morning, like every Sunday, Andy left for church at seven-thirty. Molly encouraged Abbey to go with the Darrells at nine, as she normally did.

"We'll be all right until you get back," Molly assured her.

It was true that Molly was moving more skillfully with her broken leg, and she was able, now, to change Emily's diapers and put her in a stroller. Molly was even warming Emily's bottles and fixing light meals with Abbey.

Paul struggled to maneuver with both his broken arm and ankle, but he was improving, too.

Neither Paul nor Molly could manage to go to church, today, but it wouldn't be long before they could.

Abbey quickly dressed—and a few minutes later, she was startled. There in the living room, dressed in a suit and holding her coat, was Mac. Abbey blinked to make sure of what she was seeing. Yes, it was true! Her father-in-law was going to go to church with her.

Mac feigned gruffness at her surprise but said nothing. Molly and Paul watched wide-eyed in silence, too, as if they were afraid to break the spell.

Abbey recovered from her astonishment and slid her arms into her coat. Mac opened the front door.

The Darrells were in the driveway, waiting. They welcomed and made room for their extra passenger. Mac said a simple thank you, and Abbey introduced him. She knew this was all new to Mac.

At the church, Mac declined Sunday school. Instead, he sat in the sanctuary, and he made Abbey and the Darrells promise not to tell Andy he had come. Abbey had a hard time keeping Mac's secret, because the news that Andy's dad was in church was exploding through the membership like the Fourth of July.

Abbey couldn't believe that with all of the tongues wagging, Andy's first realization of his father in the pew was after Andy had taken his place on the platform and the organ prelude had begun. Abbey had skipped choir and was sitting next to Mac about halfway back in the center section.

When Andy saw them, tears welled up in his eyes, and Abbey hoped her husband would be able to preach. She was relieved when Andy closed his eyes and smiled. When he opened his eyes, again, Andy looked away. He would not look at her or his father again—Abbey knew he didn't dare. She knew he had to imagine they weren't there.

Mac stood woodenly through the hymns and fidgeted a bit during the choir number, but then he listened intently to his son's sermon.

As printed in the bulletin, Andy related the story of the day that Bartimaeus regained his sight. Andy read from Mark 10:46 about the blind beggar who cried out for the passing Jesus to have mercy on him. Bartimaeus not only called out, but he addressed

Jesus as the 'Son of David,' a term reserved exclusively for God's promised king who would restore Israel.

"We read that the people in the crowd shouted for the beggar to be quiet," Andy said. "Perhaps his cries made it hard for them to hear what Jesus was saying as He walked along, or maybe some felt the beggar's shout to Jesus as 'Messiah' was blasphemous. In any event, it is interesting that Bartimaeus is the first person in the gospels to give Jesus this title. It speaks of his belief in who Jesus was and his faith in what Jesus could do for him.

"We read that in spite of the rebuke from the crowd, Bartimaeus called out even more loudly, and Jesus responded (in verse 52) by saying 'Go, your faith has healed you.'"

Andy loved this Scripture passage, and he loved explaining that, just as Jesus could open physically blind eyes, he could also open spiritually blind eyes.

"Jesus continues to heal souls, today," Andy said. "When we call out to Him, He is able to give us spiritual sight and to heal our sin blindness."

As Andy finished speaking, Abbey noticed for the first time that the order of service for today included an invitation—as it often but not always did. Opal had prepared the bulletins on Wednesday, days before their family discussion about the night of the fire. Andy could not have known, then, that he would be extending the invitation to his father, today.

Andy did not look in their direction when he invited those in the congregation who wanted to give a public testimony of a spiritual life-change to come forward and meet him for prayer.

But as the congregation opened their hymnals, and Marilyn Ingraham led the singing of "Just As I Am, I Come," Mac stepped out from the pew and Andy looked up to see him resolutely make his way to the front of the sanctuary.

Andy began to weep. There was no way, now, that he could restrain his emotion. His shoulders shook and sobs overtook him.

It was Danny Hart who stepped in to finish the invitation. Danny came down from the choir loft and put his arms around Andy, and he welcomed Mac with a handshake. Danny prayed briefly with Mac, and then he helped Andy into the front pew with his father.

As the singing of the rest of the hymn's verses continued, Abbey came to sit with them. Then Amanda Smith came, then Ivey Webb, then Bob Parks, then the Darrells... Soon, the entire church family was crowded around the front pew, holding hands and patting shoulders.

Because Andy was still unable to speak, Danny Hart announced what the church people already knew—that Andy's father had come, today, to affirm his faith in the salvation of Jesus Christ. Danny then gave the closing prayer and pronounced a benediction.

In a grand postlude, the organ fanfare nearly lifted the roof from the building.

CHAPTER THIRTY-NINE

AMEN!

Mac was bewildered by the outpouring from the church congregation. He had virtually no experience with churches, and he hadn't expected such a response to what he had thought was between him and God—and Andy. The love he felt that morning in the sanctuary was staggering.

Mac wondered: is this what Andy has been a part of all these years?

———◦◦◦———

Andy understood his father's reticence at the parsonage, that afternoon. Everything about his spiritual conversion was new to him. It would take time for his dad to grow into his relationship with God and his new relationship with his family. Andy remembered, very well, what it had been like for him when God had intervened in his life and called him to embark on a new life journey. Andy had not known God or other believers, until that time. Everything had been strange to him but also strangely compelling. He recalled the Gentle Hand that had led him to those who could explain his salvation more fully. And he had found a hunger for God's Word. Best of all, God had given him Abbey! It was his adventure with Christ and Abbey that had helped him grow into the role of spiritual leader for others. How Andy loved it that his journey had led to the First Baptist Church of Cherish!

Content in his calling to be a pastor, Andy had longed for his parents to understand and share the new life he had found. He had prayed for their peace and had made overtures to them, but nothing had seemed to have any effect—until now!

In God's timing, He had brought Mom, and now Dad, to Himself. In just a short few months, God had completed His miracle in the Garrett family!

Andy wasn't sure where God was taking his father, but he trusted God's perfect leading. And he prayed that perhaps his dad would stay in Cherish or Harmony and that he and Abbey, and Molly and Paul and Emily, could embrace him more freely. Andy prayed that his dad could grow stronger as a Christian through the ministry of the First Baptist Church.

"Heavenly Father," Andy whispered in prayer, "You have done an awesome thing! And I trust You, now, to complete it."

Andy was tired. It had been a long day, and Abbey was already under the covers and possibly asleep. Andy hurried into his pajamas and turned out the end-table light in the television/ guest room.

As he lay on the sofa-bed in the dark, Andy marveled again at how God had used the loss of Grannie and then his mother to stir a need in his father's heart. And God had transformed a near tragedy into a way to heal wounds from a greater tragedy from the past. What a wonder that God could use a fire and little Emily to demonstrate His vast and eternal love for a man who had lost his way!

"*A little child shall lead them,*'" Andy whispered into his pillow.

Abbey overheard, and she understood the reference from Isaiah 11:6. She whispered back another King James Scripture passage, from Luke 2: 11-12: "'*For unto you is born this day in the city of David, a Savior, who is Christ the Lord. And this shall be a sign unto you: Ye shall find the babe wrapped in swaddling clothes, lying in a manger.'"*

Abbey snuggled closer to Andy and said, "Won't this Christmas be heavenly?"

THE END

NOTES FROM THE AUTHOR

For those who grew up in the church, as I did, getting to know Christ is like growing up with an old friend. For some, like my husband, finding Christ is a dramatic introduction to an awesome new acquaintance. For others (like certain characters in *Cherish: Behold, I Knock)*, it is an engagement in a defensive battle, fought fiercely, until they realize who the true enemy is and find that it is not God. I hope that however you have come to Christ, you have indeed come. His friendship is a forever friendship—and a new, healed life with Him always starts NOW.

ABOUT THE AUTHOR

In her fiction series about a pastor in a small Midwestern town named Cherish, Debby L. Johnston illustrates eternal truths and brings to life characters and situations like those in the churches that she and her husband, Scott, served in their forty-year ministry. Debby and Scott currently reside in Ohio. Visit Debby's author site at www.DebbyLJohnston.com and her Facebook Page at Debby L. Johnston.

Debby L. Johnston

CHERISH: BEHOLD, I KNOCK
READERS' DISCUSSION GUIDE

1. Before Jeff Archer came into his office, Andy Garrett may have wondered why God had let him experience a life without Him for so many years. And Andy may have wondered why God had allowed cancer to threaten his life. When Andy began sharing with Jeff, however, Andy realized how his past had made his testimony to Jeff possible. Have you ever looked back and seen where God has used the difficult things of your life in ways you hadn't expected?

2. When God worked in Andy's life, He immediately took away Andy's desire for alcohol and cigarettes. But even though God had come into Jeff's life, Jeff still had to go through all of the challenging work of drug withdrawal. Why do you suppose God doesn't always work the same way, twice?

3. When Jethro Peters passed away after years of struggle with ALS (Lou Gehrig's disease), his wife was sad, but Emma also rejoiced that, in Heaven, her husband was finally free of his infirmity. How can knowing what lies at the heavenly finish line help us run our earthly race with confidence?

4. Abbey's experience as a substitute Sunday school teacher with little Alan Horn and Brady Shook made her wonder if she was cut out for children's Sunday school work. Is it possible that God would lead you into a new ministry, even though it might be difficult at first?

5. Grannie was a pivotal character in Andy and Molly's lives. Who in your life has had that kind of impact?

6. When Andy's parents broke Abbey's irreplaceable antique lamp, Abbey struggled to forgive them. Later in the story, we learn that Mac had a hard time forgiving God for his experience in losing Little Mac. Are there things in your life you have had a hard time forgiving? Does forgiving mean that you have to open yourself up to being hurt again in the same way? Have you ever sought help with forgiveness from your pastor or another Christian counselor? Have you been able to give the offense to God and let Him help to heal you?

7. When Andy and Abbey were snowed in on Thanksgiving, it was hard not to resent the change in their plans. But when the storm's delay gave Andy time to prepare his funeral message, it was a help to him. Have you ever had

a wrench thrown into your plans? Were there good things that came from the disruption?

8. Grannie created special childhood memories for Andy and Abbey, especially when she allowed them to stay up late to watch wrestling and have popcorn with grape juice in goblets. Do you have any special childhood memories?

9. Andy was terribly disappointed when what he shared at Grannie's funeral about accepting Christ seemed to have no spiritual impact on his parents. It wasn't until much later that Andy knew how that message had been working on his mother and father. Have you ever witnessed for Christ to someone and felt as if you didn't get through to them? Is it possible that you planted a seed that God can bring to fruition later?

10. Do you think that, without the onset of her illness, Rachel would have begun to seek God? Do you think God sometimes allows difficulties as a way of moving us closer to Him? Have you ever seen the William Holman Hunt painting of "Christ Knocking" and realized there was no door knob or latch? Have you opened the door of your heart to Jesus?

11. There can be lots of decisions to make when parents age. It is easy to get pushy and force them into situations for which they aren't ready. Mac was not ready, at first, to come to Molly's. But when the time came, he made that decision on his own. The Bible tells us to "honor our mother and father." How have you been able to do that, whether your parents are still young or whether they are aging?

12. Andy's unresolved anger and childhood fear of his father eventually changed to pity and concern for his father's soul. Often the people who hurt us the most have been affected by hurts, themselves. When Andy finally knew the reason

for his father's anger and his parents' fights, the power of their anger and arguments to harm him dissolved. Have you ever let your bitterness over something in your life color your relationship with someone else?

13. What does it mean that we live in "a broken world" (as Andy tells his father)? What does it mean that Jesus lived "an unbroken life in a broken world?" How did Jesus' unbroken life (a perfect life, without sin), His sacrificial death (dying for the sin of the world), and His resurrection (that proved His power over sin's judgment) make His spiritual healing from brokenness for others possible? Can we ask Him for that spiritual healing in our lives?

14. Secrets can be destructive. The secret of Little Mac's death and the related trial haunted Mac and Rachel, and it colored all of their other relationships, especially their relationship as parents to their other children. How might things have been different if the secret had been out in the open? Are there times when it is appropriate to keep a secret?

15. As Andy shared with his mother, and then his father, about God's love and grace, and about the open invitation Jesus extends, was the explanation clear to you that God is ready and waiting for a response from everyone? Have you responded and let Jesus into your heart?

Do you have questions about what it means to let Jesus into your heart? Lift up your questions to God and ask Him to help you understand. He does hear! Also start reading His Word, the Bible—starting with the book of John. Then ask God to lead you to someone in a local church who can answer your questions about inviting Jesus into your life.

Cherish: A Still, Small Call is the first book in author Debby L. Johnston's Christian fiction series about Reverend Andy Garrett. Read the story of Andy's past—a surprising past—in this first book. Get a peek at the difficulties of Andy's childhood, but also uncover his dramatic conversion and the positive influences of people like Grannie who prayed for him, a gorgeous ninth-grade teacher named Miss Randall who spurred him to read, and a girl named Bonnie who helped him to open the Bible. Learn how Andy met and pursued Abbey Preston, the love of his life. Then follow Andy's call to serve the Cherish First Baptist Church—the endearing small-town ministry that God had in mind for him all the time!

Keep up with the latest happenings about the *Cherish* series at <u>www.DebbyLJohnston.com</u>, and link from there to Debby's Facebook page (Debby L. Johnston).

Printed in the United States
By Bookmasters